REBEL
Sweetheart

by

Sydney Canyon

Triplicity Publishing

2019

Rebel Sweetheart © 2019 Sydney Canyon
Triplicity Publishing, LLC

ISBN-13: 978-1-970042-03-0
ISBN-10: 1-970042-03-6

First Edition – 2019
Cover Design: Triplicity Publishing, LLC
Interior Design: Triplicity Publishing, LLC
Editor: Megan Brady - Triplicity Publishing, LLC

Special thank you to Megan Brady for editing my mess of elementary mistakes!

For all of the country girls who like to rock and roll!

Chapter 1

"Dennis, get serious." She leaned back in the chair, rolling her misty gray eyes at the tall man standing in front of her. "I have four cases pending on my desk. I do not have the time, nor do I have the patience for some hillbilly singer with a security problem." She turned back to her computer screen and growled, "Send Jeremy."

He set a thin manila folder down in front of her.

"Just take a look at the file, Shane. What she needs is personal protection and someone with investigative experience," he said. "Besides, her manager asked for a woman."

"Fine, but that doesn't mean anything. I'll read it later." She slid the thin file into her briefcase, before going back to the computer screen and the three-page report she was working on that was due at the courthouse two hours ago.

As soon as Dennis left the room, Shane tossed her ink pen against the closed door. She hated being told what to do, and it very rarely happened anymore. The only time the agency owner ever pushed an assignment on her, it was serious and she was his handpicked choice. Otherwise, she'd be drawing from the same pool of cases as the other two private investigators at the firm, despite having a much fancier resume. She'd wanted it that way, or she wasn't taking the job. She ran her hands through her unruly and short, dark hair as she stood to stretch her tired body. At five-eight she was slightly above average height, with a trim waist and a lean, but well-toned frame. She often turned the heads of both sexes with her androgynous, chiseled features. The day Dennis had met her, he'd asked her if she was Greek, but she was unsure since she had been adopted as a baby.

***

Hours later, Shane was sitting in her riverfront apartment, sipping a glass of bourbon, when her mind loosely drifted towards the file in her briefcase. Carelessly, she opened the folder, expecting a hillbilly or a redneck in a cowboy hat, but what she saw literally took her breath away. Saliva caught in her throat, threatening to choke the life out of her when she tried to swallow. A picture of the seditious singer with long, wavy blond hair hanging in loose curls and deep bluish-green eyes, was staring back at her. *My God.* She coughed and took another sip of her drink. Shane wasn't lacking for company between the sheets, but the fine specimen looking back at her might be just what she needed to quell the flames of desire burning deep inside. "A potential bedmate is no reason to take a babysitting assignment," she chided and flipped the picture over.

Haley Nielsen was at the top of the country music charts and quickly climbing her way up the billboard music ladder in the pop category with her new album: *Rebel Sweetheart*. She was known for her raucous lyrics, smoky voice, and bluesy, country sound with a little bit of rock and roll. You typically loved her music or downright hated it, and apparently someone hated it enough to be sending her life-threatening hate mail instead of love letters.

Shane continued on to the bio page. Haley had just turned twenty-six and was barely five-foot-four. Based on the picture at the front of the file, Shane guessed she was probably a hundred pounds soaking wet with her petite build. Her marital status was single and she had an Associate's Degree in Fine Arts from the University of Tennessee. Apparently, she'd been singing for a number of years, starting out as a child performer in a local bar, and county fairs. Then, she sang in bars during her two years of college, until her first record deal, which led to a ratty hole-in-the-wall-bar tour six years ago. Now, she was with her second record label, and on her fourth album, while topping the charts with her crossover radical country music. She was currently selling out arenas all over the U.S. with *Rebellious*, her fourth tour.

She flipped back to the picture in the front. "There's something about your eyes. I feel like you really are staring back at me," she sighed, knowing she wasn't going to be able to say no. *I don't know if I can do this again.*

***

The next morning, Shane pulled her black, pristine conditioned, '64 Chevy Corvette, alongside the curb, hoping to avoid a run in with Dennis as she slipped into the office long enough to pick up some paperwork for one of her cases. She was just about out the door when she felt something pull the back of her suit jacket. She automatically reached under her right arm to the .40 caliber, sub-compact Glock pistol tucked neatly in a leather shoulder holster.

"So, did you check it out?" Dennis's deep voice bellowed in the hallway.

Shane winced and spun around to face him. "Don't you mean, did I check *her* out?" she huffed and tried to hide her trademark cocky grin as it crept up. Dennis Williams knew her well enough to know a petite blond with gorgeous eyes and an iceberg melting smile would definitely get her attention. "Just because she's easy on the eyes, does not mean I want a babysitting gig." She finally let the grin slip. "It sounds like an easy case. When do I start?"

He smiled. "I thought you didn't want this *gig*?"

"Yeah, well, Jeremy can't handle something that looks that damn good, and besides, I'm the only woman around here." She looked at his crotch and grinned again. "Unless, you have something to tell me."

"No. Nope. You're the only tits and ass in this building, babe." He smiled. "I guess you better get your open cases over to Jeremy and Randall. Your plane leaves in three hours."

"Plane! What plane? It says she lives in Nashville. It's a three-hour drive."

"Lives, yes…but, she's on tour in Louisiana at the moment, heading to Texas." He winked and walked away.

"Son of a bitch," she mumbled under her breath as she walked back to her office. This was what she got for letting her libido take over her mind. It was always a bad idea when her crotch did the thinking. She didn't even listen to country music. *This is a bad idea.*

Chapter 2

"Come on, Rich. I do not need a babysitter. We've been over this." Haley kicked her cowboy boots off and leaned back on the sofa. She'd only been on tour a month, but she was already used to living on the road. She had her own bus with two small bedrooms and a shared bathroom, while her band members shared the second bus that had six bunks and two bathrooms.

Rich Bergman, her manager for the past two years, stared across the living area of the bus at the headstrong blond in a tight, white tank top and form fitting, low-slung jeans. It had taken him close to two months to get used to being around the sexy vixen. He was close to twenty years her senior and had children her age, but he couldn't help getting cross eyed over her when they'd first met. At least until her personality reared its feisty head. Haley Nielsen generally did what she wanted, whenever, however, and with whomever. He learned quickly not to match wits with her. He'd lose. "Look, Haley, we've been over this a hundred times. We need tight security on you, and we also need someone to figure out who this asshole is before he makes good on his threats and tries to hurt you."

"What's wrong with our guys? Why are we paying for security guards at each venue if they aren't good enough?" She raised an eyebrow. The girl was definitely not the country bumpkin Rich thought she'd be when he'd first heard her smoky voice belting out a string of rowdy lines from a song on her first record.

"It's not that simple. Those guys are usually off-duty cops or whatever. They aren't with us twenty-four/seven, so they can't investigate this son of a bitch. Each jurisdiction is different, which is why we've kept this hidden from the media. All we need is another frenzy around you. The tour and the album have enough of a circus on their own. Besides, you need someone by your side like flies on shit watching everyone around you."

She raised both eyebrows. "Nice visual, Rich, and oh, such fucking language." She smiled over the cup of hot tea she was sipping. "Still, I don't need someone breathing down my neck constantly. Why can't we send the letters back to the Nashville Police, or the FBI? Whoever this dickhead is, he hasn't bothered to do anything so far."

"Exactly. Haley, we have no idea when or even if this guy will strike, but your safety is my biggest concern. Just do this for me. Try it for a month, and if you can't deal with it, then we'll try something else." *Come on girl, compromise here.*

She tucked a strand of her wild, wavy hair back over her shoulder and smiled slowly. "Fine. One month, Rich. One Month. Now get off my bus." She finished her tea and walked to the stateroom at the back of the bus.

He let out a long breath, thankful she went with his plan…finally. He'd been there for over two hours talking to her after her last show. The buses needed to be on the road, headed to the next town, and he needed to get some sleep so he could pick up the new guard at the airport in the morning, before driving to the next venue since it was too close for him to fly.

***

Haley peeled out of her sweaty, performing clothes that were stuck to her like a second skin. She was furious that Rich had bombarded her with this crap about more security as soon as she'd stepped off the stage. He was a sneaky bastard, but she trusted him. *One Month Rich, then you can go fly a kite in a lightning storm.* "Ugh!" She huffed and stepped into the hot spray of the shower just as the bus began rolling down the road.

Chapter 3

Shane stepped off the plane and stretched. She hated flying. At least there was leg room in the first-class seat she'd been in, and the flight was only an hour and a half. She grabbed her briefcase from the overhead compartment and made her way towards baggage claim. She noticed a balding man with a thin gray goatee, holding a white sign with CROWLEY written on it. She rolled her shoulders and walked towards him.

"Bergman?" she asked. He nodded. "Shane Crowley." She stuck her hand out. He shook back as he slowly eyed her up and down. She raised an eyebrow and cocked her head to the side as he finished his appraisal. "Do I pass inspection?" she asked sarcastically.

He coughed and turned a light shade of red. "It's nice to meet you. I only heard a little bit about you from Mr. Williams."

She spoke professionally, but nonchalantly. "Well, I'm sure he gave you all of the facts in my resume. I spent a little over six years as a deputy marshal in the United States Marshal Service, and I've been with Mr. Williams' private investigation and security agency for the past year," she added, grabbing her bag from the carousel. She looked up to meet his questioning brown eyes.

"What made you leave the Marshals?" he asked shakily as he led her towards the parking garage.

She shrugged, then lied. "I guess I was tired of it. I wanted something a little more stable."

Shane tossed her bag and briefcase in the back seat of his rented Escalade and slid into the passenger seat. She'd spent some time on the plane rereading the case, not that she'd missed anything the first time, but she wanted the facts ingrained in her memory. She avoided the picture the second time around, though.

"So, I guess you want to know why I went through all of the trouble to hire you, am I right?" he asked as he maneuvered out onto the expressway.

Shane hoped the drive wasn't long, but then again, she had no idea where they were going. "Well, there isn't much to go by in the file, so—"

"Haley Nielsen is…a bit eccentric, if you will. She sort of does what she wants to do and says what she wants to say. She is day and night compared to most of the country music industry. Apparently, she's made a few enemies along the way. Someone keeps sending her hate mail and the threats are escalating. Her safety is my main concern, but at the same time, I want to catch this bastard."

Shane stretched her legs and stared at the passing cars. "Do you have any idea who may behind the threats?"

He sighed angrily. "No. Not one fucking clue."

"Do you have copies of the letters?"

He finally took his eyes off the road and glanced cautiously at the woman sitting next to him. "I have all of the original letters. We didn't get the police involved since she's on tour and in a different city every night. That would just be one big cluster fuck. I want it handled privately."

Shane had to agree with him. She could imagine all of the different jurisdictions fighting over the case. "As soon as we get to wherever we're going, I would like to take a look at everything you have and send it to the private lab we use. They'll dust for finger prints and swab for DNA. Whatever they find will be uploaded to CODIS and NCIC which are the police and FBI databases. With any luck, we'll get a hit on a match. Even if it's a partial, it's still something to go on."

"Sure. Whatever you need, just let me know. Oh, and we're almost there. The buses arrived in the middle of the night so we'll catch up with them at the arena." He paused and took a deep breath. "We should probably get down to the details. I know you're familiar with personal protection, but you should know, Haley isn't going to be happy. She knows I hired someone to lead her security, but I haven't given her the details yet. She's like the queen bee and I'm about to kick her nest. Don't get me wrong, she's a sweet girl once you get to know her."

"I can understand that, she's used to having things her way and having her space. Anyone would have a little bit of a problem with a bodyguard walking around constantly. I'm well trained, Mr. Bergman. She'll know I'm there, but I can be discreet."

He cleared his throat and turned off the exit. "That's where it gets hairy, Ms. Crowley. I'm sure you will assess the situation and do what you feel is necessary, but you will need to be at her side. The reason I requested a woman is...well...because, you'll be living on her bus with her. The band shares the second bus, and the third and fourth buses are for the road crew."

Shane's jaw hit her lap. *Living together? Damn it, Dennis!* She raised an eyebrow and turned to face her companion. "What is the need for cohabitation? I was under the impression I'd be...uh...somewhere else until she was in the public eye."

"We're here," he announced, pulling into the parking lot of a large arena, ignoring her question as he cut across the numerous parking lanes towards a group of four buses and two semi-trucks which were parked next to the back doors of the building.

Chapter 4

"Richie Rich, you missed our dry run. I thought you'd be here hours ago," Haley called from the center of the stage to her manager as he walked in.

Rich rarely missed their warm ups. Noticing that he had someone with him, Haley jumped off the stage, tossed her long blonde curly waves over her shoulder, and sauntered up to them. When Rich moved to the side, Shane stepped into her line of sight. Haley started from the ground up, noticing the shiny shoes and expensively tailored black suit. She could tell the body beneath the suit was female based on the slight curvature of hips. Her dark brown hair was somewhat curly and cut short. Blue-green eyes locked onto gray ones, and for a minute, the room was silent.

"Haley Nielsen, meet Shane Crowley, your new personal bodyguard, and the private investigator that's going to catch our letter writer."

Shane felt the breath leave her chest. The picture in the file was no comparison to the petite blonde standing a few feet away, dressed in a tight, white tank top, threadbare jeans, and scuffed, brown cowboy boots. Her long hair hung halfway down her back in slightly unruly waves. Turquoise was the only color Shane could think of when describing the bright eyes boring into her. *She's beautiful.*

"It's nice to meet you, Ms. Nielsen." Shane stepped forward, sticking her hand out to the smaller woman. The heat from Haley's hand penetrated her skin like flames licking a fire when they touched for the first time.

"Likewise, Miss…Crowley, was it?"

"Shane," the taller woman said with a grin.

"Fine, call me Haley." She turned to the balding man next to her who was scratching his goatee. "I have a few minutes before we do another run. Shall we get this over with now or later?" Haley's voice was light and smoky, and very sexy.

Shane felt her knees knock together.

Rich cleared his throat. "I guess now is fine. I need to get Ms. Crowley settled on your bus and—"

"Excuse me?" Haley raised an eyebrow. "Come again."

"Uh…I need to get Ms. Crowley settled—"

"Yeah, I got that part," she growled.

Oh, here comes that feisty temper. Shane thought to herself.

"Haley, she has to share your bus, we've been over this. You need personal protection."

"That doesn't mean I need someone sharing my bed. Does she have to stand in the stall while I piss too?" she said sarcastically. "Put her on the bus with the band."

"Now, Haley, come on. If I won't put one of those guys on your bus, what makes you think I am going to put her with all of them? That's why I hired a female."

"Damn it, Rich. One Month!" she spat and walked back to the stage.

"Sorry. She'll get used to it," he sighed, looking at Shane.

She raised her eyebrows and nodded. This assignment was getting crazier by the minute.

Chapter 5

The band was still on the stage rehearsing, so Shane used the extra time to get acquainted to the tight confinement of the bus. There was a couch and a loveseat across from each other when she walked inside. The galley was next to the loveseat with a sink, stovetop, microwave, and refrigerator/freezer combo. The handful of cabinets above the sink had various boxes of food scattered across and a handful of bottles of liquor. The cabinet under the sink was full of dishes, as well as pots and pans. Across from the galley sat the small bench-style dinette table. The doorway in the wall between the galley and dinette led to a small hallway with a washer and dryer on one side, and the door to a small stateroom with a single bunk on the opposite side. The door to the shared bathroom was on the other end of the hall, with what she assumed was Haley's large stateroom taking up the back of the bus on the other side.

Shane tossed her bag onto the twin-sized bed in the small stateroom. Instead of having a window above where her bed was, the folding doors on the wall opened into a hanging closet that ran the length of the bed, which went from wall to wall in the tiny compartment. The nightstand next to the bed doubled as a desk with a small pullout chair under it.

She decided to go ahead and check out the bathroom since she was alone. The toilet was on one side of the room behind another doorway with a tiny sink across from it. The opposite side of the room had the large vanity and glass enclosed shower. She stepped to the side and opened the door to what she assumed was Haley's room. A queen-sized bed came off of the wall to the right with nightstands on both sides. A narrow dresser ran the length of the opposite wall with a large flat screen TV on top of it. A full closet ran the length of the other wall.

***

Shane sat at the dinette table, holding each letter with a pair of tweezers as she read it. Rich was across from her, watching like a little kid at a magic show.

"Well?" he asked.

"You can't see finger prints unless they are in something like ink or paint but, maybe he slipped up and touched the paper, or licked the envelope. Whoever it is, he's definitely progressing. These letters go from an unhappy fan to threats on her life in a matter of six weeks. What happened during this time?" She raised her eyes to meet his.

"I'm not sure. Her new album came out about four weeks ago, which is why she's on tour now. At first, we thought it was someone who didn't like her new album, but this is going a little too far."

"No, I agree with you. I'm sorry, I'm not up to date on her music. I'm not...I don't generally listen to..."

Rich laughed. "You don't like country music. You're not the only person in the world. To each his own and all."

"Yeah well, I need a copy of this album. Actually, you better get me all of her albums. I'll start there."

"Okay. Do you have an iPod? I'll load them."

Shane shook her head. "Not with me. I left it at home."

"No problem. I'll have one for you after the show tonight with all of her music loaded onto it. Speaking of the show, I'm surprised Haley's not back yet. She usually takes a power nap and loads up on some kind of carbs before she goes on stage." He checked his watch. "The show starts in three hours."

"Maybe you should take off for a little bit and let me talk to her alone," Shane suggested.

Rich sat back against the cushioned bench and regarded her seriously. "Are you sure?"

Shane flashed her cocky grin. "Yeah, if the bus starts shaking, you might want to check things out, but I think I can handle her attitude. She's a little pissed off, you would be too."

"Well, okay, if you think you can calm her down then…" He waved his hand. "By all means, give it a try. You don't know her very well." He smiled and hurried off the bus.

***

Shane was putting her clothes in the narrow closet above her bed when she heard the entrance door of the bus. She stepped out of the room and ran head on into Haley coming down the hall.

"Oh, you're still here. Wonderful!" Haley growled sarcastically.

Shane backed up to let her pass by.

"When you get a minute, we should talk."

"About what?" Haley asked with a raised eyebrow as she walked through the bathroom.

"I know the show starts soon. I plan on being close by until the minute you take the stage. While you're up there, I'll be on the side so you'll be in my line of sight at all times."

"Don't you need to be discussing this with the security guys?" Haley huffed.

Shane stepped closer to her. "No, those are rented guys that get paid eight or ten bucks an hour to stand around and look buff. I'm responsible for your safety, and you and I need to be on the same page. Now that your rehearsal is over, I'm going to go brief your band and road crew. Here's my cell number, call me when you're ready to leave the bus. That's the best we can do for now." Shane stepped back and turned to walk away.

"Don't think you're calling all of the shots here. I come and go as I please. I'm not scared of some jackass who doesn't like my music." Haley slammed the door to her stateroom. *Damn you, Rich. This is going to be a very long month. Why the hell did you have to put tall, dark, and handsome on my bus!?*

Chapter 6

All of the road crew and band members were sitting on the edge of the stage when Shane walked in. Twelve pairs of eyes stared her up and down.

"Gentlemen, this is Shane Crowley. She's Haley's new personal bodyguard. As you know, we're beefing up security because some fans aren't exactly happy with the new album. Ms. Crowley is here to keep Haley safe for the remainder of the tour, or until things calm down. What she says goes, and if any of you disagree with her..." Rich turned around. "There's the door."

"Thank you," Shane said, stepping closer to the stage. "As Mr. Bergman stated, my job first and foremost, is to keep Haley Nielsen safe. At the same time, I plan to make sure there is a fully functioning security detail for the entire operation." She paused. "Going forward everyone will have a two-way radio to communicate with each other as well as with me. I know Mr. Bergman hires temporary security at each venue, but these guys do not have prior knowledge of our situation, and most of them are glorified rental cops at best. They don't care about Haley and what happens to her. This is a side job to earn a little cash. Plus, one of the guys could easily be our letter writer," she finished, waiting for Rich to pass out the small radios.

"I know you gentlemen have a routine that you are used to following, and I don't plan to change that, although I may make a few adjustments here and there. If, and when the next letter arrives, it goes straight to me. If anyone is asking to see Ms. Nielsen, they talk to me first. Last but not least, Ms. Nielsen doesn't go anywhere without me at her side. Is that clear?" Shane waited for some kind of answer. She turned around when she noticed all of the guys fidgeting and looking behind her. Haley was standing on the other end of the arena, listening. *God damn it! What part of don't go without me doesn't she get?*

"You might as well join us, Ms. Nielsen," Shane called out as she turned back around. "Are there any questions?" she continued. "This will take a few days to get used to. I'll do my best not to step on anyone's toes."

"Except for mine," Haley sneered over her shoulder.

"Well, on that note, let's get back to work. Have a great show tonight guys," Rich said as he walked up next to Shane. "Everyone will come around, eventually. You just pissed in the proverbial cookie jar."

"No shit," Shane mumbled under her breath.

***

Haley was sitting on the couch when Shane stepped back onto the bus. She couldn't help looking a little too closely at the blond, curled up like a Cheshire cat. Shane shook her head as she sat on the couch across from Haley. Once again, blue-green eyes met gray ones in a standoff.

"I know you have a problem with me being here, and we just got started. Mr. Bergman said you're giving me a month. If you keep defying everything I ask of you, this is going to be a hell of a long month." Shane never broke eye contact as she spoke.

"I don't need to be babysat, and I damn sure don't need to be told what to do," Haley sneered.

"I'm sorry if I made it sound like I was telling you what to do. How about we start over? I'm here to keep you safe and find out who is threatening you before he makes good on his promise to attack you."

"You don't even know me!" Haley growled.

19

Shane raised her voice. "You're right, I don't!"

"Then why? Why the hell do you care about some guy sending me hate mail? Why do you want to protect me so badly?"

Shane closed her eyes. *I have no idea.* When she opened her eyes, she simply said, "Because it's my job."

Silence filled the bus like a thick morning fog. Shane stared at the floor. She couldn't trust herself to look into the eyes burning a hole through her. *I can't even stand this headstrong pain in the ass. Maybe I should just call Dennis and tell him to fuck off. She's straight anyway, that makes it even more of a bore to babysit her.* Shane was lost in thought when her two-way crackled to life on her belt. Haley saw the gun strapped in a shoulder holster resting under her right arm when she lifted the side of her suit jacket to grab the radio.

"You carry a gun?" Haley gasped.

Shane furrowed her eyebrows in question, then nodded as she keyed the radio.

"Ms. Crowley, we'll be ready for Haley in five minutes."

"Ten-four."

"Ready for me? What the hell? Who is that?" Haley snapped as she stood.

Shane stood a foot away. "Calm down. That's one of your road crew letting me know that the backstage security checks will clear in five minutes and you can safely walk through."

"I really do not like this."

"Haley, it's not for you to like. Just cooperate with me and with any luck, I'll catch this bastard and be out of your hair soon." Shane checked her watch. "Are you ready?" She swallowed loudly as she ran her eyes from

Haley's scuffed boots, to the tight threadbare jeans, and across the thin black tank top barely covering her torso and perky round breasts. She shivered when their eyes met.

"I'm fine. Let's go," Haley huffed as she stomped passed Shane and shuffled down the stairs of the bus.

Shane was right on her heels and slightly to her left, scanning the tops of the buses and semi-trailers, as well as the rooftop of the building just before they entered. She wasn't touching Haley, but she swore she could feel the heat coming from the feisty, petite woman. As soon as they were safely under the stage with the crew, Shane tucked the radio earpiece into her right ear. She then stepped up onto the side of the stage behind the side curtain so she could scan across the crowd and keep an eye on Haley.

A minute later, the crowd roared as the moan of an electric guitar echoed around the arena. Shane watched the drummer start his slow staccato as the base and lead guitars joined in behind him. Soon after, she heard Haley's bluesy, smoky voice, slowly draw out the words to her chart-topping song. The stage opened, and she rose up on the platform from the floor with the microphone in her hand and her guitar behind her back. When the floor closed, she snapped the mike into the stand and slung her guitar around to strum the chords of the chorus and pick the song up to its faster pace.

Shane felt her foot tapping to the beat. Her eyes glued to the back of Haley as she ran up and down the stage, playing her guitar like a begging lover in need of release. Her singing voice reminded Shane of a country drawl version of Janice Joplin, although it was a little more blues and smoky, and definitely sexy as hell. Haley Nielsen's country music was unlike any country music she'd ever heard.

***

An hour and a half later, Haley ran down the staircase on the back of the stage. She was full of energy, hooting, hollering, and high-fiving her band members and stagehands. Shane dove off the stage, landing like a gymnastic cat next to her with her eyebrow raised and a cocky grin on her face. Haley rolled her eyes and continued celebrating the great show all the way to the exit doors of the arena.

Shane was taken aback by the enormous crowd outside between the building and bus lot. "Holy shit!" she yelled, grabbing Haley and pulling her tightly against her. She muscled her way through the crowd with two of the road crew guys behind them, keeping the stray hands from grabbing at Haley. "What the fuck was that?" Shane rasped as she slammed the door to the bus. The hired security finally began crowd control and were able to get everyone backed away from the bus lot.

"That's what happens when you rock the roof off the house. The fans go crazy." Haley smiled brightly and flopped down on the couch. "Get used to it. It's like this every night."

"Do me a favor and do not leave this bus," Shane said, then turned back around. "There's a two-way radio on the table over there. If you need to leave for any reason, call for me." She paused to meet blue-green eyes. "Please."

As soon as Shane stepped from the bus, she dialed Rich's number on her cell phone. "When were you going to fill me in on the god damn attack mob outside?" she yelled when he answered.

22

"Ms. Crowley? I'm sorry, I had no idea it would be that bad here. I should have warned you."

"How do you expect me to protect her when you don't give me the full story? We both could have been killed tonight. I'm in charge at the next venue, or I'm out of here." She ended the call and felt like throwing her phone against the side of the bus as she ran a hand through her unruly short curls. She wanted to hit something or shoot someone, but what she really needed was a glass of bourbon on the rocks. She paced around outside of the bus until she felt calm enough to go back inside.

***

Haley was sipping hot tea from a mug when Shane finally boarded the bus again. Gone were her boots and tight jeans. She'd changed into a pair of little, black shorts. A tiny sliver of her smooth skin showed between her tank top and shorts when she raised the cup to her lips. Shane felt sweat run down her back, and it wasn't from the Texas heat. She removed her jacket, placing it on the opposite sofa on her way to the small kitchen area. She rummaged through the liquor side of the cabinet and frowned when she didn't see anything but rum, vodka, and tequila.

"What are you looking for?" Haley asked softly.

"Whiskey. Bourbon to be specific." Shane called over her shoulder and settled for a light beer from the refrigerator.

"Send Rich to the liquor store before we pull out tonight. He owes you, you know."

Shane turned around, pressing her back against the counter as she regarded the woman sitting on the couch with her legs curled underneath her. "Yeah, well, you didn't exactly fill me in on the mob crowd either." She let out a deep breath. "What time do we leave?"

"We usually don't leave until sometime in the morning. It takes the guys two hours to tear down."

"I see."

"Can you take that thing off?" Haley eyed Shane's chest where the shoulder harness connected, holding the gun tucked under her arm. "I'd prefer if you didn't wear it in here."

"I forget it's even there most of the time," Shane said as she walked to the door of the bus and slid the lock closed. She set her beer on the table and grabbed her jacket on her way to her room down the hall.

"How's the driver going to get in?" Haley called out.

"I don't know. I hope he has a key," Shane yelled back as she slid her shoulder harness off and tucked it into the drawer of her small nightstand with the handgun still snapped in place. She then unbuttoned her cuffs and rolled her sleeves back before walking back out to the living area.

Chapter 7

Shane awoke to a loud noise. She shook off the initial disorientation from being in a strange bed. Someone was on the bus yelling, to be exact Haley was yelling and more than likely at someone that didn't deserve the brunt end of her temper.

She pulled on a pair of navy blue chinos and a baby blue button down shirt with the sleeves rolled up on her forearms and slid into her shoulder holster, nonchalantly checking her guns clip before stepping out of her room to see what all the commotion was about.

It was already ten in the morning. She had no idea how she'd slept so late. Then again, it was after three a.m. when she'd heard Haley playing her guitar in the living room. The bus was just taking off towards their next destination. Close to five a.m., she'd heard Haley slam her bedroom door, obviously unhappy with the song she was working on. With that thought, Shane realized she probably only had about four hours of solid sleep. No wonder the loud yelling had woke her. Nevertheless, she shuffled into the living room bright eyed and bushy tailed, as if she'd had ten hours of sleep and a nice hot shower. Neither of which she was privileged to. She still managed to look like a GQ model in the pressed clothes with her short, dark curls, stormy gray eyes and chiseled features. The gun holster under her right arm fit her like it was permanently molded to her body.

"Damn it, Rich. We have been over this a hundred times! I cannot work with her on this bus. If you are so hell bent on keeping her here, then put her somewhere else!"

Haley spat from her seat on the couch. Rich sat on the loveseat directly across from her.

"It's temporary, Haley. You agreed to give it one month."

"Move her in with you then!" she yelled.

He sighed. "You just have to get used to the new arrangement. No one expects uninterrupted bliss here. I'm only asking for a smooth transition. Your safety is my number one concern, and honestly, it should be yours too."

"This is bullshit," Haley growled.

"He's right," Shane said from the entrance to the hallway a few feet away. Neither of them had noticed her presence.

"No one asked you," Haley spat.

"You didn't have to."

"I'm sorry we woke you. Haley is having a little conflict that we are trying to work out," Rich said with apologetic eyes.

Shane poured a cup of coffee from the machine and sat down next to Rich.

"So I hear," Shane replied with a raised eyebrow.

"How was your night?" Rich politely asked.

"It was fine," she answered and turned her eyes to the woman across from her. Haley was wearing impossibly short, cutoff jean shorts and a tight white t-shirt that left nothing to the imagination. Her long unruly blond waves hung forward over her right shoulder.

"What he is saying is true. What does your life mean to you?" Shane sipped from her mug and waited.

"My life is none of your business. You're here to catch some lunatic who is writing me letters."

"Quite the contrary, Ms. Nielsen. I am here to *protect* you. That means your life *is* my business. And my business means a hell of a lot to me."

"Your psychobabble bullshit isn't going to work on me, Shane Crowley." Haley pierced her with fiery blue-green eyes and quickly stormed off the bus. Shane jumped up and ran after her.

"Haley, Haley, Haley!" a guy in a black t-shirt and jeans was running towards her shouting her name from a short distance away. He had his arms around her in a bear hug, picking her up off the ground before she realized what was going on.

Haley screamed and kicked, but he had a very tight grip on her.

"Let her go or I'll spread your head all over the pavement." Shane's deep voice was steady and powerful.

Haley saw the black gun pressed against the side of the man's head.

"Now!" Shane yelled.

He let his arms loose, and Haley fell free, barely catching her feet on the ground. She quickly stumbled away towards Rich who was standing between them and the bus twenty yards away. Shane took a step back with her gun still trained on the stranger's head.

"On the ground! Move it!" she shouted and dove on him as soon as he hit the ground. She snatched his arms back and cuffed him before he could take a full breath. "Get her on the bus Rich, and call the authorities," she said without turning around to see them.

Haley visibly shook as she was rushed back onto the bus. Everything had come about so fast, she wasn't even sure what had actually happened. One minute she was walking, trying to blow off steam and get the stuffy, good-looking bodyguard off her mind, and the next, she was being squeezed and lifted up off the ground. Within a split second, Shane was a foot away, pointing a gun in her direction.

"What the hell was that?" she mumbled, looking at Rich as he handed her a glass of something strong.

"Your letter writer, I believe," he said, sitting down next to her. "Thank God Shane is quick on her feet and knows what the hell she is doing. She may have just saved your life."

"Are you sure it wasn't just a fan?" she asked, sipping the burning liquid.

He shook his head. "I don't think so."

Chapter 8

Shane interrogated the man before the Dallas Police Department arrived and took over the scene. She found out his name was Leroy Marvin, and he had no clue about any letters. He was just a ticket holder for the evening concert. He had decided to go to the venue early in hopes of catching a glimpse of the woman he claimed to be in love with. Shane believed he really was a lovesick hillbilly with a warped version of a celebrity crush. She explained what happened to the police and rode behind them to the station to make sure she got a copy of his prints and arrest record.

***

It was after five p.m. when Shane arrived back at the venue. The early rehearsal and last-minute run-through had both been completed. Haley was eating dinner on the bus when Shane walked in the door. Gray eyes met turquoise ones as Shane strode past her without a word. She put her shoulder holster and gun in the nightstand drawer in her room, and shed her clothes while the shower water warmed up.

Twenty minutes later, Shane was freshly showered and dressed in jeans, a pressed black t-shirt that stretched across her athletic upper body, and Doc Martens. The ever-present shoulder holster clung to her body under her right arm. She was glad she'd packed as many pairs of jeans as she had suits. This job had just taken a major turn for the worse. She was hoping she wouldn't have to get physical, but the rules of the game had changed and she needed to be prepared.

Haley was rinsing her dishes in the sink when Shane walked down the hallway. "I—" she started as Shane walked past her.

"I don't want to hear it," Shane said as she grabbed the two-way radio from the table and clipped it to her belt.

"Was it him?"

"No." Shane spun around and faced her. "The next time you jeopardize your safety because you are rebelling against my protection, I will get on a plane and never look back. Do you understand me? Because the next time…it will be him." Shane grabbed the black windbreaker from the arm of the couch that had SECURITY written across the back in white letters, and walked out the door.

***

Rich was standing next to the stage, talking to the hired security for the night. "Ah, here is our head of security now," he said, seeing Shane appear near the back of the stage, walking the path Haley would take. He watched as she circled the full stage, looking for suspicious packages or objects that were out of place. "I was just filling these guys in on this morning's events," Rich said.

"We need to set up a perimeter around the bus line and the entrance/exit of the building, now. No one goes in or out of the perimeter without my authority." Shane pointed to five members of the rented team. "The rest of you will spread out between the entrance/exit point and the stage." She waited for them to take their posts before she spoke again. "Rich, we have a serious problem."

"I know." He blew out a long breath. "I just don't know how to get a handle on her temper."

"That's not what I'm talking about. This morning her security was breached and her safety was seriously compromised. That could have easily been the letter writer, here to make good on his promise. We need to beef up the hired security into three groups. One should be in a one-hundred-yard perimeter around the bus line and the path to the entrance/exit point. No one comes within one hundred yards of that area. The second group needs to secure the path from the entrance/exit of the building, all the way to the stage by twenty yards on either side, if possible. The third group will surround the stage. These three groups need to be your personal hired security members. The venue security staff can cover the rest of the building. No one gets near her again without my authority, Rich. Never." She stared straight into his brown eyes.

"Not a problem. Our next venue is Little Rock. I will call tonight and step it up to a minimum of twenty-five hired security members. They are usually off-duty or retired police officers."

"Make it thirty."

"I don't know if they have enough people available on such short notice," he rebutted.

"If they don't, then contact the local armed security companies."

"Alright. I'll also call ahead to the rest of the venues and get the ball rolling. After tomorrow, we start traveling further out, so our stops will be sometimes two or three days apart." Rich bit the inside of his cheek. "Has she said anything?"

"No. She tried, but I didn't want to hear her excuse. Her attitude should not have been the cause of today's problem. If we'd had the security perimeter set, then that guy would have never gotten close enough to even notice her."

"That's why I hired you. You know how to outsmart her and keep her safe."

Shane shook her head. "It's not about outsmarting her. I am to blame. I should have known there was no perimeter protection and had it taken care of when I arrived yesterday."

"It was a little hectic yesterday, especially with Haley in full battle mode. We were all a little distracted. It was the first day."

"No excuses, Mr. Bergman. Excuses get people hurt or worse…killed." Shane checked her watch. "I will be in radio contact. I also have my cell with me. Let me know when she is ready," she said, before walking away to continue her rounds of checking all the points of contact.

Chapter 9

Shane watched the show from her position on the side of the stage behind the curtain. Haley was sitting on a stool, singing a soulful ballad about a broken heart. She quickly kicked the stool out of the way and jumped right into her next song, a fast, ass-kicking jam about a cheating lover. Shane smiled and shook her head at the jagged words about finding her man in bed with a bimbo, shooting them both with the shotgun, then driving off with a bottle of tequila in his brand-new four-wheel drive. Haley was an amazing entertainer. The crowd cried at her ballads and stood in their chairs singing along to the fast songs. Her voice alone caused the hair on the back of Shane's neck to stand on end. The petite, hotheaded blond was beautiful and dangerously sexy. Add in the sultry smoky voice and the package became borderline illegal.

Shane's mind wasn't far from the events earlier in the day and she wouldn't let them pass until Haley was safely back on the bus, and they were once again on the road. She silently cursed herself for taking this assignment, especially because they were only ten stops into a fifty-stop tour. She hoped this guy would pop up soon. Haley only promised to cooperate for a month, if her actions could even be called cooperating. Shane had no idea how much worse it would get after a month had gone by, and she had no ambition to hang around for another couple of months until the tour was over.

"Shane?"

She heard her radio crackle. "Go ahead."

"I'm not sure if you have the show schedule down yet, but she wraps in two songs. The next one is the final, but there is a one-minute break and she goes back for the encore."

"I'll be ready," Shane replied, glad Rich had radioed her. She'd only seen one performance and had missed all of the rehearsals and run-throughs so far.

***

The crowd outside was further away than the one from the night before. They weren't in reaching distance, but still way too close for Shane's nerves. She wrapped a protective arm around Haley's small frame and raced her quickly to the bus. Once they were close to the bus Haley pulled away from her.

"You know, at some point I'm going to have to stop and give autographs," Haley growled.

Shane held her tongue and waited for Haley to board the bus. Then, she closed the door and turned back towards Rich.

"Everything okay?" he asked.

"Peachy," Shane replied sarcastically. "Did you happen to take care of my request?"

"No. It was hectic around here once you left with the cops this morning. Why don't you post one of our extra hands with a radio by her bus door and come with me."

"Where to?"

"Relieve some stress." He grinned.

"Huh?"

"Do beautiful, naked ladies offend you?" he asked, hoping he was right.

She raised an eyebrow. "No."

"Good. There is a very upscale place not far from here where we can have a little business meeting. If the buses pull anchor we will catch up to them."

"Sounds like the best thing I've heard in three days. Let me do a sweep of her bus and post a couple guys out here until they are ready to roll."

Fifteen minutes later, Shane met Rich at the waiting SUV. She had checked over the bus while Haley sat on the couch, steaming with a raised eyebrow. She'd also posted three of their extra road crew outside of her bus, one of which was the backup driver for Haley's bus.

"Ready?" he asked.

"Yeah," Shane said, sliding into the backseat. The rented car service quickly pulled away from the arena parking lot.

"Did she say anything?"

"No. Her attitude seems to be back in full swing though. You would think she'd be a little worried about what happened today, but honestly, I don't think it affected her," Shane sighed.

"I'm not sure. She went into her room and didn't come out for a couple of hours. She barely said two words."

Shane sat in silence watching the city lights go by. Minutes later, the car service pulled up to a large building that looked like the Bellagio in Vegas. She was glad she'd changed into a black suit and stowed her gun on the bus.

"Welcome to The Palace," Rich said as he stepped out of the SUV and led her towards the VIP door.

Shane had been to her fair share of entertainment clubs, but this place was like the icing on the cake. The club had three tier levels with a live jazz band. Playboy quality, topless dancers were posted on numerous stages around each level, with a large, main stage for one single performer at a time. Crystal chandeliers and sconces cast diamond shards of light around the open club. Each table had a marble top and was adorned by heavy wooden leather covered chairs.

"What do you think?" Rich asked with a grin.

Shane smiled. "Great place for a business meeting."

They sat at an open table on the second-tier level, close to one of the smaller stages. A beautiful, topless, mocha-skinned waitress greeted them. She gave Shane the once over with a wide smile.

"Would either of you care for a beverage?"

"Shane, you drink whisky, right?" Rich questioned.

"I'm more of a bourbon drinker than single malt."

Rich turned towards the beautiful young woman with the perky breasts. "A couple glasses of ice and a bottle of Jameson Limited Reserve." When she smiled and walked away, Rich turned back to Shane. "Wait until you give this a try."

Rich noticed many of the women watching Shane, who was oblivious to the attention. "I've only been to this place one other time, about five years ago. Haley was still fairly new and opening for one of country music's superstars. His manager brought me here."

"It's a very nice place. I'm not a frequent strip club patron, but I have been to my fair share." She grinned.

"What was the story on our man-handler today?" he asked.

"Not a whole lot. Leroy Marvin is a fan with a crush, I'm afraid. He swore he knew nothing about any letters and even gave us his fingerprints without hesitation. I'm pretty sure it wasn't him. The guy we are looking for is not currently a fan, and not lovesick either. He's more of a loner. He could be married, or perhaps single, but he has what he believes to be deep values and ethics. Haley has somewhat come out of her music shell, and her songs have gradually changed to a style that is more original, and this guy doesn't like the turn her sound has taken." Shane paused for the waitress to deliver their drink order. Two dancers stood behind her waiting to offer services to the table while never taking their eyes off Shane. She smiled and politely refused.

"I see what you're saying," Rich said as he opened the bottle and poured the liquor into their glasses.

"Wow," Shane murmured.

"You like it?"

"It's good, smooth." She smiled. "Not what I was expecting at all," she said, taking another sip.

Rich grinned and took a long swallow of his own glass. "This is very different from traditional Jameson. It's actually a three whisky blend that's aged in bourbon barrels."

"I like the mix of vanilla and almond with the charred wood from the barrels. It has a nice taste," she said, taking another long swallow.

"Do you think there will be more letters?" he asked.

Shane nodded. "I'm sure our letter writer will contact her again. He's unhappy with her, and he wants her to know it."

"What's your plan?" Rich asked.

Shane took another sip and sat back in her chair. She glanced at the sultry brunette moving seductively on the stage close to their table. "At the moment, I am waiting on his next move. I don't think he is ready for real contact, but I'm not letting my guard down either. My plan is to stay close and watch everything around her while she is vulnerable to danger of any kind." Shane took another sip.

"Mr. Bergman, catching a stalker is like playing chess. One of you always has a hand up on the other during the match, until the other player figures out your next move and blocks you."

"Hmm…are you a religious person, Shane?"

"Not really. Why?"

"Just curious. Philosophy major maybe?"

Shane laughed. "Hardly. I am merely an investigator. Criminal intelligence and profiling skills generally come with the territory."

"Why did you leave the U.S. Marshals?"

Nice try. Shane finished her drink. "I'm afraid that's too long of a story for this business meeting." She smiled politely. "Let's just say I needed a change."

Chapter 10

Haley set her guitar next to her on the couch when she felt the bus come to a stop. She'd been trying once again to work on a new song, but the lyrics just wouldn't come to her. She couldn't clear her mind long enough to let them.

A minute later, Shane appeared in the doorway, stumbling onto the bus just after three a.m. She knew she should have stopped after the third glass, but the whisky was good and went down like water. Besides, with all of the bullshit she had to deal with recently, she deserved a few hours full of liquor and sexy women.

To Haley, she looked professionally...drunk. "What are you doing here?" she snapped.

"Huh?" Shane hadn't noticed Haley sitting on the couch, until she was standing inches away. She gave Haley a very long seductive once over and grinned.

Haley raised an eyebrow and backed up a step. "Damn it, I thought maybe you'd quit or at least got moved to another bus."

"Nope."

"Ugh!" She rolled her eyes and growled. "You reek of alcohol and smoke." She realized the spot on the collar of Shane's shirt was actually make-up. "Where the hell have you been?"

Shane was not in the mood to go another round with 'Miss Attitude'. "I don't have to answer to you," she said as she stepped past her and walked down the hallway.

"Then don't expect me to answer to you either. I don't need your fucking services, and I damn sure don't want you sharing my living quarters if you're out all night getting drunk with some floozy while you're being paid to *protect* me!" Haley yelled to her retreating back as she followed her down the hall.

Shane spun on her heels and Haley ran into her. She bounced off the tall, solid body and backed up a step to look up into the fiery, smoky gray eyes staring down at her. "First of all…" Shane's voice was low and deep. "I made sure you were safe before I left. My *job* is your safety. If you think I am not needed then take a real hard look at what happened twelve hours ago." Haley opened her mouth to argue but Shane kept talking. "As far as tonight goes, I went out with Rich Bergman for a meeting. What happened at that meeting is none of your business." Shane stepped closer to the blond. "If you ever accuse me of *not* doing my job again, I *will* quit, and you can let some ten dollar an hour rental cop protect you." Shane walked into her room and slammed the door shut.

Haley stomped back to the couch, fuming with anger. She was furious with Rich, and seriously contemplating firing him in the morning. Still, her mind wandered back to Shane's smoldering eyes. She swore she could feel them caressing her body as Shane eyed her slowly from head to toe. *I know I didn't imagine that. Damn you. Get out of my head!*

Chapter 11

Shane was sitting at the dinette table drinking coffee, when her cell phone rang. She looked at the caller ID and smiled.

"Hey sweetheart," Dennis said when she answered. "How's it going?"

"Wonderfully. Couldn't be any better. It's good to hear from you sweet cheeks."

He laughed. "That bad, huh?"

"Oh, honey, you have no idea. None whatsoever. Trust me," she replied sarcastically with a huge fake smile on her face.

"Can you talk?" he asked seriously.

Shane was sure Haley was still asleep. She hoped she wasn't stupid enough to leave the bus alone. But, she didn't want to be overheard talking about the case. "No not really."

"Okay. I'll let you know when I get the package you sent. I should have the CODIS and NCIC results by the end of the day if FedEx arrives on time." He was waiting on the fingerprints and bio information on Leroy Marvin, as well as all of the original letters.

"That's fine. I'll wait to hear from you then." She hung up just as Haley stepped into the kitchen.

"Good morning," Shane said, looking at her back.

Haley poured honey into her hot tea and turned around with a raised eyebrow. "What's good about it?" she huffed and padded over to the couch.

"I don't know. The sun is shining, you're alive…" Shane shrugged sarcastically. She was still pissed at Haley for the ungrateful attitude the night before.

"Yeah, well, what you call good…I see as miserable. What is good about getting nothing done? For the past two nights, I have tried to work and I get nothing…absolutely nothing…done with you around," she growled and sipped her tea.

"I plan to be out of your way soon, until then, we need to cooperate with each other." Shane finished her coffee and checked her watch. "I'm meeting with Rich in a few minutes. Are you planning on leaving the bus anytime soon?"

Haley rolled her eyes and let out a deep breath. "Oh great, I can only imagine what today's meeting will accomplish compared to last nights." When Shane didn't take the bait she said, "No, not until the noon run through."

"That's fine. Make sure you—"

"I know. I know. Call you before I leave. Damn it, I am so sick of being babysat. Tell Rich to get his ass over here when he is through with your little meeting," she spat and snatched up her guitar.

***

Shane hit speed dial on her cell phone when she stepped off the bus. She had twenty minutes before her meeting with Rich inside the venue building.

"What do I owe the pleasure?" Dennis joked as he answered.

"Hey. I'm free to talk."

"What's your honest opinion of this Leroy Marvin?"

"It's not him. Too easy. No, the guy we want is not looking to marry her and have babies. He's angry with her. He disagrees with her choices and wants her to come to his side of thinking."

"Yeah. How's she taking it?"

Shane laughed sarcastically. "Dennis you have no idea. You've seen the picture, which does her no justice by the way. She's hotter than a fire poker, with the razor-sharp claws of a bobcat in heat."

"Wow," he laughed.

"She's the most self-centered, egotistical bitch that I have ever met."

"Tell me how you really feel," he said, still laughing.

"Man, I am not kidding. She's flat out mean. Oh, and to top it all off, she doesn't want me around, doesn't want protection, and rebels anything and everything I tell her or even simply ask of her. She talks to her manager like he's a piece of shit. Hell, she attacks me every chance she gets too."

"She looks so sweet and innocent in her photo, and her music isn't half bad."

"Ha! Try living with her."

"What?"

"You heard me pal. We're cohabitating."

"Just the two of you?"

"You got it."

He laughed again. "No wonder this is so difficult. I figured you would be somewhere else I guess."

"Yeah, me too. It's like living with a rattlesnake." Shane paced outside of the venue building with her eyes on the bus line in case Haley decided to bolt again. "You know, to a certain extent, I understand why she is upset. I mean, she's used to her space and having the utmost authority over anything and everything, including her life. Then, I come in and turn the entire show upside down. She chewed me out this morning because she can't get any work done with me on the bus."

"What kind of work?" he asked.

"She stays up late at night writing songs. I've heard her playing her guitar every night. Apparently, my mere presence is a problem. I don't know. I'm not a musician or artist. I don't know how that shit works. All I know is, I'm being paid to protect her and all she does is pitch a fit and do whatever the fuck she wants."

"Sounds stressful. No one ever *enjoys* having a bodyguard, but I've never heard of someone rebelling so much. You would think with everything that happened yesterday she'd change her tone a little bit and be at least somewhat thankful you were there. Even though he isn't your guy, he still could have easily hurt her."

"Exactly. She hasn't said a word about it. She's extremely ungrateful." Shane ran a hand through her short locks. "I can guarantee you, this is one of the most focused assignments I will ever be on. I am ready to catch this guy and get the hell away from here."

Chapter 12

Haley sat on the edge of the stage, strumming her guitar and humming along to the melody. No one else was in the arena. She had finally found a place to be completely alone. She stopped every couple of notes to write on a plain white piece of paper lying next to her. She wasn't known for ballads. Slow songs took too long to write, too long to sing, and they brought her down from the high she rode during her performances. She was a wild child and that's what made her famous. The kick ass and take names motif, and the lyrics that pushed the limits were what people knew her for, which was why she was wondering what the hell she was doing sitting there writing a heart wrenching love song. She didn't even know what love was, she'd never been in it. She'd only experienced the bullshit that goes with corrupt relationships and one-night stands that fueled her hit songs. She strummed a few more bars and added another line of lyrics as they came to her in her head.

"I always remember the passion, we share at night in my dreams. But like any good love affair, it ends when a new day begins," she sang softly, feeling the words as her fingers picked the strings of her guitar.

***

Shane sat in the upper deck of the arena with her feet up on the seat in front of her. She'd already been in the arena doing a security walk-through, when she got word that Haley was ready to leave the bus early. Shane had allowed one of the security members to walk her inside. She quickly took a seat and watched as the fiery blond sat on the edge of the stage, strumming on her guitar. She couldn't hear the words she was singing, and barely heard the echo of the beautiful melody in the huge arena because the guitar wasn't plugged into an amp. However, Haley looked like she'd finally found the peace she was cursing Shane for taking from her. Shane wondered what inspired an artist like her, someone who walked the fine line between wild and reckless.

An hour later, Shane's phone vibrated in her pocket. She was far enough away that Haley wouldn't hear her so she picked it up.

"I'm assuming you're with her," Rich said.

"Sort of. What's up?"

"The last time I saw her, she had her claws out and one of the security guys informed me that he escorted her inside on your orders, but left her alone."

"She doesn't know I'm in here with her."

"Oh, really. Boy is she gonna be pissed when she finds out."

"I don't plan on telling her. I think she's finally working on her music, and there is no need to disturb her."

Rich checked his watch. "The band should be there in half an hour to do the run through."

"When they come in, I'll make an appearance. I've already pissed her off today, so I plan on keeping my distance until the show."

"You pissed her off? Shit, you should have seen the verbal ass whipping she gave me this morning for keeping you out all night and bringing you back drunk with 'whore' perfume and make-up on your clothes. I honestly thought she was going to fire me for real this time. She's threatened before, but I don't think I've ever seen her that mad. So, as you can see, I'm avoiding her too."

Shane laughed. "This is going to be a very long month."

"Just think, we're barely one week into it."

"I can only imagine what the next three will be like," she said before hanging up.

Chapter 13

Haley's smoky voice filled the arena as she belted out the words to one of her hit songs, while her fingers flew up and down the strings of her guitar as if they were on fire. The band behind her chimed in on the background vocals of the chorus. Shane felt the hair on the back of her neck stand up as she watched Haley in her element. Her long, wild, curly hair hanging over one shoulder, paired with the low-slung, tight-fitting jeans that had threadbare holes, and the tight black tank top covering her torso and inching up enough to reveal the velvety smooth skin of her abdomen, only encouraged the hormones racing through Shane's body. She turned away from the stage as the band continued practicing. *Lord have mercy.* She thought as she walked away. She couldn't help her attraction to Haley. She might be the meanest, most ungrateful person Shane had ever met, but the young woman was the poster child for sex appeal. She was hot enough to melt the soles of your boots if you got too close.

Shane stretched her back and wiped the sweat from her brow.

"Radio or call me when she's ready to go back to the bus," she said to Rich as she walked by him on the floor of the arena.

***

Shane was asleep on the couch in the bus when Haley returned. She startled awake when she heard the door slam and looked up to see blue-green eyes staring daggers at her. She sat up quickly.

"Wow, so this is what you're doing while you're being paid to protect me," Haley said loudly. "It's not enough that you stay out all night with whores, but then you sleep on the fucking bus all day."

"I haven't been lying here sleeping all day. I just got back here less than an hour ago. I must have dozed off. As for last night, I thought we were passed that?"

"I haven't seen you all day. Aren't you supposed to be up my ass as my brave protector?"

"I thought I was getting in your way? I tried to give you some space, and now you're giving me shit for that too? What is your problem with me, because it's obviously me and not just the situation?" Shane countered.

"You're right, you are the problem. I don't want you here, and I don't need you here. Then, you're not even where you should be, so tell me what the fuck I am paying you for?"

Shane stood up from the couch, stretching to her full height over the smaller woman. "First of all, I told you I wasn't in here sleeping all afternoon. As a matter of fact, I gave the order for you to be escorted to the arena by security. I sat in section three-twenty on the upper level and watched you for hours while you worked on your music. Then, I gave the order for you to be escorted to the bus and back again for your run through. So, don't say I'm not doing my job. I've been less than a hundred yards from you the entire day and you had no idea. I did it to give you some space, so you would quit screaming at me constantly and blaming me for everything. I see that backfired in my face, so expect me to be as you put it, up your ass again." Shane spun on her heels and left the bus before Haley could reply with what was probably another round of yelling expletives at her.

***

"Damn you. You make me crazy!" Haley spat as she flopped down on the couch, alone. The cushions were still warm where Shane had been lying asleep, and the scent of her light balsam and citrus cologne lingered in the air, making Haley's senses tingle. "This is never going to work," she sighed, wishing she could clear her mind and work. Her concentration had been broken since the moment she'd found out about the whole bodyguard situation. She hated being told what to do, and felt like she was being treated like a child. She was a rebel who had spent her entire career fighting to get to the top, fighting to stay at the top, and fighting against the naysayers who told her she would never make it with her music and her sound. She never conformed for anyone, making it all the way to the top on her own. Now, it seemed like conforming was all she was doing lately...except when she was on the stage. That was something no one would ever be able to take away from her. It was the one place she always had complete control. Walking the line was all new to her, and she didn't care for it at all. She wondered if it was the whole concept, or the person behind it, causing her more frustration.

***

Shane walked the perimeter twice, checked the holding area under the stage a handful of times, and paced outside of the bus on the path leading to the arena entrance. She was hungry, tired, and needed to change her clothes, but there was no way she was getting back on that bus. She never noticed Haley watching from the slightly open curtain. She finally decided to go get a chilidog from one of the vendors preparing for the arrival of the concert patrons. She would most definitely have heartburn within an hour, but that had to be better than the headache she'd get if she stepped foot on that bus any time soon. The doors to the arena were opening in a handful of minutes and Haley was set to take the stage in one hour. She was probably getting into her character, or whatever she did before a show, and Shane didn't dare mess with that routine.

"Did I just see you with a hotdog?" Rich said to Shane when he saw her step out of the shadows between the buses.

"Yes. I was about to starve to death."

"I sent a big spread to Haley's bus an hour ago for the whole band, with you included of course."

"Yeah, well, she and I aren't speaking at the moment, so I am better off with a hotdog for dinner."

"She'll come around…eventually." He smiled.

"Yeah, when I leave." Shane smirked. "If I may be blunt, maybe she needs to get laid."

Rich laughed so hard he almost choked. "She's very secretive about that subject, and until we had this situation where she needed a bodyguard, I couldn't tell you what happened behind the closed doors of her bus or with whom. She's no saint, that's for sure, but I don't really get into that part of her personal space."

Shane nodded her head. "Maybe you should." She grinned. "Send her a stripper, or better yet, a whole pack of male dancers."

"I would definitely be fired," he laughed.

"She might actually get that sharp stick out of her ass," Shane said just before her radio crackled to life.

51

"I'm walking off this bus in five minutes," Haley growled.

Shane looked at Rich. "I guess I'm being summoned."

Chapter 14

Shane wasn't surprised to see the mob of people outside waiting for Haley's autograph as they walked towards the waiting bus line. Haley's show was downright ferocious with crazy pyrotechnics and her signature rowdy vocals. Hundreds of people were screaming her name and reaching for her as Shane shuffled her away.

"I need to sign some autographs," Haley said as she began to pull away.

"It's not safe out here, you're in the wide open," Shane replied.

"Nothing is going to happen if I sign my name a few times. Give me a break. Besides, I haven't gotten a letter in almost a month." Haley pushed away from her security detail and walked over to the group of cheering fans.

Shane shook her head and stormed after her, making sure to stand next to Haley, scanning the crowd for suspicious male figures while she signed autographs. Shane actually wished Leroy had been their letter writer so she could go on with her life and leave this hellfire to her own runaway train she called a life, but after the call she'd received earlier in the night, she'd be stuck there a while longer. Leroy Marvin had nothing more than a few speeding tickets on his record in the last ten years. He wasn't their guy. Shane knew it was an extremely long shot, but she could leave no stone unturned when it came to threats on someone's life.

"That wasn't so bad was it?" Haley snickered, feeling a little less constrained as she walked past her towards the waiting bus.

Shane wanted to smack some sense into her when they stepped onto the bus; she settled for slamming the door closed instead. She went straight to her stateroom without looking back and quickly shed the jacket she'd been wearing to cover her handgun. She put the gun and shoulder harness in the nightstand drawer and kicked her shoes off. She was so used to working in suits that she actually felt uncomfortable in jeans and a windbreaker.

After splashing water on her face, Shane checked her watch and decided she really wanted a glass of something strong, but Haley was more than likely sitting on the couch and still wound up from the show. It usually took her hours to unwind, which was why she always stayed up working on new music, at least, until Shane came along and invaded her space. She decided two drinks would do, one to calm her nerves and one to deal with Haley and her attitude. It would be at least another hour before the buses pulled anchor.

***

Haley had changed from her jeans and boots to short, cotton shorts and bare feet. She sat on the couch with her legs stretched out and her guitar in her lap strumming a light melody that was similar to the one Shane had heard her playing when she thought she was alone earlier that afternoon.

Shane stood at the edge of hallway, watching as she flung her wild blond curls over her shoulder. The innocent gesture made her smile. There was no denying the fact that she was attracted to Haley. The woman was beautiful…but she was like gasoline on an open fire. Shane had no doubt Haley would rock her world and leave her with a broken heart. If she wasn't such a huge pain in the ass, she might actually think twice about going a round or two with her between the sheets. Shane adjusted her position to try and relieve the pressure building between her legs, but the slight noise was just enough to grab Haley's attention. To Shane that was like waking a sleeping dragon.

"Sneaking up on me will get you nowhere quick," Haley said without looking up.

Shane stepped into the small living room area and sat on the couch across from her. "I wasn't sneaking up on you."

"You were watching me."

"I was listening to you play," Shane countered.

Haley shrugged. "Same thing."

"He's still out there. The guy we apprehended barely has a speeding ticket on his record. I'm almost certain it wasn't him." Shane spoke without enthusiasm. Her voice sounded very plain and to the point, mostly because she was tired. Tired of babysitting a grown woman, tired of being treated like a piece of shit, just plain tired.

Haley set her guitar down and raised her eyes to the woman across from her. Shane's dark hair had gotten slightly longer and her gray eyes looked haunted. Haley was angry at herself for finding the reserved woman attractive. She'd been on her mind since the moment they'd met. She didn't want to think about her, dream about her, want her. She hated the situation, and the mere presence of this woman was making her nuts. She reached for the empty glass that had been full of vodka and juice at one point. Frustrated, she turned her eyes back to Shane, only to be met by a questioning gray gaze. She swallowed the lump growing in her throat and stared into those eyes for what seemed like minutes. Finally, she got up and refilled her glass and snatched her guitar off the couch. "You make me so," she mumbled in frustration. "Never mind," she sighed heavily as she walked away.

Shane shrugged, watching her back as she retreated. The short, cotton shorts barely covered the tight little ass under them. Shane wanted to bang her head on the wall. She had to catch this guy and soon before she either had a nervous breakdown or worse, a sexually charged meltdown. She needed to get out of this stuffy environment and wished she could take a weekend to go home and hit the town. A night of dancing in her favorite bar, followed by a romp in the sheets with a hot body, would clear her head.

Chapter 15

A few days later, Shane was busy reading the security checks and walking the perimeter at their latest stop on the tour. No one had bothered to alert her when a flower box had been delivered for Haley, until it was too late and she heard Haley screaming her name into the radio. Shane ran towards the bus in a full sprint.

"What happened?" Shane said as she stormed onto the bus.

Haley and Rich were sitting at the dinette table across from the galley. Haley had dried tear lines on her face and a blank look in her eyes. Rich slid a card towards the edge of the table.

Take a long hard look at the flowers in this box. They were once beautiful like you, now they're dead, and soon...you will be too.

Shane was careful not to touch the note. She peered into the box full of two dozen wilted roses. She had a feeling this would happen sooner or later. He wanted to let her know he was still out there, still watching, still waiting. Shane put her hands in her pockets and took a step back.

"I'm sorry, Haley. I can't say I didn't warn you. This guy is a lot more than the crazed fan you all think he is. I'm not here to play games. My job is to protect you when he decides to make good on his promise." She turned to walk away and looked back over her shoulder. "Rich, seal all of that in an evidence bag; the flowers, box, card, everything and ship it to the same address you sent the other letters to. Try not to touch it without gloves."

"Really, Rich? I just got a box of dead flowers and a letter saying I'm going to be dead and she just walks away? What the fuck?" Haley yelled when Shane stepped off the bus.

"What do you expect, Haley? It's not like she's going to sit here and let you cry on her shoulder. She has a job to do, and as far as I'm concerned, she's damn good at it."

"Oh, if she's so fucking good, then why did I get these?"

"That's probably what she's addressing right now. I have a feeling she will be hiring a whole new security staff for tonight," he said.

"That's not good enough, Rich," she huffed as she stormed to her room and slammed the door.

***

Shane was sitting in the front row across from the stage with her head in her hands when Rich caught up to her. She looked up, hearing the approaching footsteps.

"How is she?" Shane asked.

"Pissed and upset."

"I fired the security agency and hired a dozen off duty cops for tonight."

Rich sat in the chair next to her and grinned. "It's not your fault."

"No. I never said it was. Still, when we have to 'rent' security at every venue, it can be dangerous. You never know when someone will slip something past me because they don't understand the seriousness of the situation, or better yet, one day he could be hired as a security guard and we would never know it."

"Maybe he made a mistake this time."

Shane looked at him. "I doubt it. He's smart and he's getting brave. He will make his move soon." She sighed and stretched her legs. "Do you play chess, Rich?"

"No, not really."

"Well, in the game of chess you have multiple pieces that move in very different ways, but they all have one common goal, checkmate. Stalker killer minds operate like a chess game. They make different moves, each one a little bolder than the last until they get close and see an opening, then...checkmate."

"Do you think he will try to kill her?" Rich wiped the sweat from his brow.

"There is no doubt he will try. He won't succeed, that's what I'm here for. The question is...when." She stood and turned towards Rich. "He may have just found an opening with his latest move."

***

Haley slid her feet into the scuffed, pointed toe boots she always wore on stage and added a small, black, leather vest that she kept open over her tight white tank top. When she walked into the living room area, Shane was sitting on the couch talking on the phone. Haley had no idea she was back aboard the bus. She took a second to look at the woman a few feet away. She was wearing loose fitting jeans, Doc Marten shoes, and a black t-shirt with her shoulder holster pulling it tightly over her small breasts. Her gun was tucked under her right arm.

"I'm ready when you are," Shane said, hanging up the phone and slipping on the black, short-sleeved dress shirt she'd started wearing to cover her gun instead of the windbreaker that had been causing her to sweat to death.

Haley liked this look better, but wouldn't give her the satisfaction of letting her know that. At least she'd stopped wearing the stuffy suits that made her look like a secret service agent. Her heartbeat sped up when she smelled the familiar floral and spice scent that lingered when Shane stepped in front of her and led them off the bus. Haley walked next to her, close enough to rub arms as they walked. Once she was secure under the stage, Shane took her post up on the edge of the stage where she could watch the crowd from all angles.

At the first strum of her guitar the crowd went wild. Haley's elevator hadn't moved yet to lift her to the center of the stage, and the sold-out building was already rocking. The fireworks went off as she appeared, already a few bars into one of her hit songs. Her long blonde hair hung loosely in wild waves that slung back and forth as she played her guitar. Feeding off the energy of the crowd, she belted out the lyrics like she was six feet tall. Her sexy smoky voice was light and cute with a southern twang when she talked, but it was a smoky blues sound when she sang. The drastic difference made her unique. She was a totally different person when she was on that stage.

Shane watched the people in the first row reaching as far as they could, trying desperately to touch her, even if only for a split second. There was no way that would happen. She'd made sure there was three feet between the crowd and the edge of the stage. She laughed out loud, wondering what these people would think if they knew how mean Haley really was.

***

A few songs later, Haley slowed things down. Sitting on a stool in the center of the stage alone, she picked her guitar and sang from someplace deep inside where Shane was sure no one else was allowed to go. The gentle melody rolled off her tongue like butter, capturing the hearts of everyone around her.

Shane leaned against one of the stage pillars, watching her intently. The vulnerability she heard in her voice as she sang made Shane want to hold her close and never let go. *I could listen to that voice whispering in my ear all night long.* Taking a deep breath, she pulled her eyes away from Haley's grasp and moved to another area to scan the crowd.

As she finished the song, Haley turned and looked towards the side of the stage where Shane had been standing, before rushing into another fast song full of wild and reckless abandon. The people in the crowd stood on their feet, singing along at the tops of their lungs as Haley ran around the stage, spouting razor sharp lyrics like a spitfire.

"One minute she's the sweetheart of country music, the next she's a rock n' rolling rebel, burning up the stage," Rich said.

Shane turned to see him standing close by. "Yeah," she muttered in agreement.

***

When the show ended, Shane fell in step next to Haley as she came off the back of the stage and maneuvered through the arena tunnel system that led outside.

"Great show," Shane said as her eyes scanned all around.

"I didn't think you saw it," Haley said, sounding slightly sarcastic.

Shane grabbed her hand and stopped her. "Just because you don't see me doesn't mean I'm not there. I was less than a hundred feet away from you for the entire show."

Already hyped up from the buzz of the show, Haley looked up into the gray eyes staring down at her. Gone were the snappy comebacks as blood raced through her veins. She felt herself leaning closer to the moist lips beckoning her...just before Rich rushed up and wrapped his arm around her, pulling her away.

"Fantastic show!" he said. "The roof nearly blew off this place!"

Shane walked along behind them. She wasn't sure, but her body told her Haley had been about to kiss her. Which only twisted her even further. She had no time to analyze what that even meant as the sound of the screaming crowd outside grew louder. She cringed knowing it would be a nightmare getting Haley to the bus.

The rented security guards were doing the best they could to hold back the hundred or so people who had decided to wait for an autograph near the bus area, but the people were pushing and shoving, cheering Haley's name.

"I have to sign autographs," she said.

"Two minutes," Shane replied, moving in front of her before the doors swung open.

Haley sauntered over with a huge smile on her face. "Did you guys like the show?"

"Haley, we love you!" one person yelled.

"I love you guys, too!" she laughed.

Shane stood right beside her as she took selfie after selfie and signed her name on everything from pictures and CD cases to t-shirts and human skin. Once two minutes had passed, she wrapped her arm around Haley's shoulders. "We have to go," she whispered, pulling her away.

Haley gritted her teeth, but smiled brightly at her fans. "I gotta go, folks! I hope you all enjoyed our show!"

Shane ushered her away with two security people following behind them. Haley turned around, waving at the crowd as she boarded the bus. The doors closed behind her and Shane went back to manning the security detail who was trying to get the people to leave. The buses wouldn't be pulling out for a few more hours, and they didn't need obsessive fans lingering about.

She never saw Rich walk by behind her and board Haley's bus.

Chapter 16

"You weren't up for any awards because your album just came out and your tour just started. I hadn't expected you to attend," he said. "However, it's an honor to get asked to perform."

Haley sat across from him on the sofa in the small living area, shaking her head.

"It's Country Music Television, Haley."

"I know that, but do you think it's a great idea to detour the entire entourage for a last-minute performance at the CMT awards because another act pulled out? They didn't invite us to perform in the first place. That chaps my ass enough, but to be their backup…" she shook her head. "I won't do it."

"I don't think you were the backup plan. I believe they've been trying to reach me, but with us out on tour, it's been hectic."

"That's bullshit, Rich. And you and I both know it," she growled.

"They've also asked you to present," he said carefully, waiting for the blowback.

Haley laughed. "You're kidding me?"

"Uh…no. No. They want you to present best newcomer with Tucker Miller."

"Wonderful. Country music already has rumors going around that we are an item. Why not force us to present together at the awards?"

"I need to get an answer to them now because I have to book you, along with the band, and Shane on a flight out—"

"Excuse me?" Shane said. Neither of them had heard the door open during their heated conversation. "We're flying somewhere?"

"The CMT awards tomorrow night. Haley's been asked to perform and present an award. Obviously, you'll need to be with her."

"Okay...why are we just now hearing about this?" she asked, leaning against the kitchen counter, sipping a bottle of water from the fridge.

"Because I'm the sloppy seconds," Haley grumbled. "We're not going, so don't worry about freaking out over security."

"Haley, I think that's a bad idea. You should go and promote the new album and the tour," Rich countered. "It doesn't have to be a huge production. Play the new single. It's slower, and you'll only need guitars if you do it acoustically. You'll arrive late and miss the red carpet, so that won't be an issue," he added, looking at Shane.

"I can deal with that," she said.

"You've also been asked to collaborate with three or four other artists to sing some of Calvin Baldwin's music. He's being inducted into the Country Music Hall of Fame this year and they are doing a tribute to him."

Haley peeked through the curtains at the dark parking lot. The mass of fans was long gone and the buses were awaiting Rich's word to hit the road. "Fine, but I'm not changing my music. We'll need a drum set for Vince, and a keyboard for Eddie. Joey, Stiles, and I will travel with our guitars."

"I'll get it done," Rich said, jumping up quickly and getting off the bus so they could head out.

"This is going to be a shit show," Haley said as the door closed behind Rich. The bus rocked as it began rolling down the road. She grabbed her cell phone and called one of her band members. "Put me on speaker," she said when he answered.

Shane walked down the hall to her room, giving Haley some space to talk with her band about the sudden change of plans. She dialed Dennis's number and sat down on her bed with her back against the wall.

"Hey, stranger!" he answered. "You're still alive, and more importantly, still working, so I guess you figured out how to live with a rattler!"

"Funny. I'm headed to Nashville, so I'm getting closer to home."

"I thought the tour was mid-west?"

"We were in Austin, Texas tonight. I believe the next venue is in Oklahoma. We're working our way north."

"Why are you going to Nashville, then?"

"She's performing and presenting at the CMT awards," Shane said.

"Have things gotten any easier?"

"I wouldn't say that. A little better, maybe. I'm no closer to figuring out who is doing this than when I arrived. I hate to say it, but I hope he strikes again. That may be my only chance in catching him."

"I agree."

"She's a last-minute addition to the show, which she's extremely pissed about, but it's a good thing. He won't know she's there until it starts."

"Are you hungry? We're stopping at some barbecue joint," Haley called, knocking on Shane's door.

"Dennis, let me go. I'll call you in a few days." Shane hung up the phone and walked out of her room. She was still wearing her jeans and tight black t-shirt, but her shoulder holster and gun were gone, as were her shoes.

Haley eyed her up and down as her mind drifted back to their almost kiss in the tunnel of the arena. *You make me crazy. I can't believe I almost kissed you. Hell, maybe I should sleep with you. Then, I might be able to get some work done.*

"Everything okay?" Shane asked, watching her eyes.

Unable to find her voice, Haley simply nodded.

Shane felt the bus roll to a stop and quickly turned her head down the hall towards the living area.

"Dinner," Haley said, clearing her throat as she walked away.

"This can't be a good idea," Shane mumbled, slipping her Doc Martens on and grabbing her shoulder holster with her gun.

"Where are you going?" Haley asked as Shane rushed towards the door.

"I need to make sure this place is secure before you get off this bus."

Haley laughed. "Calm down Robo Cop. No one is getting off the bus."

"Huh?"

"Either Rich or one of the road crew will bring out menus. Everyone writes down what they want, then they place the order. Once it's ready, they bring it to us and we head out."

"What about the drivers?"

"I assume they eat while we are waiting, that way they are finished and ready to go. This is the fourth or fifth time we've done this, so don't freak out and change everything. The system works fine as it is."

A knock on the bus door got Shane's attention just as she was about to sit down. She walked over, grabbing the menu from one of the drivers who was distributing them. Haley was already ready with a piece of paper and a pen when she turned around.

They each perused both pages and wrote down a meal with sides. Shane wondered if they would actually sit at the dinette table and break bread together. So far, they'd managed to eat at completely different times.

***

While they waited for their food, Haley sat on the couch with her legs folded Indian style, strumming her guitar and humming along to the melody. Shane stayed in her room, hoping to give her some space.

"Damn it," Haley growled, tossing her pen across the room. It bounced off the window and landed on the loveseat.

"Barbecue for two!" the driver yelled, pounding on the door.

"Thank God," Haley muttered, setting her guitar down beside her as she started to stand up.

"I've got it," Shane called, walking briskly through the bus.

"Seriously?" Haley huffed, crossing her arms. She could see through the one-way glass of the window. "It's Fizzy. He's not the damn letter writer. Ralph Fizzuto, known as Fizzy to anyone who knows him, has been my main driver for every one of my tours. He's family. Hell, they all are."

"I understand that. I'm just being cautious," Shane stated, walking to the door.

"Here you go," Fizzy said, handing her the bag. "It wasn't on the list, but I got a couple of slices of warm apple pie with ice cream. It's Haley's favorite."

Shane nodded and thanked him before closing the door. It was his night off, so someone else was their driver for that evening. "He got us pie," she said, carrying the two bags over to the dinette table.

"I love that man," Haley chuckled, grabbing one of the containers of pie and vanilla bean ice cream. She opened the lid and walked down the hall towards her bedroom as she took the first bite.

"Guess I'm eating alone," Shane uttered, trying to decide what to do with her dessert. The ice cream would melt in the fridge and the pie would freeze in the freezer. "Oh, to hell with it," she growled and flopped down on the couch with her socked feet crossed at the ankles and the dessert in her hand.

***

In the middle of the night, Haley walked into the living area with her guitar and found Shane asleep on the couch, still dressed in her jeans, t-shirt, and socks. She quietly set her guitar in the stand and sat on the loveseat across from her. Even in slumber she was poised for protection with a rigid body and scrunched face.

Haley watched her chest slowly rise up and down as a slow staccato of rain drops pelted the windows. The bus gently rocked with the rolling hills of the highway. She knew she was invading Shane's personal space, but she was drawn to her like a moth to a flame. She grabbed her pencil and note pad and began writing down the words that came to mind.

Midnight in Amarillo
Closed my eyes and you were there

She couldn't believe she was actually writing as she eyed her guitar. Knowing it would wake Shane, she thought better of it and decided to hum the melody instead.

The taste of your lips
Your fingers in my hair

Haley's break from writer's block shattered to pieces when the bus hit a pothole and jarred. Deep gray eyes popped open, scanning the room like a street cat ready to pounce on whatever moved first...until they landed on her and began to soften.

"What time is it?" Shane said, groggily as she sat up.

Haley shrugged as she closed her notebook and sighed, turning her attention to the pouring rain outside.

Shane wiped the sleep from her eyes and thin line of drool from her chin as she sat up, checking her wrist watch. It was three-thirty in the morning. "How long have you been there?"

"Not long," she said, unsure of the truth. "I came out here to work and found you passed out. Don't you have a bed in your room?"

Shane ignored her and stood up, stretching the sore muscles in her back from the couch. She hadn't intended on falling asleep. She wasn't tired when she'd sat down on the couch with a glass of whisky and milk, hoping it would ease her laboring mind long enough to let her get some rest.

It must've worked because she dozed off effortlessly, which was very unlike her.

"You can have the couch. I'm going to bed," she said, standing up and placing her empty glass in the sink.

"Never mind," Haley mumbled, grabbing her guitar and heading back to her room.

Shane shrugged and shook her head. "I can't win with you, can I?" she mumbled.

***

The bus finally came to a stop in Tulsa, about fifteen miles from the local airport. Shane was sitting at the dinette table drinking coffee, and Haley was on the couch, reading a magazine when Rich boarded.

"I was beginning to wonder when you'd arrive. You know I have three rehearsals to get through, plus get ready."

"I'm aware of that," he said, sitting across from her. "Macy West is handling your wardrobe, and Southern Belle Cosmetics is supplying and staffing the hair and make-up department for the entire show."

Haley nodded and smiled. At least she wouldn't look like a street walker in borrowed clothes. "Macy West...you must've pulled a few strings."

"A little more than a few. We'll get to that another time. You'll be in the audience until you present about midway through the show. Then, you'll stay backstage until you perform. After that, you'll go back out to the audience. Shane, you have the seat next to her."

"Great, so it's going to look like she's my date for the night," Haley growled.

"She pretty much is," Rich replied. "Enjoy the night. It's a big awards show for country music, and people love your videos. Anyway, we need to get on the road. Your plane is wheels up in two hours." He looked into the kitchen area. "Shane, do you need anything before we take off?"

She shook her head no and took one last sip of coffee. She'd laid out her black suit and dress shoes when she'd gone back to bed and been unable to sleep again earlier in the morning.

"Great. I'll take you all to the airport. There will be an Escalade limo waiting when you arrive in Nashville. After the show, you'll have a few hours before the plane leaves again. The limo will be waiting around, so call this guy when you're ready," Rich said, handing the driver's information to Shane. "The rest of the entourage will go get set up in town for tomorrow night's show here in Tulsa. Haley, the only protection you have for the entire night is Shane. Please listen to her and do what she asks. If for nothing else, do it for your own safety."

"That letter-writing lunatic has no idea I'll be there tonight," she huffed.

"Actually, the commercials are advertising you as a performer. I'm sure he knows."

Haley sighed and threw her hands up. "Fine."

"Everything good on your end?" he asked, looking at Shane, who was washing out her glass from the night before and the coffee mug.

She looked back at him and nodded. "Yes."

"I'm going to go get the band. We're on the road in ten minutes." He patted Haley on the top of her shoulder. "Your new single is going to light that arena on fire!"

"This better be worth it," she uttered as he left the bus.

"I'll be ready in five minutes," Shane said, leaving her alone in the living area.

Haley went to her own room and put her guitar into its case and grabbed a couple of other necessity items she wanted to take with her, before closing it up. She quickly changed into ripped jeans and a white tank top with a silver bedazzled design on the front. Then, she pulled on her worn, pointed toe boots and grabbed the hanging bag that contained her vintage, black waistcoat with tails, which she'd planned to wear with her ensemble on stage. It gave her a steam punk meets rock and roll country look that she thought would go great with the new single she was singing. She set the guitar case down, and laid the jacket over it so it wouldn't wrinkle. She spun around on her heels when she heard Shane coming out of her room. She was dressed in a black suit with a white button-down blouse under her jacket, and matching oxford dress shoes. Her dark hair was in need of a cut, so the short style had given way to a few extra curls.

Haley cleared the lump from her throat and grabbed her guitar case and hanging bag. "Let's go," she mumbled, hoping she didn't have to turn back around as she headed for the door. Shane made her crazy. Seeing her dressed like Johnny Cash, and looking just as striking, only made it worse.

Chapter 17

Haley, along with her band mates Joey, Stiles, Eddie, and Vince, sat on the couch-style seat, playing their guitars and singing the song they were doing for the show, as well as practicing the one she was doing for the tribute, while the private plane flew towards Nashville.

Shane sat across from them in a comfortable, soft leather seat, looking out the window. She'd hung her suit jacket in the closet, but still had her shoulder holster on, with her handgun snapped inside of it, and tucked under her arm.

Haley would do anything to keep her eyes off of Shane, even if it meant singing for the next hour, compromising her voice for the show…but she didn't have to. A full spread of food was served during the flight, and the band kept her attention discussing the upcoming tour stops.

By the time the plane landed, she'd all but forgotten about the aloof bodyguard sitting nearby. Shane looked a million miles away when Haley chanced a glance in her direction. Sighing, she grabbed her guitar case and stood up.

Shane exited the plane first, checking with the limo driver to make sure they had the correct person. Then, she waved for the band to exit, leaving Haley for last. Shane walked over to the gangway stairs, standing beside them as Haley stepped down. Vince had carried her guitar and hanging bag, and Joey and Stiles had their own guitars.

"Is this really necessary?" Haley muttered.

Shane ignored her as she got into the back of the limo with her band mates, then she walked up front to the passenger seat beside the driver.

74

Rebel Sweetheart

***

The drive from the airport to the arena took about thirty minutes. Shane instructed the driver to pull around to the loading docks instead of the red-carpet entrance at the front where a lot of the country music stars were entering. Then, she got out and opened the back door. Haley was the first person out, and Shane casually fell in step beside her. Joey and Stiles got out behind her, carrying the guitars and Eddie had her hanging bag. Vince walked behind them.

"Haley Nielsen," one of the assistant program directors cheered, rushing up to her. "We're so happy you could make it. Follow me and I'll show you to your dressing room. We have everything set up for you."

"I'm glad to take a night off from the tour to be here. The CMT awards are country music video royalty," Haley beamed. She knew she wasn't welcomed with open arms. She was one of the black sheep of country music because she did things *her* way and made the music *she* wanted to make. A lot of the record companies and old school producers shunned her for it, including many of the higher ups at her current label. When her latest album released a few weeks ago and immediately topped the charts on iTunes and Spotify, and her first single going to number one for a few weeks, the radio stations had no choice but to play her songs, which moved them up the Billboard country charts. The same situation had happened with her previous two albums.

"Here we are," he said, after taking them on a tour of backstage. "I believe Macy West sent over a few pieces for you to choose from. After your rehearsal, let me know

75

as soon as you're ready and we'll have hair and makeup come in."

"Wonderful," she replied with a smile.

"We'll make sure your band members know your call time for the performance. They'll be in the green room until then. Shall we head over to the stage for your rehearsal?"

"That's fine with me," Haley said, "let's get it over with."

***

Shane watched from the side of the stage as Haley and her band warmed up, then played through her performance song twice. Then, she and a male singer did a duet of a song for the tribute, which they ran through two times. After that, she was escorted back to her dressing room to get ready.

The assistant director turned to Shane. "Would you like me to show you to your seat?"

"I'm Ms. Nielsen's personal security. I'll be backstage until she joins the audience."

"Okay," he said, clearing his throat awkwardly before walking away.

"I'm pretty sure I can get dressed on my own," Haley said, pinning her with a stare.

"I'll be around," Shane said, exiting the room. She knew all of the workers had all been through extensive background checks, but the letter writer could be anyone, including someone with no criminal record.

While she waited, Shane scoped out the best vantage point backstage for both performances, as well as when Haley was presenting.

***

Haley unzipped the three leather hanging bags. The first contained a baby blue colored pantsuit with beautiful rhinestones down the sides of the legs and across the collar of the low-cut, double-breasted jacket that was meant to be worn with nothing under it but a bra. "Maybe," she said, not really liking the color.

The second bag had a long red dress made of chiffon. It had a low V cut in the front, a slit up the side, and long sleeves made of see-through, veil-like red material. "Come on, Macy. This isn't the first time you've dressed me, girl," Haley uttered, shaking her head as she put this one to the side.

Her eyes lit up as she unzipped the bag for the last garment, revealing a beautiful crème colored, satin, halter style dress. It was ankle-length with a split up the front of her left leg to her thigh. The front was cut into a U-shape that ended just below her breasts, and the back was fully open. Matching strappy heels went with it, as well as sparkling platinum and diamond earrings and a matching bracelet.

***

"Haley is being called to her seat," the assistant director said to Shane in passing as he rushed around.

She nodded and walked the short distance down the hall, knocking on the dressing room door. "Haley, it's time to take your seat."

The door opened a second later. Shane stepped back as Haley walked out of the room wearing the crème colored dress and heels. Her long wavy hair was full of bouncy curls that cascaded across her back and forward over one shoulder.

Shane held her breath as her eyes raked over the beautiful woman in front of her from the gorgeous curls, to the silky-smooth skin between her breasts, and down the thigh peeking out from the open slit, and back up to the blue-green eyes staring back at her. She moved closer, leaving little space between them.

Seeing the half-lidded look of desire burning in Shane's eyes made Haley's heart pound in her chest. Scorching blood coursed through her veins. She held her breath, trying desperately to swallow. Shane's lips were even closer because she was wearing heels. If she raised up on her toes just a little…

If things were different, I'd kiss you like you were the oxygen my body needed to breathe, Shane thought, as they stared at each other. "Not that it matters," she said softly, finding her voice, "but you look stunning."

She was close enough for Haley to smell the mint she'd been chewing, on her breath. It tickled her nose. "Thank you," she said, wrapping her hand around a strong arm as Shane moved to the side, holding out her elbow.

It was a short walk from backstage to the rows of seats filling the large arena. Shane avoided the eyes staring at them as they walked across the stage and down the stairs towards the aisle in front of the rows of seats. Haley stopped to say hi to several other musicians while Shane stood off to the side. Haley had let go of her arm as soon as they'd navigated the stage steps and were on flat ground.

"Haley! I thought you were on tour," a popular female singer said, walking over and hugging her slightly so they didn't mess each other up.

"I am, but I couldn't say no when they asked me to perform and present."

"Well, you look gorgeous!"

"Thanks! So do you!" Haley replied, walking up towards the fifth row.

Shane moved into the row first and took the second seat, leaving Haley the aisle seat.

"These things are the biggest dog and pony show you'll ever see," Haley whispered, leaning over towards Shane. The fresh, clean scent of her cologne sent shivers down her spine.

***

The show opened with a performance, then the emcees took over, cracking jokes and talking about country music. When they mentioned Haley and her saucy new album, the TV camera in the aisle cut directly to her. Shane stared straight ahead, hoping to avoid the spotlight while Haley smiled brightly, winking at the camera.

It wasn't long before Haley was called to the back to get ready to present after the next commercial break. Shane stayed by her side as she was escorted to the waiting area.

"I'll be off stage to your left," Shane said, walking away from her.

Haley simply nodded.

"Who's the shadow?" a male voice said.

Haley pulled her eyes away from Shane's back to see Tucker Miller standing beside her. "What was that?" she asked.

"You look dressed to kill," he said, taking a long look up and down her body.

"Are you looking to be my victim?"

"I'll be whatever you want me to be."

Haley laughed and shook her head. "Tucker, it's never going to happen."

"Why not? You and I together is like Johnny and June."

"You're nothing like June," she replied with a smirk and walked out on stage with a Hollywood smile plastered across her face.

Tucker quickly rushed up beside her and began reading from the teleprompter.

Shane stayed behind the curtain, out of sight, but she stepped out enough to watch the presentation for the hottest video of the year. She rolled her eyes and shook her head when the guy next to Haley made a stupid comment about her latest video being steamy. "Dumbass men will do anything to get into a pretty girl's pants," she mumbled, shaking her head. "Good luck with that one, she has razor sharp claws and I'm pretty sure she bites."

Haley laughed off Tucker's inappropriate comment and continued with the words they were supposed to be saying as she revealed the winner. As soon as they handed off the award, Haley walked back stage.

"I'm not sure what part of 'no' you don't get, but I'm not into you, Tucker, and I never will be. You're a pompous ass who thinks he is God's gift to women. Don't you ever put me on the spot with a sexist remark like that again, or I'm going to nail you to the wall," Haley growled and headed off to get ready to perform.

Shane stood a few feet away, but close enough to hear the tongue-lashing Haley gave him. Then, she followed her down the hallway.

"I can change clothes on my own," Haley snapped.

"I wasn't coming in," Shane replied, stopping outside the door before Haley slammed it closed.

God help the person who does win her over. They'll be in for one hell of a ride," Shane thought, sighing as she crossed her arms and leaned back against the wall.

***

When the show came back from commercial, Haley was center stage, dressed in her steam punk country outfit, with her band members behind her. The electric guitar moaned as Joey played the first few chords. Haley's raspy, blues sound cut through the music like a hot knife through cold butter, firing off one country twanging lyric after another. Much to her surprise, the audience clapped and sang along during the chorus. The wild blonde waves of her hair bounced all around as she jammed on her guitar, capturing the attention of everyone in the massive room. She had a demanding presence unlike anything Shane had ever seen.

By the end of the song, most of the crowd was on their feet, and Shane was nodding her head to the beat. Haley waved and smiled like a kid in a candy store before leaving the stage as the show cut to the side stage for the next award presentation.

"We blew the roof off this mother!" she cheered, high-fiving her band mates.

"Hell yeah we did," one of the guys said.

"I don't know about you guys, but I'm ready to get back to Oklahoma. What do you say we head on out of here and skip the rest of the show?" she said.

"That's fine with me," Joey replied.

"Me too," the others added.

"I'm going to grab my stuff out of the dressing room. I'll meet you where we came in. The limo should still be outside." As she turned to head down the hallway, she tripped over an extension cord.

Shane, who had been nearby the entire time, reached out, quickly grabbing her and pulling her close. For a split second, their eyes met and time felt like it stood still. Their lips were a couple inches apart at most.

It would be so easy to kiss you, Shane thought before helping her stand back on her feet.

No words were spoken, but the blood pounding in Haley's ears as her heart raced was deafening.

"I'm sorry," Shane finally said, letting go of her and taking a step back.

Haley didn't say a word as she headed into the dressing room, still holding her breath. She was certain Shane was about to kiss her, and her body had wanted her to. Shaking the thought from her head with an audible sigh, she walked over to the vanity and looked at herself in the mirror. "Get it together, girl. The last thing you need to do is get involved with someone like her," she muttered, removing her jacket. That's when she noticed the white envelope propped up against the mirror with her first name written across the front of it. Figuring it was an invitation to one of the many after parties that she couldn't attend, she tore it open.

A loud shriek came from her mouth as her eyes focused on the letter that flew from her hands and slowly sank to the floor like a feather in the wind. "Shane!" she screamed at the top of her lungs.

***

Shane checked her watch. They had to be back at the airport in an hour and she estimated it would take at least thirty to forty-five minutes to get through the downtown Nashville traffic. She watched other country artists walking around and talking to one another backstage while the crew worked diligently to close the show. All of the singers and groups who had performed also had dressing rooms to change clothes if need be, so most of the rooms along the hall were occupied.

She was only about thirty feet from the door to Haley's dressing room, but the shrill sound of her screaming Shane's name sounded as if she were standing right next to her. The hair on the back of her neck stood up as her body went into protection mode. She took off running and smashed the door open.

Haley was standing near the vanity with tears streaming down her cheeks. She didn't have to ask what had happened. A quick glance around the room was all she needed. A white, half folded piece of paper was lying on the floor, and a white, torn envelope was on the vanity counter.

Shane rushed over, wrapping her arms around Haley. The familiar smell of her floral scented shampoo and conditioner was stronger than ever. Shane closed her eyes and breathed in slowly, burning to memory the feel of Haley's warm body against hers. If she moved her head slightly, her lips would press against Haley's forehead in a gesture that meant so much more than she was willing to let herself feel. Instead, she kept her position and held on until Haley was ready to let go.

Haley threaded her arms around Shane's waist and laid her head against her collar bone where her chest and shoulder met. The steady cadence of her pounding heart soothed Haley enough to stop the tears. She took a deep breath, inhaling the fresh and clean mixture of Shane's soap and cologne. Feeling much calmer, and in a position that was starting to kick start her libido, Haley casually backed away.

Shane released her hold and searched around for something to use to touch the letter and envelope. Haley stepped away to wipe her wet cheeks and pull herself together. "Can we please get out of here?" she said softly.

"Absolutely," Shane replied, wrapping tissue paper around the envelope and letter as she folded it. She shoved it into her coat pocket and walked over, pulling open the door.

"Do you think he's still here?" Haley uttered, looking around the hallway.

"I can't say for sure," Shane answered honestly as she moved closer.

Together, they walked side by side through backstage towards the side exit door. The limo was idling next to the loading dock with her band members already inside.

"Everything okay?" Joey asked as they climbed inside.

"Yeah. I got stuck talking to a few people," Haley replied with a quick smile that vanished as soon as the door was closed.

Chapter 18

The plane ride was uneventful. Haley barely touched the lavish meal that was served for dinner, and Shane spent most of the flight texting back and forth with both Rich and Dennis about the new letter. She hadn't read it yet, but all that mattered was he'd somehow gotten into her dressing room, or at least had it delivered there.

By the time they were back in Oklahoma, Rich had found out that the envelope had been delivered around the start of the show and was put with other after party invitations and gifts that were placed in the dressing rooms. The stage crew had assumed that was where it belonged. No one remembered how it arrived at the arena and there was no camera footage showing the delivery.

With nothing else to go on, Shane was right back to square one, which only frustrated her more. She was ready for this case to be over. She didn't mind protection detail and she lived for the thrill of solving a criminal case. What bothered her was Haley. She was unpredictable; headstrong and uncooperative; and the most beautiful woman Shane had ever met, all rolled into one red hot ball of fire that burned Shane in more ways than one.

***

Haley boarded her bus and went directly to her bedroom. Shane shrugged out of her jacket, placing it over the arm of the seat and she sat down at the dinette table with the tissue paper covered letter and envelope. Using utensils from the kitchen drawer, she unfolded everything. The envelope had Haley's first name written in block letters across the front of it. The letter had two words cut out of a magazine picture and glued onto the paper: Welcome Home. Shane studied the paper, then pulled out her phone and snapped a picture of it, which she sent to Rich and Dennis. Even if they tracked down the magazine they came from, there could be a hundred thousand people with a subscription to it. The only thing she had to go on was his choice of words. *Welcome Home.*

***

Haley spent most of the next day with the band in the arena, while Shane went back and forth with Rich over the phone. He'd been unable to get any more information out of anyone working for the awards show or the arena the night before.

"Forget it," she said, "it's a dead end anyway. I doubt there will be any prints, either. I hate to say it, but he's going to have to come after her for me to catch him."

"I know. I've thought the same thing. Do you need me to come back you up?"

"No. There's no room in the entourage, and I have no idea where the hell we are going at any point in time."

"Alright. We'll talk soon."

Shane ended the call on her phone and pushed off the rail she was leaning against in the upper section of the arena.

Haley was down on the stage, alone. She'd run through the full show twice already and was pretty much just sitting there with her guitar.

Shane's phone rang a second later with a call from Rich. The tone echoed through the massive open space, drawing Haley's eyes directly to her.

"Damn it," she growled, answering as Haley snatched up her guitar and stormed off the back of the stage towards the prep area below. "Let me call you back," she said, rushing down the stairs to the lower section where she could swing herself over the railing. "Haley! Wait!" she called as she ran across the arena floor.

"I can't do this anymore!" Haley snapped as Shane caught up to her. They were completely alone in the dimly lit space below the stage.

"Do what?"

"Work! Write music! Sleep! Anything!" Haley yelled, wanting to smash her guitar against the metal rafters holding up the stage as she leaned it against one of the beams. "You have to go!"

"I'm not going anywhere," Shane growled. "I've given you plenty of space."

"You were just in here spying on me! How the fuck is that space? How long were you here? Did you watch the entire rehearsal? How long did you sit there and watch me when I thought I was alone? Damn you!" Her body hummed with energy fueled by a hunger unlike anything she'd ever felt. Which only made her madder.

"It's my job to protect you. I try not to be seen for your own benefit...to give you the God damn space you need so badly!"

"I can't. I just fucking can't anymore!"

"You have no choice! Someone is trying to hurt you! Can't you see that?"

"You don't think I know that?" Haley stepped closer, moving to within a foot of her. "You're fired. I'll hire someone else to do the job. It just can't be you!" she said through gritted teeth.

"Why? Because I actually *want* to protect you?" Shane snarled back.

Haley glared at her, then reached up with one arm around Shane's neck and the other tangled in her short hair, and pulled her close, pressing her mouth against Shane's soft, inviting lips. She briefly tasted mint as their intense kiss quickly turned into a fierce battle of tongues fighting for dominance. Shane wrapped her arms around Haley's waist, pulling their hips together before sliding one hand down to her ass and the other up her back under her long, wavy locks.

The whimper of desire escaped one of their mouths in a faint moan as their bodies grated together, breast to breast, hip to hip, each urging the other to go further. Haley pushed into Shane, pressing her back up against one of the metal beams. Shane quickly spun Haley around, taking control as they continued ravishing each other.

The lustful kiss seemed endless until some blood made its way back into Shane's head from between her legs. She let go of Haley, feeling the air sting her sensitive lips as she backed away. She knew they either had to stop or take the next step, and having meaningless sex with Haley would only make matters worse, not to mention anyone could've walked in on them at any time.

"We can't do this," she said, meeting Haley's eyes.

Haley stared back at her with a raw, carnal look in her hazy blue-green eyes. Shane searched her brain for something to say, but Haley turned and stormed off like a scorned woman. She didn't go after. She knew the paid security personnel was right outside and would escort her back to the bus.

Space was something they both needed if they were going to survive another encounter.

***

Shane was standing twenty yards from the buses, talking to the rented security about after the show. She'd replaced her short-sleeved over shirt, to hide her gun and shoulder holster, with a long-sleeved one. October had arrived and so had the fall weather with cooler temperatures. The warm Texas sun was long behind them.

When one of the bus doors slammed open, all heads turned as Haley immersed, dressed in light-colored, threadbare, blue jeans with holes at the knees and slits across the thighs. They were slung low on her hips and held up by a wide black belt with a large silver buckle. Worn, pointed toe boots stuck out below the boot cut leg openings. A tight white T-shirt with a large American flag across the front, showed off her small, lithe frame and the curves of her round breasts.

Bob Seger's song *Her Strut* played in Shane's head as she watched Haley walk. Her swagger was full of independence and self-confidence as she moved. Her long blonde waves bounced up and down along her shoulders and back, and her hips rolled in a steady side to side motion. Metal-framed aviator sunglasses hid her eyes from the fading sun, but that didn't matter. All eyes were on her backside, watching her ass move under those tight jeans.

"Oh...she's a rattlesnake ready to strike. Who pissed her off?" Rich muttered.

"That would be me," Shane sighed.

"If you survive the night, it'll be a miracle," Rich mumbled, walking away.

"That's why I stopped," Shane whispered. Haley Nielsen was unlike any woman she'd ever met. If she loved as passionately as she hated…God help the person she fell in love with. Shaking the thoughts from her head, Shane picked up the pace and joined the group who was escorting Haley.

"I thought I fired you," Haley sneered, catching a glimpse of Shane out of the corner of her eye just before they entered the building.

"Not likely," Shane replied. "I told you I wasn't going anywhere."

The roar of the crowd was loud in the tunnel leading under the stage. Shane's blood pressure rose slightly as they passed by the spot where just four hours earlier, they'd shared a kiss hot enough to melt the rafters around them. She quickly turned and headed towards a staircase that would take her up onto the side of the stage behind the curtain. Her foot tapped to the beat as the band began the first song.

Haley rose up on an elevator lift, already playing her guitar. The screaming crowd became impossibly louder as she grabbed the mic and went to town singing the first song of the night.

Shane had worried in the beginning about Haley tripping over the various items people always seemed to throw onto the stage, but as usual, she put a boot to them, sending the objects flying off to the side and out of her way as she walked back and forth, sawing the chords of her guitar.

Tearing her eyes from the singing bombshell, Shane scanned the massive audience, but the only people she could truly see were in the front two rows. Most of everyone else was darkened by the bright stage lighting.

***

At the halfway point of the performance, Haley grabbed a shot of tequila that had been sitting by her guitar stand. "Here's to you; here's to me; here's to the party you came to see!" she shouted and slung it back. Then, she traded her acoustic style guitar for her custom Telecaster guitar and stepped up to the mic.

Shane raised a brow. She'd never seen Haley drink shots on stage, and she usually jammed on her Telecaster at the end of the show when she covered a couple of rock and roll songs.

"I feel like doing things a little different tonight. What do you say Tulsa?" Haley asked with a huge grin on her face. Then, she turned and nodded at Vince on the drums before playing the first ten or so chords of Deep Purple's *Smoke on the Water*. The crowd roared with cheers as she adjusted the switch and changed the tune to tease them with the opening of Guns N' Roses' *Sweet Child O' Mine*.

Shane had never heard a crowd so loud. Enthralled, she waited, eyes glued to Haley and the cherry red electric guitar in her hands. The initial surprise wore off quickly as Shane watched her work the stage and the crowd while jamming on the guitar. The country spitfire was also a pretty badass rock and roller, and the tens of thousands of people in the arena absolutely loved it.

Stiles jumped in, playing with her first the first few chords of ZZ Top's *Sharp Dressed Man*, while Vince continued riffing with her on the drums. Then, the band went silent once more. The spotlight closed back in on Haley as she played the intro to Aerosmith's *Walk this Way*.

"What do you think guys? You want more?" she yelled into the microphone.

The crowd continued screaming at the top of their lungs. Haley smiled from ear to ear and went right into the beginning of *T.N.T.* by AC/DC, then finished with Ted Nugent's *Cat Scratch Fever.*

"Alright. Alright," she laughed. "Enough teasing!"

The spotlight faded and slowly, the whole band came back into view as Haley and Stiles traded chords once again, this time to Led Zeppelin's *Whole Lotta Love.*

Haley stepped up to the microphone. "You need coolin', baby I'm not foolin'," she sang. "I'm gonna send you, back to schoolin'."

People in the front row fought security, trying to get onto the stage as Haley continued singing.

Shane stood frozen, utterly mind blown when Haley played the guitar solo in the middle. Watching her jam on that guitar and belt out rock and roll lyrics, was one of the sexiest things she'd ever seen. The only time Haley had let loose like that however, was once in a while in rehearsal. This was the first time she'd done it on stage in front of a crowd, and they were eating it up.

By the time the song finally ended, the entire arena was on their feet screaming, standing in their chairs screaming, and jumping up and down in the aisles screaming. They were just plain loud.

"What the hell was that?" Shane asked, leaning over towards Rich when he stepped up next to her.

"She loves to jam, but usually in rehearsal and rarely on stage. I've never seen her like this. I'd say she was having a blast out there, and it looks like she is…but she's been hell on wheels all afternoon."

Shane pursed her lips and nodded.

Haley turned her back to the crowd as Vince played the beginning drum solo of Joan Jett's *I Hate Myself For*

Loving You. Then, she spun around, her fingers working the chords of the electric guitar as she stepped up to the microphone. "Midnight gettin' uptight, where are you? You said you'd meet me, now it's quarter to two," she sang.

Rich looked at Shane. "Whatever you did…I don't think it was a good idea," he said, shaking his head.

Shane turned back towards Haley. No, it hadn't been a good idea.

"Whatever is going on, either this is how she's getting it out of her system, or you better hold on for a wild ride."

"There's nothing going on…at least not—"

Rich held up his hand. "It's none of my business."

Shane growled in frustration. *Great. Now her manager thinks we're sleeping together.*

After the song ended, Haley set the electric guitar back in the stand and walked back to the microphone. "Tulsa, did we bring the party, or what?" she laughed.

Shane looked around, but Rich had once again disappeared. She wondered if he had A.D.D., or really was insanely busy.

***

Haley had slipped easily back into her country music, wooing the crowd even more with her chart-topping hits for the last thirty minutes of the show. Shane waited away from the side of the stage for her to finish.

As soon as the encore ended, Haley exited the stage and waited for her band members to finish out the song and join her. Her eyes met Shane's in the dim lighting. They were only a few feet away from where they'd stood, locked in each other's arms while passionately kissing, earlier in the day.

Shane opened her mouth to speak, but the music went quiet, and her band members appeared.

"We rocked the hell out of this place!" Haley yelled, high-fiving the guys as they celebrated together.

"That was insane!" Stiles exclaimed.

"You're such a badass!" Joey added, causing Haley to laugh.

"Come on, party's on my bus tonight!" she cheered as she headed off towards the exit where a couple hundred fans were gathered, hoping for an up close glimpse of the blonde bombshell.

Shane rushed to catch up to her, falling in step at Haley's side as they walked out of the building. She watched cautiously as Haley snapped selfie pictures and signed autographs. She hated this part. She knew the arena's all had metal detectors, so it was somewhat safer for her on stage. Out in the open, anyone in the massive crowd could get to her.

When she'd had her fill of the fans, Haley said goodnight to them and walked off towards the buses with Shane never leaving her side. "I thought you were supposed to be like a shadow...out of sight, out of mind?" she mumbled as she opened the bus door.

"I am, now that you're away from the masses of people out there," Shane uttered, watching her board.

The other band members got onto the bus after Haley and Shane closed the door behind them.

***

Outside, Shane hoped to ignore the ruckus going on in the living room of the bus. She was sure the tequila was flowing. She knew they needed to talk, but now wasn't the right time. Everything was still too raw and emotional. Haley's over the top, wild behavior was a testament to that.

Shane rubbed her hands together before shoving them into her jeans, wishing she'd grabbed her jacket. She didn't mind the cold, but the long-sleeved dressed shirt over a t-shirt wasn't exactly feasible for a fifteen-degree temperature drop.

"Looks like we might get some snow tonight," Fizzy said, lighting a cigarette.

"Where are we off to from here?"

"Omaha. It's about a six-and-a-half-hour drive."

Shane nodded and checked her watch. The show had ended at ten, which meant the road crew would be busy tearing down the set until one a.m.

"I heard she rocked the house tonight," Fizzy said, smiling and shaking his head. "She blew my mind when I met her right before her first tour. She was just starting out and green as goose shit, but man that girl can play the hell out of a guitar, and she has pipes like no singer I've ever heard. I'm sorry I missed it. Sometimes I sneak into rehearsal just to listen." He smiled.

"Yeah." Shane nodded. "She's definitely something else, that's for sure." She glanced around, looking for Rich to discuss the next venue. "Have you seen Rich?"

"I believe he hopped a flight already. I saw him leave not long after I got up. There's

pizza and wings. I'm sure they're in there pigging out," he said, nodding towards the bus.

"Wonderful," she muttered, wondering what she'd be eating for dinner because she wasn't getting on there any time soon.

***

The party on the bus had only lasted about a half hour. After that, Shane watched the band members leave Haley's bus and board their own.

"As soon as the road manager gives the all clear, we're out of here," Fizzy said.

"Sounds good."

"Goodnight," he said.

"See you in the morning," she replied, pulling the door open.

***

Haley was sitting on the couch with her socked feet curled up under her, when Shane entered.

"We should talk," Shane said, sitting down across from her. She was happy to be in the warmth of the bus and out of the cool night air.

"Not tonight," Haley replied, without looking up from her notepad.

"Fine with me," Shane shrugged, getting up. As she walked past the kitchen area, she snatched the pizza box from the table and kept going. "Your show tonight was on fire, in case you give a shit what people think," she called before going into her room.

***

"Enjoy your cold pizza, and it's not like I asked anyway," Haley uttered. It had been a great show. One of the best she'd ever done. The kiss with Shane had still been reeling on her mind like a bleeding cut during the final rehearsal, so she'd made a sudden change, a shift in the temperament of the show. She needed to let loose; to free herself and feel the music; even if it was for only a few minutes. The couple of tequila shots afterwards had helped even more. She was by no means drunk, or buzzing for that matter, but she felt warm inside. Her mind was in a good place finally after hours of mayhem, and she wanted do to nothing but write. However, writing only brought her right back to where it all started...the kiss. "Damn it!" she growled, tossing the notepad across the bus to the loveseat.

Chapter 19

Haley had finally cleared her head enough to find the words she was searching for. The cavalry had long pulled out of Tulsa. The bus was quiet, except for the faint sound of her strumming her guitar and scratching notes on a piece of paper.

Two a.m. in Tulsa
you're the reason I can't sleep

She strummed a couple of chords, then continued.

We toss and turn, tearing at the sheets
the fire burns
between you and me

She was about to begin another line when all of a sudden, the bus jerked and swayed all around. Tires skidding and a loud smashing sound were heard, before everything lurched forward. The cabinets opened, spilling their contents, and Haley flew airborne, almost suspended in the air as the bus swerved to miss an oncoming car that had veered in its lane, before smashing through a guardrail and going over an embankment. The furniture shifted, pummeling down on top of Haley as the bus came down on its nose, smashing into the ground and crushing the first seven feet like an accordion with twenty tons of pressure, before flipping over onto its roof, then finally coming to rest on its side.

***

Shane had been thrown from her bed, to the floor, then slammed hard against the wall. When she opened her eyes, she had no idea how long she'd been out. It was pitch black, and she was disoriented. Nothing was where it used to be, and she was standing on the closet instead of the floor. "What the fuck," she mumbled, frantically searching for her gun and a pair of shoes. Thankfully, she'd fallen asleep on top of her covers with her clothes still on. *Haley*, she thought. "Oh God!" she felt around, trying to locate the door, which was now above her head. Moving the bed frame, she was able to stand on the edge and reach up for the door. She never found her shoes, but nothing else mattered. She had to get to Haley. The smell of diesel fuel permeated the air as she crawled on her hands and knees on what used to be the hallway wall.

"Haley!" she called, trying to get her bedroom door open. Something was wedged against it, most likely the queen-sized bed or dresser. "Damn it!" she yelled. "Haley! Can you hear me?" She pounded on the door with her fist, but heard nothing. The sour fuel smell was getting stronger and stronger. Realizing she may be able to get to her from an outside window, she headed the other way down the hall, falling into the kitchen around, in the midst of pots, pans, and dishes.

"Fucking, damn it, ouch!" she yelled, scrambling to get out of the mess. There was zero light. She had no idea where the living area furniture had ended up, as she continued crawling around, searching for the exit door.

"Shane," Haley called out softly.

"Haley!" she exclaimed. "You're in here?"

"Shane," she said again.

Shane quickly began pushing and pulling whatever she could grab a hold of. The diesel fuel had made its way to her location and was now stronger than before. *I have to get her out of here!* She wedged herself under what felt like the couch and used every ounce of strength she had to stand up, and she was able to get it moved to the side. Reaching down, feeling her way around the jumble of furniture, she finally felt a soft, warm hand.

"I'm going to get you out of here, Haley. Are you hurt?"

"I don't know," she said, frightened and trying to hold back tears.

With adrenaline flowing through her veins, Shane continue heaving furniture until she found Haley on the very bottom. She reached down, grabbing her around the waist. Haley put her arms around Shane's shoulder's and neck as she pulled her free. They fell backwards with Haley half on top of her. "Come on," Shane said. "We have to get out of here, now!"

"What about Fizzy?" Haley called, trying to feel her way around.

"Haley, the front of the bus is smashed flat. I'm sorry." She wrapped her arms around the sobbing woman as Haley began to break down. "This thing is going to be on fire any minute. Please, Haley. I have to get us out of here." She felt around for the door, but it was in the part of the bus that was crunched inward. Feeling along the wall, she realized the window was smashed. Thankful she'd fallen asleep with her shoulder holster on, so she used the butt of her gun to break it the rest of the way, allowing the cold night air to fill the interior of the crumbled bus.

Moving back towards the spot where she'd left Haley, she searched around, grabbing her hand. "Are you hurt anywhere?"

"No. I don't know. My whole body hurts like hell," she said through tears.

Shane pulled her to her feet and helped her over towards the open window. She grabbed Haley from behind, and pushed her up and out, onto the side of the bus. Then, she heaved herself up and out as well. Together, they slid down the top, landing in a pile of dirt and freezing cold grass.

Faint light from the half-moon cast eerie shadows along the black metal roof of the bus. Shane put her arms around Haley's waist and pulled her further away from the wreckage. Leaving her in a seated position on the ground, she walked over towards the front. The windshield was gone, and Fizzy's body was crushed between the dash and wall section behind his seat, and hanging limply to the side. She reached in, checking for a pulse, but there wasn't one. Feeling around, she realized his neck was completely broken, with his head lying on his shoulder.

She made her way back over to Haley and huddled closely with her to share their body heat, trying desperately to keep warm in the near freezing temperature. "Fizzy's gone. I'm sorry."

Haley turned into her. Huge drops trickled down her cheeks, wetting the front of Shane's t-shirt as she cried.

"Help will be here soon. The rest of the group had to have seen the accident."

"You don't think they crashed too, do you?" Haley mumbled.

"I don't know. I don't even see a road. I think we went over the side of the mountain or something."

"Oh my God," Haley cried.

"It's okay. We'll be okay. We don't seem to be really hurt," Shane reassured, pulling Haley further into her.

Within minutes, the back of the wrecked bus began to spark. Shane watched as a tiny flame appeared. They'd gotten out just in time as the fire began a slow burn.

***

Shane had no idea how much time had passed before she heard the sirens in the distance and the faint thump of a helicopter. Within minutes, a spotlight lit up the two of them, and rescuers were lowered down on cables. The entire back of the bus was engulfed in flames that were quickly working their way forward.

"Are you hurt?" one man said, rushing over to them.

"We don't think so," Shane said, letting go of Haley as they began to check her out.

"Is anyone else on the bus?" another guy asked.

"Yes. The driver. He's deceased, but please pull his body free before it burns," Shane said as the guy began assessing her for injuries. "I'm fine!" she yelled. "Please get him out!"

Two of the rescue workers rushed over, pulling Fizzy's limp, crushed body away from the bus. A minute later, the entire wreck was engulfed in flames.

Both women had IV lines pumping warm saline into their veins, along with limited pain meds, and were wrapped in warming blankets before being loaded onto backboards for precaution, then rushed over to the helicopter that had landed nearby. Once they were secure, the rescuers put Fizzy's body into a bag and brought him inside before lifting off.

***

It was dark and quiet. The only sound was a slight beeping noise. Shane squinted, trying to see her surroundings. She immediately froze, feeling as if she were trapped in the bus all over again. "Haley," she croaked through a dry mouth. Her body felt like she'd been beaten with a wooden baseball bat.

"She's okay. They have her down the hall in a more secure room," a male voice stated.

What? Shane pried her eyes open a little further. "Dennis?" she squeaked, seeing him sitting beside her.

"Do you know where you are?" he asked.

"We got out...the bus...fire," she mumbled. Finally, it started coming back to her. "Haley!" she said, trying to sit up. "Ugh," she grimaced.

"Just relax. You're fine. The bus was in a bad accident. You and Haley are both okay. You both have concussions and a lot of bumps and bruises."

"I feel like I was hit in the head with a two by four," she sighed.

"I bet," he sympathized. "The doctor said you'll both be able to get out of here today. Rich has arranged for the entire entourage to stay in a nearby motel."

Shane felt around the arm of the hospital bed, searching for the button to lift her head up. Lying nearly flat wasn't working for her. As the bed began to raise, she lulled her head to the side, finally seeing a streak of light peeking through the closed blinds. "Why is it so dark in here?"

"The light will make your head hurt worse. Trust me."

She nodded. "What about Fizzy. The driver?"

"He was DOA."

"I know that. Has he been sent home to his family?"

"I don't know the specifics. Rich is handling everything. I only came because of you. Look, Shane. I understand if you're done. He can hire someone else. You can come to Memphis with me and get back on regular private investigator cases."

She stared at the slit in the blinds, then rolled her head to look at the beeping monitor next to the bed. "I can't leave her. Not now," she sighed, shaking her head.

"Are you sure? You're lucky to be alive, Shane."

"I know. But, that's my answer."

"Alright," he said, dropping his shoulders.

"What caused the accident?"

"A deer ran out on the opposite side of the road. The guy swerved to miss it and clipped the bus. Your driver tried to avoid hitting him head on, which ultimately saved the guy's life, but he hit a patch of black ice and skidded out of control. You went over the side of a very steep embankment and dropped nearly a hundred feet down into a dry river bed. It's a miracle the bus didn't explode."

"Holy shit," she mumbled.

"I think it shook Haley up pretty good," he said.

"She was trapped. I don't even know how I got to her and got her out, honestly."

"Adrenaline is the most powerful drug money can't buy."

"Yeah," she agreed. "Haley and Fizzy were pretty close. I think he'd worked for her for quite some time. He was a stand-up guy." She shook her head. "Does he have any family? A wife or kids?"

"No idea."

"I want to go check on her," Shane said, willing herself to sit up and swing her legs over the side.

"You're plugged up to this machine."

"I don't care. It's on wheels. I'll drag it behind me." It hurt to stretch and move, but it also made Shane feel a little better once she was less stiff. She grabbed a hold of the IV pole with her left hand, and held her hospital gown closed with her right. "Can you grab the door? I'm a bit preoccupied."

"Wouldn't want you to let go and flash the nurses' station," he laughed, grabbing the handle.

***

"I've arranged for Fizzy's body to be sent back to Nashville later today on a private plane. His family has already been in touch with a funeral home. I let them know we would cover all of the costs," Rich said.

Haley sighed and shook her head as more tears slid down her cheeks. "I'm going to pay out his death benefit to them as well. The insurance company can cut me a check when they finish their investigation. I'm not leaving his mother and wife with nothing while they hem and haw over the crash details."

"Okay."

"Also, make sure you get the information for the funeral," she said through tears. "The entire crew and band will be there."

"As will I," Shane said from the doorway.

Haley turned to see her making her way into the room. "Hi," she said softly.

"I'm going to go make some calls. I'll check back in with you in a little while," he said to Haley, then turned to Shane and mouthed 'Thank you.'

Shane nodded and stepped closer to the bed. Haley had the back raised as high as it would go, obviously trying to get comfortable. She had a bruise on the left side of her forehead.

"Do you think maybe we could have that talk now?" Shane asked, sitting down in the nearby chair.

"I'm pretty sure my life flashed before my eyes. At least, what I remember of it anyway. Some things are still a little faded."

"Yeah, same for me."

"I do know you got me out. So, thank you."

"You're welcome," Shane said. "I—"

"If you say you were just doing your job, I'm going to strangle you with that IV line sticking out of your damn arm!"

Shane shook her head and grinned. "Life flashes before her eyes and nothing changes," she muttered.

"I just don't want to hear any macho bullshit."

"Have I ever said any macho bullshit to you?"

"You use your job as an excuse a lot, so yeah."

"Touché." Shane nodded. "I was going to say I'm glad you're okay. We could've both been so much worse."

"I know. I still don't understand how you even found me," Haley whispered, hanging her head as a tear rolled down her cheek.

Shane reached out, grabbing Haley's warm hand in hers.

"Good news," Rich said, coming into the room.

Shane quickly let go of Haley's hand.

"You're both being discharged. We can head over to the motel as soon as you get dressed. Oh, and Shane, Dennis left you a package in your room. He said he'd be in touch."

"Okay," she said oddly as she stood up with ease and pushed the IV cart out of the way. "I can't wait to get this damn thing out of my arm."

"You look like you're moving a lot better," Haley said.

"Yeah, well, I have to get back to work. You know, macho bullshit and all," she teased before walking out of the room.

"What was that all about?" Rich questioned.

"Nothing. I tried to fire her, but she won't leave."

"That's because I hired her. You have no authority. I made that pretty clear the first day in case you decided to fire her then. I'm surprised you waited this long to give it a try," he laughed.

"Rich," she sighed.

"Yes?"

"Piss off."

He laughed. "Let's get you out of here. We're in the middle of nowhere, literally. The band is all worked up and chomping at the bit to see you. I made everyone stay at the motel."

***

Shane walked back into her room to find a black duffle bag on the bed with a note lying on top of it.

Shane,

You're the hardest working person I have ever met. I knew the minute I heard about the accident and found out you were not only alive, but pretty much uninjured, you'd be right back to work as soon as your feet touched the ground. Call it old man intuition. Anyway, I had to come for myself to make sure you truly were okay. Now that I know you are, I can leave you with this. I raided your place and packed you some clothes along with your Deputy U.S. Marshal identification because that was all that I could find, and a new phone. The notebook computer has the latest information on your stalker loaded on it. I figured you'd need that too, because yours was probably fried. Hopefully, this is enough to get you going. Oh, and I added a credit card I found as well, in case there are other things you need. Just send me the bill when all is said and done. I'm glad you're okay, my friend. I'll be in touch.

PS. I took the car for a drive. You know, since it hasn't moved in a couple of weeks.

"Wow," she mumbled, unzipping the bag. There were a couple pairs of jeans, a couple t-shirts, a pair of black tactical boots, a couple of long-sleeved shirts, a pair of socks, and a black, zip up hoodie. "Really? You went through my entire bedroom and this is what you come up with? At least you threw in a pair of underwear," she grumbled, shaking her head. "And we both know you didn't drive my car," she laughed.

Chapter 20

"The same room, Rich? Really? It was difficult enough sharing a bus. Now, we have to share a bed?" Haley growled.

"They only have three rooms available, and it's two to a room. You two are the only females, and you're not sharing a bed. You're sharing a room."

Haley snatched the key out of his hand and headed off in the direction of room 215.

"For the record, I'm with her on this one," Shane added, following behind Haley.

"We're only here for the night," he called to their backs. He'd already sent the road crew back to Nashville as soon as he found out Haley was okay, and had gotten word they'd be arriving the next morning. He'd put the band up in the motel, and booked an extra room for himself, which was how they'd ended up with the remaining open rooms. Once he'd found out Haley was being released, he'd booked the first available private plane out of Topeka, the closest airport. However, they had to wait until the next day.

***

The small motel room had two full-size beds with a nightstand in between them, and a rickety desk and chair against the wall in the corner. A sink and counter top were along the wall outside of the closet-sized room where the worn tub and toilet were located.

"This ought to be fun," Haley muttered, stepping inside and walking over to the bed nearest to the door, where a couple of bags were sitting.

Shane followed her in and tossed her duffle bag onto the other bed.

"What the hell?" Haley grumbled, emptying the contents of the bags. A pair of dark green sweatpants fell out of the first bag onto the bed, along with a baggy white t-shirt with a cat on the front of it. The second bag had a package of ladies brief underwear and a brown jacket that looked like it was from the seventies.

Shane turned her head to hide her laughter. It honestly wasn't funny. They were in a horrible situation that took the life of a good person, as well as all of their personal belongings. Still, she couldn't wait to see Haley in her new outfit. As it was, she was dressed in the sweatpants, matching sweatshirt, and brown snow boots with fuzzy lining that Rich had rushed out to get so she could leave the hospital.

"You can sleep outside in the cold if you'd like," Haley sneered, shoving the items back into the bags.

"Come on. Rich has great taste," Shane replied, trying desperately to keep a straight face as she turned on the TV. "Oh, look. We're on the news."

"What?" Haley spun around, gasping when she saw the charred remains of what used to be her tour bus, lying on its side in the dried river bed.

Country star Haley Nielsen narrowly survived a horrible accident last night on Highway 75 when her tour bus swerved to avoid a head on collision and crashed through a guardrail, landing down in what used to be the Tomahawk River. She was reported with minor injuries and has been released from Memorial Hospital. Her driver, Ralph Fizzuto, 55, out of Nashville, Tennessee, died at the scene. Another passenger, former Deputy U.S. Marshal

Shane Crowley, survived with minor injuries and has also been released. Reports say Ms. Nielsen was headed towards Omaha, Nebraska, where she was set to play tonight on the next stop of her Rebellious Tour. The tour has been postponed until further notice.

"That didn't take long," Haley sighed, wiping a tear from her cheek. Seeing the remains of the bus brought the horror of the night into the light of day.

Shane pressed the button on the remote to turn it back off. Then, she walked over to her duffle bag and unzipped it. "I don't know what size you wear, but these might fit," she said, tossing one of the fresh pairs of jeans onto the other bed.

"How do you have clothes and stuff?"

"My boss, who's also a very good friend, flew here as soon as he got word of the accident. He stopped at my apartment first, bringing a few things he thought I might need. I have an extra t-shirt, too," she added, tossing it over to her. "Unless, you want to be a cat lady."

"Very funny," Haley said sarcastically.

"There's nothing I can do about the granny panties, however. He only packed me one pair of underwear. Apparently, men don't change them daily or something."

Haley rolled her eyes and chuckled slightly.

***

Later that night, Shane was sound asleep, albeit moving around restlessly. Haley sat in the desk chair, watching her through the moonlight cascading in between the shabby curtains. She had her knees curled to her chest and the motel complimentary small notepad and pen in her hands.

She didn't have to think hard to remember the lyrics of the song she'd been working on. She began humming the tune and writing as they slowly played in her head. By the time she'd finished, she'd completed the final verse, which she'd been working on just before the accident. She tore the paper off and stuffed it into one of her fuzzy snow boots so she wouldn't lose it.

Shane made a few noises, almost like she was talking in her sleep. Then, she flopped around, either trying to get comfortable, or fighting with the blanket and sheets. Haley wasn't sure. She moved between their beds. Hesitating at the side of hers, she turned back towards Shane. "What is it that makes me want you so bad, and want to run from you at the same time?" she whispered. "You make me crazy," she sighed, shaking her head and getting into her own bed.

***

Shane focused on the open notebook computer in her lap, instead of the beautiful woman sitting across from her. Haley was slightly disheveled and certainly out of her element, but she looked sexier than ever wearing Shane's oversized clothes with her hair falling wildly around in loose spiral waves. She was curled up in a pair of seats, and nearly asleep as she stared out the window at the clouds they were flying over.

Bringing her focus back to the computer, Shane read over all the notes she'd sent to Dennis, along with the new updates he'd added. At first, she'd thought the magazine angle was a long reach, but Dennis had a note about the latest letter that Haley had received at the CMT Awards. Both words on the paper had come from the same magazine: *Beloved From Above*, a monthly Christian publishing with thousands of subscribers. She had no idea how he'd found this out, but it was something, when all they'd had previously was nothing. None of the other letters had solid words from a single page. They all had individual letters cut from multiple pages and glued together on the paper to form words. He'd obviously taken his time on each one. The newest letter had two full words cut from the same magazine, indicating that he'd most likely been rushed. *I bet he saw the commercial the day before, or perhaps even the day of, showing Haley performing at the show. Until that point, she wasn't listed at all.* "The post mark is fake," she said loudly, startling everyone on board.

Haley nearly jumped out of the seats she was slumbering in, and Rich squeezed the cup of water he was holding, causing it to go everywhere.

"I'm sorry," Shane said, reaching for the cell phone Dennis had left her with. She fumbled from screen to screen, looking for the contacts, finally finding the only one listed, Dennis's number. She quickly pushed the call button.

As soon as Dennis answered, Shane said, "He's local."

"Huh? Shane? Is that you? You sound like you're in a rabbit hole or something."

"I'm thirty-thousand feet up. Listen, I was looking at my notes. I saw what you added about the magazine. Are you able to get a hold of their subscriber list?"

"Yeah, but there are thousands of households in Tennessee. I'll be honest with you, very few of them are men."

"Shrink the net to the Nashville area, maybe thirty miles outside. He's local, Dennis. The postmark on the envelope was fake. He hand-delivered that letter. He had to because he didn't have time for it to go through the mail. He found out she'd be there in less than twenty-four hours," Shane said, trying to pull up a map on the computer, but the WiFi wouldn't connect. "Damn it," she huffed. Looking up, she saw all eyes on her as if she were a circus act about to perform.

"I sent a request. I'll forward it to you if I get it," he said.

"Good. We'll be landing in Nashville shortly."

"Are you coming home at all?"

"I don't know. I need to, but—"

"Stay with her. She's safer with you than anyone else, especially if he's in Nashville. Text me a list of what you need. I'll get it and have someone bring it to you."

Shane hesitated for a second. "Rich," she called.

"Yeah," he answered, staring at her like everyone else.

"Is it possible to change our flight plan?"

"Ugh…yeah, sure. I guess."

"I need to get home," Haley countered.

"I know," Shane said, meeting her eyes. "Do you trust me?"

"What's that supposed to mean?" She crossed her arms.

"When you touch down in Nashville, everyone is going to want to interview you. You'll be all over the news. He doesn't need to know you're home, until we want him to."

"Are we back to that again? I honestly don't give a shit about this letter writer guy. Fizzy is dead! I'm going home to bury him and figure out how to get my tour back in line."

"About that…I think you should take some time off. Not necessarily cancel, just a long postponement, or maybe play some small venues to make it easier to control your surroundings. At least until we've caught him."

"I agree," Dennis said through the phone.

"Shit," Shane mumbled, forgetting he was still on the line. "I'll call you back," she said, ending the call.

"I'm not stopping my tour or anything else. You've lost your mind."

"Now, Haley. She has a point."

"No way, Rich. I'm not doing it. The tour will continue. Find me a damn bus, already."

"I don't mean the tour, although playing some smaller venues before we head back out isn't a bad idea. We're dead in the water at the moment anyway, so we have the option to make changes. No, I agree with you not going back to Nashville. At least not with all of the pomp and circumstance. What's your plan?" he asked, turning back to Shane.

"Drop us off in Memphis."

"Memphis?" Haley huffed. "What the hell for? That's three hours away."

Ignoring her, Shane continued. "I live there. I can get what I need from home, and drive us to Nashville. No one will know she's coming home. We'll arrive later tonight."

"What about the band?"

"No one knows she was coming home on this private jet. You can still proceed as planned. We just didn't want someone to see her and alert the press."

"No one knows what we look like anyway," Joey laughed.

"Hey, that's not true," Haley said. "You're my band. I don't go anywhere without you guys."

"I like it," Rich said, calling the stewardess over. "Have the captain divert to Memphis for a quick layover."

"Yes, Sir," she stated with a smile, then walked away.

"This is crazy," Haley said.

"You'll be home tonight, it'll just take a little longer than expected," Shane replied.

Haley folded her arms a little tighter and forced her eyes back to the window. *This is bullshit!*

***

Shane waited for the plane to touch down and roll to a stop before removing her seatbelt. She grabbed her duffle bag and moved towards the exit door.

"You have my new cell number," she said to Rich as she checked her watch. "We should be in town just after dark."

"Drive safe. I'll be in touch."

Haley hugged her band members, then walked over to Rich. "You can keep the clothes."

He smiled.

"Just so you know, I'm over all of this shit," she added. "Right now, all I want to do is bury my friend and grieve with his family."

He nodded in agreement. "I understand. Let's get through the next couple of days and go from there."

Haley sighed and stepped through the open doorway. Shane was waiting for her at the bottom of the

116

staircase, and a black SUV was parked nearby with Dennis standing just outside the driver's door.

"This is Dennis Williams. He's the owner of the private investigation security firm I work for. He's also the one who brought my stuff to me in the hospital," Shane said. "Dennis, this is Haley Nielsen."

Haley smiled politely and shook his hand.

"It's a pleasure to meet you, Ms. Nielsen."

"Please, call me Haley. And thank you for picking us up."

"My pleasure," he replied, opening the rear passenger door for her.

Shane slid into the front passenger seat. "Did you get what I asked for?" she said as she buckled her seatbelt.

"I'm still working on it. It may take a couple of days. There are a lot of strings to pull," he replied, putting the vehicle in gear before driving across the tarmac towards the airport's rear exit.

Shane still had connections with the Marshal Service, but they weren't in Tennessee. Even so, she would only use them as an absolute last resort.

Chapter 21

Haley watched the scenery through the window as they drove across town. The nearly silent drive took about twenty minutes, and ended when they turned into a high-end apartment complex on the north end of Mud Island, the peninsula between the Mississippi River and Wolf River Harbor.

"Let me know if you need anything," Dennis said, pulling to a stop in front of one of the buildings. There were three levels and a row of single car garages side by side across from the unit, similar to town houses.

"Thanks," Shane replied, shaking his hand.

As she got out and walked around the back of the vehicle, Dennis looked up into the rearview mirror at Haley. "I know it's not the best of circumstances, especially right now, but you'll be safe. If there is one thing that woman won't do, it's let something happen to you."

Haley smiled thinly and nodded as she opened her door. Shane was already waiting in position, scanning the rooftops, then back and forth, an instinct she'd grown accustomed to. As soon as Haley shut the door, Shane fell in step next to her.

"This way. I'm on the third floor," she said, leading her towards the staircase. "We won't be here long," she added, pulling her key out of her pocket as they reached the second level and continued upwards.

***

Shane's apartment was about what Haley had imagined: small, only one bedroom and bath, sparsely furnished, and very orderly. All of the walls were the same crème color with white trim. There was light, tan-colored carpet in the bedroom, but the rest of the place had dark wood floors. The kitchen had stainless appliances with a matching sink and faucet, and dark stone countertops. The bathroom sink had the same stone counter. The tub was white porcelain, and the large tiles surrounding it were white with a dark swirl pattern.

The dark gray couch in the living room had a chaise lounge on one end, while the other end reclined. Across from it sat a black TV stand, with a modest sized flat screen TV on top of it. The bedroom had a queen-sized bed with matching nightstands and a long dresser, which were all black wood.

"How long have you lived here?" Haley asked, standing near the French doors that looked out at the river. Joggers ran and walkers passed by on the concrete path along the bank. It was a gorgeous view. Haley could see why she'd chosen that location.

"A year," Shane called from the bedroom as she packed a suitcase that matched the one she'd lost in the accident.

Haley raised a brow, wondering if she was ever home because the place didn't look lived in at all. In fact, it looked like the model unit they would show people or take pictures of for the property website.

"It came furnished. The only things that are mine are what's in the closet…and the towels and sheets," Shane added, walking out of the bedroom with her suitcase and a hanging bag that contained a black suit for the funeral. "I'd offer you something to eat, but obviously, I haven't been here in quite some time. I have bottled water, though."

"I'm fine."

"Okay. Give me a few minutes to get the rental car ordered, and we'll be on our way."

"Rental car?" Haley questioned, finally walking away from the serene view. "You don't have a vehicle?"

Shane pursed her lips, hesitating for a second. She knew the apartment was stuffy. It had reminded her of an expensive hotel suite when she'd first seen it, but it was easy to maintain, and she liked easy. She was new to town with nothing but a couple of suitcases, and liked the tranquility of Mud Island, so it was a winning situation. Throwing caution to the wind, she went back into her room and walked out with another set of keys. "Come on," she said, nodding towards the door.

Haley raised a brow, but followed along as they took the stairs all the way to the ground floor. Shane took a precautious look around, then walked over to the row of garage doors, stopping at number 318. She used one of the keys to unlock the door, then pressed the button on the key ring to make the door rise up.

Haley's jaw nearly hit the floor when she saw the classic muscle car parked inside. It was black and chrome and hand-polished with a mirror shine. The soft top was down, so she was able to see the two light-gray, low-back leather seats and matching door panels, along with the black leather and chrome steering wheel and the eight ball on the end of the chrome gear shift lever. The rest of the interior was black, except for the glove compartment door. It was light gray and had the word Corvette on it. The gauges were also black with chrome rings around them. Black exhaust pipes ran down both sides under the doors between the custom wheels, which had tires with thin white walls.

"You look a little surprised," Shane laughed.

"A little?" Haley squeaked. "Holy shit."

Shane smiled and shook her head.

"This is your car?"

"Yep."

"What year is it?"

"1964."

"We are definitely taking this. Forget the rental," Haley said with a low whistle as she walked around, checking out the car.

"You really want to ride 200 miles in this?"

"Hell yeah," Haley said with a big smile.

Shane wasn't too worried about the mileage. The car barely had ten thousand miles on it. "Alright," she agreed with a shrug.

***

After the suitcase and hanging bag were loaded into the small trunk directly behind the seats, Shane put the soft top on, then climbed down into the driver's seat. She looked over at Haley, who still had a huge grin plastered on her face, and turned the key. The small block V8 engine thundered to life inside of the garage. Then, it idled with the throaty sound of any old muscle car as she slipped the gear shift into reverse and let off the clutch. The car rolled slowly out, glistening in the sunlight. Shane pushed the clutch in, and put the car in neutral while she waited for the garage to close. There was no sense in using the extra locking system because the car wouldn't be inside, so as soon as it was down, she pushed the shifter into first gear and drove away.

As they made their way out of the complex and onto Island Drive, Shane barked the tires while changing gears.

"Whoa…Deputy Crowley's a badass. Who knew?" Haley said, smiling.

"Former deputy," Shane corrected. "I used to drive a Tahoe every day, but this became my daily driver a year ago."

"Why did you leave the Marshal Service?" Haley asked.

Shane stared straight ahead, avoiding the questioning eyes looking at her. "We have a long drive. Let's save that one for later," she replied, turning on the radio, which had been upgraded to a much better sound system when the car was fully restored. It was tuned to the local classic rock station which was currently playing Bon Jovi's *Bad Medicine*.

Haley gave her a sideways look.

"Sorry. I don't listen to country music," Shane said, "at least I didn't until we met."

"Uh huh," Haley laughed, reaching for the knob to turn the volume up. "Bad medicine is what I need!" she sang. "Shake it up, just like bad medicine!"

"This is going to be a long ride," Shane mumbled to herself as she crossed the bridge onto the mainland and took a side road towards the interstate to avoid going through downtown.

"Are we anywhere near Graceland?" Haley asked. "I've always wanted to see it."

Shane shook her head. "No, it was out by the airport. We can take a detour if you want," she said, downshifting as they came to a light. The entrance to the interstate was just on the other side.

"No," Haley sighed. "I need to get home. Maybe another time."

When the light turned green, Shane got onto the interstate, but instead of going north, she headed south. Haley paid no attention to the road signs, as she was too busy singing along to the radio.

When the song changed to Whitesnake's *Still Of The Night,* Haley belted the lyrics and played the air guitar with her fingers. *You're so beautiful. If only you weren't so damn mean and feisty,* Shane thought, fighting hard to keep her eyes on the road. Haley was only inches away in the small cockpit of the car, and she looked sexy as hell rocking out in Shane's clothes that were a couple of sizes too large.

"You're clearly a rock and roller. Why do you sing country music?" Shane said.

Haley laughed. "Country will always be my first love. That's where my roots are. You can take the girl out of the country, but you can't take the country out of the girl, know what I mean? Rock and roll is just fun. Sometimes you need to let loose a little and rock out."

"I see," Shane chuckled.

"You're obviously not from Tennessee," Haley said. "Let me guess…up north somewhere."

"No," Shane grinned and shook her head. "Arizona…Phoenix to be exact."

"Really?" Haley crossed her arms.

"Yes."

"You don't look like you're from Arizona."

Shane laughed. "And what is that supposed to be?" she asked, downshifting and getting off one of the exits.

"I don't know…just not this," Haley said, waving her hand up and down.

Shane shrugged as she rolled to a stop at a red light. She quickly changed the radio to a different local station. Elvis Presley's *Jailhouse Rock* was just starting. The light turned green and she drove on for a couple of miles, then got into the far-right lane and slowed down.

Haley's jaw dropped when she saw the two planes behind the fence, next to a large building.

"That's the *Lisa Marie* and *Hound Dog 2*," Shane said.

"No way," Haley uttered, staring out the window as they rode past the two jets.

Shane went down and turned around, and came back down the other side of the street, driving slowly along the famous wall in front of Elvis's mansion. "Welcome to Graceland," she said, rolling to a stop in front of the gates. The huge house was slightly visible through the trees.

"Oh my God." Haley's face lit up like a small child on Christmas morning. "I thought it was out of the way?"

"It is, but I can take a different route. No big deal. Do you want to go inside?"

Haley noticed the tourists milling about. "I probably shouldn't."

"I wouldn't offer if it wasn't safe," Shane said. "No one knows you're here, so they won't be looking for the wild and reckless country star. Besides, I have a jacket and hat that will disguise you. Or…we can get back on the highway," she said, putting the car back in gear.

"Wait!" Haley squeaked. "Let's go in!"

"Alright." Shane smiled and got back into traffic so she could go park in the lot up the street.

***

After paying the fee to tour the mansion only, Shane gave Haley the thin leather jacket from her suitcase, and a pageboy hat she kept in the car. Then, they boarded the tour bus that rode up the long driveway to the mansion. As they got back off, Shane nonchalantly felt the butt of her Glock pistol in the shoulder holster under the zip up hoodie jacket she'd put on to cover it.

The people in the group were all on self-guided tours, meaning they didn't have anyone rushing them around or explaining everything. That made it easier for Shane to keep most of them away from Haley as they did their own thing. She was fairly certain no one would recognize her.

The first room they came upon was the large living room. The carpet, walls, and furniture were all stark white. There was a gorgeous stained-glass partition separating that room from the one further behind it, the music room, where a black grand piano was sitting. The blue and gold tones of the curtains and décor had a very fifties and sixties feel to them.

Goosebumps rose on Haley's skin as a wave of nostalgia washed over her. She'd heard stories about other people's experiences at the mansion, most of which she thought were just marketing ploys to get people to come there, but no…she felt it too…his presence. Haley chanced a glance at Shane through the mirror as Elvis's song *Can't Help Falling In Love* played softly over the speaker system throughout the house. She quickly pulled her eyes away when she saw Shane looking back at her.

They made their way around the first floor of the large house with the rest of the tour group, moving from the drab, dark brown kitchen that literally looked like you'd stepped into 1975, to the beautiful dining room with an Italian glass chandelier hanging over the massive oval table. The basement had three separate rooms that all represented the seventies as if time had stopped. The first, a pale-yellow room with a dark blue couch and a matching bar. Three TV sets were recessed into the wall side by side by side. The next room had pleated fabric in a floral pattern on the walls and ceiling, and a pool table with a tiffany lamp hanging over it. The final room was the jungle room, complete with green shag carpet on the floor and ceiling, wood panel walls, hand-carved wooden furnishings, fur fabric covering the cushions, and a waterfall running down one of the walls. The room was decorated with ferns and other types of greenery all around.

"Does your house look anything like this?" Shane teased as they made their way back to the main floor.

"Hell no," Haley laughed. "I definitely do not have a jungle room, but I feel like a lot of music was made right here."

Shane chuckled. "Oh, I don't doubt it. From what I've read, he sang and made music all over this house. I'm pretty sure his ghost lives on, right here in these walls."

"I believe it," Haley said, still feeling the goose bumps covering her skin.

As they made their way back to the main floor, Elvis' song *All Shook Up* was playing softly on the speakers. Haley fought the urge to sing along.

"Are you ready to get back on the road?" Shane asked, walking towards one of the tour buses that was about to leave.

Haley nodded, then reached out, grabbing Shane's hand. "Thank you," she said softly, meeting Shane's eyes.

"You're welcome," Shane replied with a smile, interlacing her fingers with Haley's to hold onto the feeling of touching her just a little longer.

"Last call for this bus," the driver yelled, breaking the connection between them.

Haley quickly let go and got on, finding the only open pair of seats. Shane squeezed in beside her, then the driver slammed the door and took off down the driveway.

Chapter 22

"That was an experience I'll never forget," Haley said once they were back in the car and heading down the road. "I can't thank you enough, and I plan to repay you for my ticket—"

"I already told you, it's not a big deal. Forty dollars isn't going to break me. I know you have nothing but the clothes on your back at the moment."

"And *they* are not even mine," Haley muttered.

"True," Shane said, smiling sympathetically at her before heading up the ramp to get back onto the interstate. "Is there anything you want to listen to? We're going to lose the Elvis station in about two miles."

"Not really."

Shane switched to the next station and Tina Turner's *Proud Mary* was just starting. She turned the volume up a bit, and left it there.

"We covered this on my last tour," Haley said before she started to sing along. The smoky blues sound in her voice was very apparent as she sang the slower lyrics in the beginning.

Shane tapped her hand on the steering wheel and nonchalantly checked the time as she watched the road.

"How much longer?" Haley asked as the radio went to commercial.

"A little over two and half hours. I have to stop in about an hour for gas. We can eat somewhere, if you want."

"I'd rather just get home."

Shane nodded.

***

Shane leaned against the car with her feet crossed at the ankle while the gas pump slowly filled the tank. Orange and red leaves were falling from the trees and blowing around in the cool breeze. The small, one light town looked somewhat familiar, causing her mind to wander back to a time she thought she'd forgotten. If she closed her eyes, she swore she could smell the sweet and playful scent of vanilla and lavender, and hear the soft, innocent voice calling her name.

"Shane?" Haley said, repeating herself a couple of times.

"Huh?" Shane said, finally looking at her as the memory faded like a ghost in the wind. She cleared her throat and pushed off the car.

"You were a million miles away."

"What?"

"The pump stopped two minutes ago."

Shane exhaled heavily and returned the spout to the pump. Then, she put the gas cap back on. She took a couple of deep breaths and shook her head. She hadn't had such a physical experience in a long time.

"What happened to you?" Haley asked, staring at her across the top of the car.

"Nothing. I'm fine."

Haley pinned her with a stare and crossed her arms, silently refusing to get into the car.

"Come on. We need to get back on the road."

"Not until you tell me what the hell that was about."

"Alright. Just get into the car," Shane growled, trying not to cause a scene. The last thing she needed was the station attendant coming outside and recognizing Haley. She'd removed the jacket and hat disguise not long after they'd gotten onto the interstate back in Memphis.

Haley got in and pulled her seatbelt on, all the while looking at Shane as she started the car, put it in gear, and headed back down the road towards the interstate.

"This isn't something I talk about…not ever," Shane sighed, avoiding her stare and keeping her eyes straight ahead on the road. "I placed someone in a town like this when I was a Deputy Marshal," Shane said.

"Witness protection?"

"Yes," she answered.

"Were you thinking about her just now?"

Shane nodded.

"Where is she now?"

Shane cleared her throat. "Green Hill Cemetery," she uttered.

"I'm sorry."

"Don't be. It was a long time ago."

"Is that why you left the Marshal Service?"

"Yes and no."

"Did you love her?"

"Are we going to do this the rest of the way?" Shane questioned, pinning her with a serious look.

"You went somewhere else back there. I've never seen you do that."

"You've known me all of three weeks." Shane's jaw tightened. "It doesn't happen often," she sighed. "In fact, it hasn't happened in several months."

"You loved her," Haley said softly.

Shane nodded. "I shouldn't have."

"Why not?"

"She was my first assignment working witness protection." She paused, changing lanes to go around an extremely slow-moving car, but more so to gather her thoughts and choose her words carefully. "She was young

130

and innocent. Her father was an anti-Semitic nutcase. Long story short, she was placed in protection while he awaited trial. It took three months. During that time, we kept her hidden. I saw her every day. We grew close...too close. I knew better. I made a rookie mistake and fell for her. After she helped put him away for life, she was relocated and given a completely new identity. It was a town like that one back there that I placed her in. I broke it off, knowing it would never work out. I had to let her go live her life. I broke her heart and my own in the process."

Haley nodded, unsure of what to say.

Shane went on. She'd come this far, she might as well tell it all. "About two years later, she married a local guy who was really good to her. She wanted a family and a real life, something she never had with her father. A little over a year and a half ago, her father broke out of prison. When she found out her father was on the loose, the fear of him finding her drove her to suicide. She left a note for her husband, and a letter for me, thanking me for getting her away from him and giving her the life she'd always wanted, even though she'd always wanted it to be with me. She said death her own way would be easier and less painful than death at the hand of her father when he found her. Then, she took a bunch of pills, went to sleep, and never woke up."

"Oh my God," Haley gasped. "I'm so sorry."

"It's okay. Like I said, it was some time ago. I took it hard. The Marshal Service gave me an extended leave, but I decided not to go back. At that point, I wasn't even working with witness protection anymore, I'd been moved to criminal investigation and was working my way towards special operations. She was the only person to die out of several witnesses whom I'd placed," she sighed. "None have ever been located, at least that I know of. During my time in witness protection, I also protected foreign dignitaries, presidential candidates, and ex-presidents when the Secret Service needed assistance. None of them were ever harmed either. Anyway, I was looking for a way to utilize my skills, but change the pace a little bit. I saw Dennis' add and moved to Memphis, Tennessee the following week. That was a little over a year ago."

"I'm sorry I made you tell me. I know how hard that had to have been."

"It's fine. I moved on a while ago and came to terms with myself. I know it wasn't my fault. I also know I couldn't have prevented any of it. I honestly haven't thought about her the entire time that I've been working for Dennis."

"It's strange how things bring up old memories you'd buried so deep, they were all but forgotten."

"Yeah," Shane mumbled.

***

Haley casually looked over at Shane from time to time as they changed interstates once again on their drive. Hearing her story had made it clear why she'd kept her distance from Haley. There were so many layers to her profound personality. She'd only seen a few. Turning her head back towards the window, she wondered what the rest were like as you slowly peeled them away, uncovering the woman inside. It was a curiosity she'd have to forget about. Just like the dreams that haunted her at night, making it impossible for her to work, and the kiss…that would be the hardest thing to forget. She was sure the feeling of Shane's soft lips on hers would be burned into her memory forever.

That thought alone made her sigh. *I may never write another song. Hell, I know I won't while she's still around.*

"You okay?" Shane asked.

"Yeah," Haley replied, giving her a quick smile.

"We're almost there according to the GPS," Shane said, looking at her phone.

Haley nodded. She'd been looking out the window and through the windshield for most of the drive, but hadn't paid much attention to where they were. The somber reason for the return home came flooding back to her. She felt horrible for Fizzy losing his life in the accident and wished she could do more than just pay for his funeral and give his employee death benefit to his family, but she couldn't bring him back. The sadness of losing a friend was overwhelming. She couldn't imagine going through what Shane had described.

Recognizing the park nearby as Shane exited the interstate, made her perk up a little. They were still a few miles away, but she was back in Brentwood, a suburb city ten minutes from Nashville, and the place she called home.

"You don't need that, I know where we are," Haley said as the GPS told Shane the next step in the directions.

She quickly turned it off and listened as Haley directed her to a country road back behind a bunch of subdivisions. It was pitch black and she couldn't see much, except cattle fencing and trees.

"Slow down. The driveway is right here on the left," Haley said.

Shane came to a stop in front of a double iron gate and rolled the window down. She looked over at Haley, waiting for the code to open the gates.

Haley moved to get out of the car and Shane laughed. "It's not like I'm going to come back and stalk you once this is all over."

"Zero, eight, one, four," Haley huffed.

Shane punched the numbers on the key pad and the gates swung open. The exterior lights were on as they drove up the drive, and around the side of the large two-story house, to the attached three car garage. "Wow," Shane mumbled, trying to get a good look at the place in the dark. It was farm-style with red brick and had a wide front porch with square pillars, and two chimneys.

"I'll use the keypad to open the last door. You can park in there. I assume you're staying here and not at a hotel," Haley said.

"That would be correct. I don't want to crowd your space, but with the funeral coming, he will assume—"

"I know. I know. It's all about the mystery letter writer. It's fine. My house is a hell of a lot bigger than that bus was," she replied, getting out and heading over towards the keypad on the wall. She entered the code for the empty third bay and the door began to rise up.

Shane pulled the classic car inside and shut it off. When she got out, she noticed a silver midsize SUV in the first bay and a blue gas-powered golf cart in the second bay. She quickly opened the trunk and grabbed her bag, along with her jacket, then followed Haley through the door and into the house.

"The bedrooms are all upstairs," Haley said, flipping a switch and lighting up the kitchen. It had a modern feel with an island in the middle and dark wood flooring, but it was antique style with crown molding that had a design etched in it. All of the colors were different aged shades of white, the countertops were dark marble, and the appliances were stainless. It looked like something out of a magazine, and certainly like no had ever made a meal in there.

The kitchen looked out over the large living room, where a crème colored couch and loveseat, and two matching chairs were all placed over a massive area rug. The wall at one end had a red brick fire place with a large painting of a light brown and white horse hanging over it. Family pictures from different generations, hung in antique wood frames on the opposite wall. Next to that wall was a wide-open doorway to the dining room. Large windows ran along the entire back of the house, looking out at the expanse of green grass and the horse pasture in the distance, with massive oak trees along the edge of the property just inside the cattle fencing.

"Come on. The bedrooms are this way," Haley said, leading her through another wide opening that took her to the front of the house where the foyer was located, along with the double front doors and the beautiful wooden staircase.

Shane noticed the crystal chandelier hanging over the foyer as they ascended the stairs that zigzagged left, then right before opening into a small open area in the middle of the second floor. Hallways ran to the left and right, and another went straight ahead to a closet and the laundry room.

"The spare rooms are down that hall to the right. The bathroom is in the middle. Take either, it doesn't matter."

"Thank you," Shane said.

"Hopefully, this doesn't last long," Haley replied, walking away.

Shane watched her open the double doors at the end of the opposite hall and step inside the master suite, before choosing a room of her own. She'd picked the smaller of the two, the one on the back of the house that overlooked the pool, but she didn't have time to take in the view, or lack thereof in the dark. She was hungry, but didn't want to just rummage through someone's kitchen. However, it was seven o'clock at night and she hadn't eaten since that morning. Her stomach had other plans.

When Shane opened the refrigerator, she found a pan of vegetable lasagna and chicken pot pie. Her mouth watered as the scent made its way to her taste buds. *Yes!*

"There's probably apple pie in there too," Haley said from the other side of the island, scaring the hell out of Shane. She nearly dropped the lasagna pan on the floor as she spun around. The look on her face was like the Grinch getting caught stealing presents. Her jaw dropped as she tried to think of a way to back pedal out of the situation. Haley stared at her with a raised brow and her arms crossed at chest level.

"I…" Shane started, then stopped herself. *I'm a grown woman. If I want to eat, I'm going to eat. I'm your damn houseguest!* she thought, then cleared her throat and said, "I'm hungry. So, unless you have other plans, there happens to be freshly made food in here."

"My maid, Emma Jean, made the food earlier today. Rich must've told her I was coming home. She does this every time I go on the road or leave for more than two days. I'm pretty sure she thinks I'm going to starve to death if she doesn't feed me. I swear, I pay her to clean my house, not be my chef. She never could have kids, so she treats me like I'm her own. Her husband Marvin takes care of my horse and keeps up with the barn and yard work around here. His nephew helps him out."

Shane simply nodded, unsure of what to do with the plate of food she was holding, all while the refrigerator was still open.

"Anyway, the plates are in that top right cabinet, and the silverware is in that drawer over there," Haley said, coming around the island to help her with the food.

"Are you sure you eat in here?" Shane asked, looking at the spotless kitchen.

"Yeah," Haley laughed. "I don't cook much because it's just me, but Emma Jean believes a house should look presentable, so she keeps the place spotless. The only rooms she doesn't mess with are my music room and the den."

"Oh," was all Shane said, surprised that they were about to sit down and have their first meal together.

"Rich just called. Fizzy's funeral is tomorrow at ten a.m. He'll pick us up at nine," Haley said as she put some food on her plate and shoved it into the microwave. As soon as she was finished, she pulled out one of the island stools and sat down. Shane did the same, saying nothing as she took a seat.

They were a couple feet apart, having their first actual meal together, but the house was eerily silent. Neither woman was really up for conversation to begin with, and until the last twenty-four hours, they'd done nothing but argue.

"This is really good," Shane said, nearly clearing her plate.

"Yeah, Emma Jean is a great cook. She's a wonderful maid, too," Haley replied, getting up and putting her dish in the sink. "Have a good night," she added, walking out of the room.

Shane had never seen her so sober. It was like the light was gone from her personality. It had been vanishing the closer they got to Nashville, and by the time they'd walked through the door of the house, it was completely extinguished. Shane felt bad for her. Coming home should be an exciting time marking the end of her tour, not a quick trip to bury your friend who died tragically…while working for you no less.

Her cell phone rang in her pocket as she headed up the stairs. She was happy to have the distraction to take her mind off Haley, if only for a few brief minutes.

"We got in a little over an hour ago," she said as she answered. "It took a little longer than expected."

"What happened?" Dennis asked.

"Nothing. I took her to Graceland."

"Really?"

"Yeah, it was a little out of the way, but not too bad. I figured she needed a break from everything for a little bit."

"How was the drive?"

"Fine. A little bumpier and more cramped than if we'd rented an SUV like I'd planned, but as soon as she saw the Vette, she was hooked."

"Get out! You drove the Corvette all the way to Nashville?"

"Yep."

Completely floored, Dennis squeaked, "Who are you, and what have you done with Shane Crowley?"

Shane laughed.

"I'll let you get some sleep. I know it's been a long day, and you're obviously delirious."

"Two hundred miles isn't that bad. I shipped it from Arizona because that was entirely too long of a drive in that car. Anyway, yes, it has been a long day. I'll touch base with you as soon as I know what's happening next," she said, ending the call.

Chapter 23

Around two a.m., Shane was awoken by the soft sound of a piano. She had no idea where it was coming from, but assumed Haley was up, burning the midnight oil, something she'd done just about every single night on the bus. Although, it seemed to be more of a struggle than anything else...wholeheartedly blamed on Shane's presence. She wondered if it was the comfort of home allowing her to work. Nevertheless, she got out of bed, pulled on a pair of joggers and a t-shirt, and walked out of her room. The sound seemed to be coming from downstairs. She crept down slowly, hoping the old stairs didn't creak. The last thing she wanted to do was disturb her and cause another riff. She navigated the first floor in the dark, letting the sound of the piano guide her. She finally came to a stop outside of what she believed was probably the music room Haley had mentioned earlier. She didn't dare go in. Instead, she leaned against the wall a few feet away from the door, listening as Haley played the melody and softly sang the lyrics of *Nothing Compares 2 U,* written by Prince and made famous by Sinead O'Connor. She didn't have to see her face to know that Haley was crying. Her usual sound of smoky blues mixed with country twang, was laced with tears. Shane squeezed her eyes closed, feeling the words cut to her soul as Haley sang them. She wished she could take away her pain. She knew all too well the feeling of being so riddled with guilt that you were broken inside.

***

When Haley finished the song, she let the piano go silent. Then, she wiped the tears from her face and put her hands back over the ivory keys once more. Before she could start playing, the wood floor creaked in the hallway, scaring her half to death. Realizing she wasn't alone, she froze like a deer in headlights, afraid to move, and nearly unable to swallow the golf ball sized lump in her throat. "Damn it," she mumbled, remembering her houseguest. "Sneaking around at night is a good way to get shot in the backwoods of Tennessee," she called out.

"Shit," Shane whispered, angry at the old board under her foot. "I'm sorry," she said, walking into the room. "I heard the piano and—"

"I seriously doubt the letter writer is going to break in and play this old thing," Haley said, getting up from her seat at the beautiful, polished mahogany, baby grand piano.

"I really wasn't trying to disturb you."

Haley nodded.

"I just…I know what it's like to lose someone close to you," Shane said softly as she moved to walk out of the room.

Haley reached out, meeting her gaze with tear-filled eyes.

Throwing caution to the wind, Shane wrapped her arms around her, taking heed at the way Haley's body fit with hers. Warm tears rolled down her cheeks, dripping onto the skin of Shane's neck where Haley's face was nuzzled against her. Shane tried not to feel the blood rushing south, but there was no use. Her mind had betrayed her as soon as she'd inhaled the lingering floral scent of Haley's shampoo and felt the warm body against her own. She tried to pull away far enough to put some space between them, but Haley's lips moved up Shane's neck, meeting hers in a passionate, yet delicately slow, kiss that made Shane weak in the knees. She knew she should stop

141

this. Haley wasn't thinking, she was just reacting with emotion. But, Shane became powerless as Haley's tongue slipped between her lips, grazing her own. Whether it was meaningless sex, a one-night stand, or the biggest mistake of her life, Shane had no choice but to let it happen. All rational thought went out the window like a trail of cigarette smoke as Haley reached under Shane's shirt. Warm hands moved up her back, removing the garment at the same time, revealing breasts that were on the smaller side, but perfect for Shane's trim figure.

Haley broke the kiss as she dropped the shirt on the floor. Her eyes traced a path down Shane's body as Shane grabbed the edge of the old Van Halen t-shirt Haley was wearing, pulling it easily up over her head. Perky round breasts, a cup size larger than Shane's, bounced free. Shane's eyes met Haley's. Her watery tears were gone, but the sadness remained. No words were spoken as her gaze lingered, waiting for Haley to either keep going or walk away. She barely waited a full second, before Haley moved into her arms once more, pressing her lips to Shane's and melding their bodies together.

Haley was too far gone to think about who she was with. She just wanted to *feel*, and Shane's warm skin felt delectably good against hers. She ran her hands along Shane's shoulders and down her sides, coming to rest at her hips and tucking her thumbs under the waistband of her joggers.

Shane followed her lead as Haley began to slip her pants and underwear off in slow motion. Without breaking their sensuous kiss, Haley pushed the clothing lower. Shane kicked out of them once the garments reached her ankles. Then, she grabbed Haley's cotton shorts, tugging them over her hips. They fell easily to the floor, revealing nothing underneath.

Haley reveled in the feeling of Shane's soft skin and a warm, naked body as she ran her hands up the front of her torso, caressing her taut stomach and cupping her breasts. Shane moved her hands from Haley's hips to her back, sliding them along her smooth skin and up under the long, wavy hair hanging down. As Haley moved her hands up to Shane's shoulders and into the short hair at the base of her neck, she pressed their hips together.

Shane wasn't used to giving into someone. This was completely new to her, but knowing this was what Haley needed, she let her keep going when she urged her backwards. She'd only taken a few lazy steps, careful not to separate their bodies, when she bumped the worn, brown leather sofa.

The kiss finally broke when Shane moved to lie down. Their eyes locked as Haley crawled on top of her, dragging her lips in a lazy path as she slowly brought their bodies fully together with her thigh slipping between Shane's legs. Itching to take control, Shane held her breath. Unaware, Haley moved to continue their fervent kissing, sliding her leg along the warm, wet folds at the same time. A tiny groan escaped Shane's mouth as Haley's hand inched lower, replacing her thigh. She was close...oh so close. It took everything she had to hold back. Needing a distraction as Haley began moving her fingers in teasing circles, zeroing in on the swollen mound in the center, Shane pushed her hand between their joined hips. She found the wetness she was looking for, but had no leverage to move her fingers. Instead, she held them still while Haley slowly rubbed herself against them, her hips matching the rhythm of her own fingers lazily working Shane's wet center.

Shane's heart pounded in her chest, trying desperately to keep up with the blood racing through her veins. She concentrated on breathing through their shallow kisses until Haley pulled her lips away, nuzzling her face against Shane's neck as she began moving her fingers a little faster and pressing her hips down a little harder.

Shane couldn't stop her body from letting go. She clenched her jaw and groaned from deep inside as the orgasm tore through her. Haley instantly shuddered on top of her, panting against Shane's skin as she reached her own climax.

As soon as her body began to relax, Haley slipped to the side between Shane and the couch, still somewhat on top of her. The coolness of the leather was like ice against her heated skin. She closed her eyes, listening to the steady rhythm of Shane's heartbeat.

***

Shane stretched in her sleep, shifting her position on the old, worn couch, causing the thin blanket covering her to slip off. Opening her eyes in the dimly lit room, she noticed the guitars in the stand nearby and the piano just beyond. She sat up, realizing she was naked and alone as everything came flooding back to her.

She quickly got up, searching the floor for her clothes. Once she was dressed, she walked out into the silent hallway. The smell of food wafting past her nose as she moved towards the center of the house, made her stomach growl.

"Biscuits and gravy are in the kitchen, courtesy of Emma Jean," Haley said, breezing past her as she headed up the staircase.

Shane simply nodded, unsure of what to say to her. Although, she hadn't expected Haley to say much either. She'd been in her position; used someone to ease her grief, but it had been a one-night stand from a bar, not someone she had to see every day. The last thing Shane wanted to do was make things awkward, so she went about like nothing had happened. It was better this way anyhow.

She made herself a plate of breakfast and sat down on the same stool from the night before. She was barely three bites in when she remembered the funeral. If the clock on the stove was correct, she had less than thirty minutes to shower and get dressed. Sighing, she dumped the remainder of the best biscuits and gravy she'd ever had into the trash and padded up the stairs.

***

Shane was standing in the foyer at two minutes to nine, wearing her black suit with a slate gray dress shirt underneath her jacket and her Glock handgun in the holster under her arm. She faced the double front door with her back to the staircase, peering out the large windows on either side through the thinly veiled curtains. To her right was a closed door, leading to a room she'd never seen. Directly opposite was the door to the room she'd woken up in that morning. She kept her focus on the long driveway, anticipating Rich's arrival. Anything to keep her mind from drifting back to that room.

Shane's back stiffened at the sound of footsteps on the stairs. She caught sight of the black Cadillac SUV pulling through the gate, before pivoting so that the staircase was on her left and the front door to her right.

Haley slid her right hand along the rail as she descended, wearing a black, knee length dress. The V in the front stopped at the top of her breasts, showing a tiny cleavage line, and wide straps went over her shoulders. A matching shawl went around her back and tucked around each arm. A black fedora hat sat atop the wild blonde waves cascading over her shoulders, and black heels put her close to eye-level with Shane. However, her beautiful blue-green eyes were hidden behind dark aviator sunglasses. Her hands came together in front of her, holding a small clutch purse.

Shane stepped up next to her and held her elbow out. Haley said nothing as she wrapped her hand around the crook of Shane's arm. Together, they walked out of the house, across the front porch, and down the steps.

The driver opened the rear passenger door of the waiting SUV and Haley slid in first, with Shane getting in beside her. Rich was seated up front, texting furiously on the phone in his hand as they drove away.

***

Haley stared out the window, her mind a million miles away. She'd been preoccupied ever since she'd woken on the couch in the music room...wrapped in Shane's arms. That night had been mostly a blur, with no rational thoughts in sight. She was lost, hurting...full of emotion. All she'd wanted to do was *feel* something, anything. Shane had been there to help ease the pain, give her what she needed, no questions asked. She'd never used anyone to physically soothe her grief...until now. It had certainly helped lift some of the pain from her shoulders, but it made sense why people turned to strangers. She wondered if her body would ever forget what it was like to touch Shane. She'd done a pretty good job of losing sight of the night before while she'd prepared for the funeral that morning, but her mind reassured her that it wasn't letting go, at least not while Shane was sitting two feet away from her. She tried to focus on the buildings passing by as the driver maneuvered through the traffic, finally turning into the parking lot of one of the oldest funeral homes in Nashville. The vehicle came to a stop under the covered area in front of the double doors. A few people dressed in black, milled about talking with one another or smoking.

Rich let himself out of the SUV, while the driver got out and opened the rear passenger door for Haley. Shane got out on her side, then walked around, quickly coming up to Haley's door before the driver was able to open it. Everyone standing outside turned their heads to watch Haley exit the vehicle. Shane and Rich flanked her sides as she walked into the building.

***

Instrumental music played lightly over the speakers as the guests walked up the center aisle to where the silver, closed casket rested on a stand with a beautiful spray of blue flowers on top of it. A large framed picture of Fizzy was sitting on an easel nearby. Several different floral arrangements were on stands all around behind the casket, and some smaller ones were on the floor in front of it. A podium stand was a few feet away with a small, upright piano behind it.

Haley kissed her fingers and placed her hand on top of the casket. Then, she put that same hand over her heart as she looked at the picture. That was the way she wanted to remember him, smiling and happy.

Fizzy's mother and wife were waiting for her as the guests continued moving in a small line, paying their respects. Haley hugged them both and wiped away tears with a tissue Shane had miraculously pulled from her pocket.

"I'm so very sorry for your loss. He was a good man, and so much more than a roadie. He was my friend, a confidant at times, and the most genuine, down to earth person I've ever met. Being on the road won't be the same without Fizzy leading the way," Haley said.

"Thank you for everything. Working for you and getting to know you as a person meant so much to him. He adored you like a father would a child," his wife said, squeezing her hands. "To him, you were family. You *all* were."

"He couldn't wait to get out on the open road every time you announced a tour. He was so proud to say he was Haley Nielsen's bus driver. He made sure everyone in town knew that," his mom added.

Haley smiled and wiped a few more tears. "This is Shane Crowley. She's been with us for most of the tour."

"I remember Fizzy telling me you had extra security because of some nutcase."

"Although I didn't know him well, I had the pleasure of talking with your husband on numerous occasions. He was always friendly and eager to help out any way he could."

"That was Fizzy. There wasn't a rotten bone in his body. If he met you once, you were friends for life," his mother said.

Shane smiled and nodded.

148

Haley gave them one more hug before moving to her seat at the front of the pews on the opposite side as the service began. Rich and Shane flanked her, and her band members sat in the row behind her, with the rest of the crew members filling in all of the pews behind them. Fizzy's family and friends filled up the pews on the left side of the room.

***

Shane stared at the wall behind the casket as the church pastor went on and on about Fizzy and his family. He led a few prayers, then he asked if anyone wanted to come up and say a few words. No one moved. He'd said enough for all of them.

"And now, we'll have Haley Nielsen sing a song at the request of the family," he added.

Haley sipped some room temperature water from the bottle Rich had been holding. Then, she walked up and sat down behind the piano. She adjusted the microphone, thinking she'd probably need it if her voice began to crack. Otherwise, her voice was strong enough to carry through the room.

Placing her hands over the keys, she started with a soft intro, then went into the lyrics of *Nothing Compares 2 U*, slowly singing, "It's been seven hours and fifteen days…since you took your love away."

Haley's rendition had a bluesy, smoky sound with a touch of country twang, instead of the sharp tone of Sinead O'Connor's voice. Halfway through the song, a few tears streamed down her face, but her voice never wavered as she kept going.

149

Listening to Haley sing from the heart sent a shiver down Shane's spine. She played the melody beautifully on the old piano, no doubt lifting the spirits of everyone in the room. Shane knew Fizzy loved to listen to her rock out on the guitar, but she had a feeling he was looking down at that moment, enjoying what he was hearing.

As soon as Haley finished the song, she rose from the bench. She held her hand to her heart while facing the family, then kissed her fingers and touched the casket one final time before taking her seat. The pastor spoke briefly, then ended the service with a prayer. Guests once again filed past the family, paying their respects on the way out of the funeral home. Rich hugged Fizzy's mother and wife, then turned to Haley.

"I have some business downtown, so I won't be going with you to the cemetery. I'm going to catch a ride with one of the road crew guys who is headed that way. The car service will follow the procession, then take you back to the house when you're ready."

Haley nodded and hugged him.

Shane shook his hand, then he walked away as they stepped up to the family.

"That was just absolutely beautiful," Fizzy's wife said. "He loved that song."

"Thank you, and if it's okay with you, I'd like to play it at all of the shows for the rest of the tour, dedicated to him each and every night. Although, I'll probably play the guitar instead. I know he used to love coming to watch rehearsals and the shows on his nights off."

"Yes." His wife smiled. "He always said you were like Janis Joplin and Johnny Cash's love child."

Haley laughed. "I've never been called that before…but I like it."

Shane smiled and nodded in agreement.

"He loved you like a daughter; he loved music; and he loved being on the open road. He died doing what he loved, Haley. It melts my heart to know you will continue to honor him for the rest of your tour. I know he'll be with you in spirit," his wife said.

"Oh, I believe she now has a guardian angel looking out for her," his mother added.

"Thank you both. That means so much to me," Haley replied, wiping away more tears. "I'll be at the cemetery service, but I want to stay in the back. Today is for honoring Fizzy and his life. We were just a small part of it."

His mother and wife both smiled and hugged her.

***

The procession to the cemetery took about five minutes, and the graveside service hadn't taken much longer. As soon as it was over, Haley and Shane made their way back to the waiting SUV, and were the first ones to leave. They'd briefly spoke about how nice the service was during the ride back out to Haley's house in Brentwood, but other than that, the drive was quiet.

Both women went to their separate rooms to change clothes once they arrived. Not wanting to crowd Haley's space, Shane pulled on a pair of jeans and a black t-shirt and padded back down the stairs after a brief conversation with Dennis over the phone to see if he had any updates. She wanted to see the music room again since the night before she'd been captivated by Haley, so full of sadness, singing and playing the piano, she'd neglected the fully decorated walls. She wished she'd taken a few extra

151

minutes to look around that morning when she'd woken, but the reality of the night before came crashing down on her like a ton of bricks. She'd dressed quickly and high-tailed it out of the room. There was also another room on the front of the house that she hadn't been privy too. Foregoing the idea of snooping around, Shane settled on the formal living room, as well as the kitchen behind it, where she'd spotted a fresh basket of plump peaches.

As she reached for one, she heard Haley's voice echoing through the house. Someone was obviously on the other end of a phone call that definitely was not going their way. She was sure the ornate cross hanging on the wall near the pictures of her family members, was rattling and would fly off at any moment due to the expletives racing out of Haley's mouth.

Shrugging, happy she wasn't on the brunt end this time, Shane grabbed a napkin and sat down on a stool, biting into the juicy peach and catching the sweet nectar as it rolled down her chin.

***

"Now listen, Haley. Tucker is only playing a few shows…until you're ready to get back on the tour. Then, you'll play a couple of shows together, and go your separate ways."

"This is bullshit, and you know it, Rich! The fucking label can't make me date Tucker Miller! I don't care what they want! I've made millions for those bastards. They should be kissing my ass, not the other way around."

"Maybe if you're seen out a few times with Tucker, they'll leave it alone. You know…get the press interested in what they think is a love story. The label will probably buy

152

into it and forget about making you play together on the tour."

"Are you serious right now?" she yelled. "Have you heard of the 'Me Too Movement,' Rich? Or perhaps, 'Times Up?' I suggest you familiarize yourself with it if you want to continue being my manager, and advise the label to get caught up on current events as well. I am not going to be forced to perform with a man on *my* headliner tour, or go out on a date with him because my label wants me to! The days of the man telling women what to do while dangling their careers over their heads is over! It's *my* tour, and I'll be back on it as soon as you get me a god damn bus! Fix this shit, Rich, or so help me, I'll be on the phone with my lawyer so fast the suits at that label will look like bobble heads!" she growled sharply, then ended the call and tossed the phone into the couch instead of the wall where it would've shattered to pieces.

"Of all the lowlife, piece of shit things to do, and on the day we bury Fizzy to boot," she grumbled to herself as she walked from the den into the kitchen. She came to a sudden stop, raising a brow as she watched Shane carelessly chewing on a peach. The wet napkin in front of her with a large brown seed in the middle of it indicated she was on her second piece of the succulent fruit. "Emma Jean is going to be pissed if you eat all of her cobbler peaches," she said.

Shane nearly choked as she turned her head. She hadn't heard Haley come into the room. "I didn't want to bother you, and its impolite to rummage through someone else's kitchen, so—"

"But, it's okay to eat their freshly picked fruit?" Haley questioned. "You're bothering me anyway, so you might as well make yourself at home. You'll starve to death if you wait on me to host meals. I eat when I feel like it. You should know that by now," she said, walking past her, through the living room and into the music room.

Shane finished the peach and tossed the remnants into the trash and walked outside onto the covered patio. The pool deck, surrounding the large, rectangle pool was just outside of it. A cool, woodsy scented breeze blew over the bare skin on her arms, causing the hair to stand on end. It was nothing like sitting outside at her apartment along the muddy Mississippi River in Memphis, which smelled like a sunbathing wet rat, especially in the heart of the summer.

She thought back to Haley's conversation, something she wasn't supposed to hear, and wished she hadn't. It was hard enough on Haley having her there, in her private home. She didn't want to make things worse by getting involved in her personal business. She was there to do one thing…keep her safe. Until there was another bus, or Haley decided to venture out, there wasn't much of a threat to her. Shane doubted whoever was writing the letters would actually appear on her property, but she couldn't be certain, so she'd taken all of the precautions by staying there with her. Although, she seemed to be failing at her job with the mysterious Emma Jean coming and going without being seen or heard. *Is she a damn ghost?*

Shane hoped the tour picked back up soon, or the guy made a mistake for her to catch him. Otherwise, she wasn't sure who was going to go stir crazy first being cooped up in that big house, her or Haley, and from the sound of yelling once again, Haley had a head start.

***

"Tucker is available to headline as many shows as you need if you want to take a little time to get everyone back on their feet, and there is no mandate that you have any contact with each other unless you wish to do so on your own."

"It sounds like they got smart real fast," she huffed.

"Let him play for a couple of weeks. Take some time to get back in the grove of things. I agree with the label on this one."

"Damn it!" she yelled. "I'm not taking any more time off the tour. We've already missed three shows. I don't need to go play in a honky tonk to get my mojo back. My fucking mojo never left. Just get me a bus, Rich. That's what I pay you to do!"

"I found one. It'll be there in the morning around nine."

"See. How hard was that?"

Rich ignored her jab. "I'll get the crew on the road tonight. St. Louis, then Chicago and Atlanta are the next three cities on the tour."

"Okay. I'll be ready." Haley hung up the phone. She needed to go through her wardrobe and pack for the road. She'd lost everything in the fire, including her favorite acoustic guitar. However, she had enough clothes to fill a small store, and a handful of different guitars in her music room.

Chapter 24

Shane was watching two birds, apparently playing tag in the air, either that or doing some kind of mating ritual she wasn't familiar with, when Haley burst through the doors. Shane raised a brow. Haley looked like she'd gone mad. "What are you doing?" she asked cautiously.

"Packing," Haley squeaked as she rushed past.

Packing? What? "Wait!" Shane called as Haley entered a door to the garage from the pool deck. "Where you going?" *Where are* we *going?*

Haley appeared a minute later with a guitar case in her hand. "What are you doing out here?" she questioned as she stepped back inside the enclosed patio.

"Bird watching," Shane muttered, still confused.

Haley lifted her chin in a slow nod, then half shrugged and went into the house.

Realizing she still didn't have an answer, Shane got up and went after her. "What are you packing for?" she asked, walking across the formal living room and through the doorway to the music room. She ignored the feelings stirring inside of her as she spotted the old, worn leather couch against the wall. Glancing around the room, Shane saw a shelf on one wall with several different awards sitting on it, and platinum and gold albums displayed around it. Another wall had three vintage guitars hanging on it, surrounded by large, framed album covers. She also noticed another couch adjacent to the one she'd slept on.

Haley was kneeling near her acoustic guitars, trying to decide which one to take. Her favorite travel guitar, a Taylor Mini, was lost in the fire. The others, sitting on the triple stand in front of her, were all concert size, which was bigger and the same size she played on stage. Two

Telecasters and one Les Paul guitar were also on a stand on the other side of the piano.

"The tour," she mumbled, choosing to take her Breedlove Pursuit, which had a beautiful dark wood finish. She placed it in the black, hard case that was lined with black plush material, and closed the lid. As she stood up, she looked over at Shane, who was staring around the room. She watched her as she moved closer to the awards on the shelf.

Shane knew Haley was popular. The amount of people selling out arenas to see her was proof of that, but she had no idea how big of a star she really was because she'd never been a fan of country music. "Is this a Grammy?"

"Yes," she replied, adding, "and that one is a CMA," as she walked up beside her. "This one here is an ACM, and those two are CMTs," she added, naming off the other music awards on the shelf.

Shane nodded slowly, looking at each of them before turning her eyes to Haley, who was standing nearby with her guitar case leaning against her. "I take it Rich found you a bus, if you're frantically packing for the tour," she said.

"That would be correct," Haley replied, picking up the case.

"Wonderful," Shane said with a half-smile, before walking out of the room behind her. The sooner the tour was over, the sooner she could get out of Haley's personal space and back into her own. Although, getting back into the tight confines of a tour bus wasn't exactly ideal either.

***

An eclectic mix of music blasted from an iPod speaker in Haley's room as she rushed around, packing for the road. Five pairs of threadbare jeans were laid out on the bed, along with several different tops, ranging from tanks to worn, tight-fighting rock and roll band tees. Two pairs of pointed toe, cowgirl boots were on the floor at the side of the bed, and various undergarments were tossed into a pile beside a couple pairs of cutoff jean shorts.

Haley walked out of the closet, singing along to *Freeway of Love* by Aretha Franklin as she tossed a wide black leather belt onto the bed, along with a dozen pairs of socks. She also added a few pairs of short, athletic shorts and baggy t-shirts.

***

Curious as to what was going on, Shane walked down the hall to the other side of the house after tidying up her suitcase. She crossed her arms and legs, leaning against the open doorway with her head cocked to the side and a smirk on her face. She watched as Haley danced and sang her way in and out of the large walk-in closet, adding more clothes to the growing pile as the song changed to *Twist and Shout* by the Beatles. She adored this playful, easygoing side of her. She'd only seen a few glimpses of it, but Haley had seemed much more carefree on their road trip from Memphis and at home than she had on her tour. Shane had a feeling this was the real Haley, not the person up on the stage or barking orders to her manager. She also realized the astronomical amount of pressure on her to perform at her best each and every night, and the toll it took on her. However, as demanding as it was, Haley seemed to live for it, as the excitement of getting back on the road was overly apparent.

"Walking into a girl's bedroom uninvited won't get you very far," Haley said, catching a glimpse of Shane out of the corner of her eye.

"I'm not trying to impose," Shane said, holding her position.

"You never *mean* to invade my space, but somehow you always do."

"It's the singing."

"Uh huh. Isn't that what drew you to my music room last night?"

"So, we're going to talk about that?" Shane asked casually.

"I have better things to do. Emma Jean should be here soon with dinner. She knows I'm headed back out, so she insists on making sure I eat a good meal before I go. She thinks I don't eat on tour."

Shane shrugged, half in agreement. "Good. I'd like to know how she is coming and going without me noticing."

"Yep. Some bodyguard you are," Haley muttered teasingly.

Shane raised a brow as if she were about to challenge her, but she turned and walked away. Haley paused her packing to watch Shane until she reached the staircase.

***

Shane stared at the large horse painting over the fireplace. She was sitting on the couch in the formal living room with her laptop balanced on her thighs, going through her notes on the letter writer. She needed to do something productive, thus taking her mind off the sphinx upstairs.

As she began reading the profile she'd put together, the door between the garage and kitchen suddenly opened, scaring her half to death. Shane nearly tossed her laptop to the floor as she reached for the gun that wasn't strapped to her. She'd gotten somewhat comfortable and hadn't been wearing it in the house.

"Whoa!" an older woman shrieked, dropping the two hot bags she was holding as Shane leapt out of the living room like a cat ready to pounce on prey. "Oh, my word! You scared the dickens out of me," she mumbled in a thick southern drawl, holding her hand to her chest.

"I apologize, ma'am," Shane said, clearing her throat.

"What's wrong?!" Haley yelled, rushing down the stairs like a herd of elephants. She shook her head when she saw the two women. "I see you've met Emma Jean. I told you she wasn't a ghost."

"What?" the woman questioned as Shane bent to pick up the bags of food.

"Emma Jean, this is Shane Crowley. She's a U.S. Marshal, and my bodyguard for the tour. She's been puzzled by you coming and going without her noticing."

"Heavens," Emma Jean laughed. "I do my best not to disturb Haley Jo. I never know if she's sleeping or working, so I come in quietly, do what I need to do and leave."

"I didn't mean to frighten you," Shane said. "I really am sorry."

"Oh, it's no bother. My ticker needs a good boost every now and then." She smiled. "So, you're a U.S. Marshal."

"Former," Shane corrected, bending down to retrieve her bags.

"Thank you. That was sweet of you."

Shane nodded and smiled.

"I'm glad you have someone looking out for you, and a U.S. Marshal at that. It's about time. I feel safer already. There are crazy people in this world you know," Emma Jean said, shaking her head as she opened the bags, pulling out the food she'd made. It was still piping hot and smelled delicious. "I made chicken and vegetable spaghetti, and cinnamon spiced apple crumb pie." She glanced at the basket on the counter. "It looks like I need more peaches," she muttered. "I'm going to jar them when I get a big enough batch, so I can make cobbler when you get home."

Haley looked at Shane and smirked. "That sounds wonderful," she said, hugging Emma Jean. "You're too good to me, you know that?"

"Oh, nonsense, child." Emma Jean shook her head. "So, Shane…is it agent or special agent with the Marshals?"

"Actually, they're called Deputy U.S. Marshal. Then, Supervisory Deputy U.S. Marshal and so on."

"Sounds like a mouthful. Tell me more about yourself, Deputy Shane. Where are you from? Do you have any brothers and sisters? What's it like being a U.S. Marshal? That must be so exciting. What made you want to do that? I love getting to know someone new, and for Haley Jo to invite you into her home, you must be someone special."

"I'm just here working, ma'am," Shane muttered.

"Uh huh," Emma Jean mumbled, waiting for her to go into her life's story.

"I live in Memphis, but I'm from Arizona originally. I graduated from the University of Arizona, and I'm an only child. I'm not in the Marshal Service anymore, but being a Deputy Marshal is nothing like you see on TV, and certainly different from the days of Wyatt Earp. I'm afraid it's a lot of red tape and bureaucracy," Shane said. "I also think you are an amazing cook."

Emma Jean smiled. "Thank you."

"You're welcome," Shane replied.

"What made you want to be a U.S. Marshal?"

"Actually, my plan was to go into the Army after college. My ambition was to become a general someday. A good friend of mine who I met at the university, her father was a retired U.S. Marshal. During our senior year, he heavily recruited me. I think he thought if I did it, his daughter would too, but she decided to become a school teacher," Shane laughed. "Anyway, that's how I wound up in the Marshal Service."

"Why did you stop?" Emma Jean asked.

Haley sat on a stool, completely enthralled in the conversation, despite knowing the real answer.

"I got tired of chasing bad guys, and protecting witnesses who were just as bad as the guys I was chasing," Shane sighed.

"Well, it couldn't have all been boring. You sound like you miss it."

"I do from time to time. I protected presidents when the Secret Service was in the area, as well as other dignitaries. And I helped catch some pretty serious criminals. So, it wasn't all that bad. I enjoy working in private service now."

"Well, I for one am I'm glad you made a career change. Although, I may be a little biased." Emma Jean smiled. "What do you think of Haley? She sings like an angel," she gushed. "I remember her running around as a child, singing and playing an old ratty guitar her father picked up at the second-hand store."

Shane laughed. "She's a very talented singer and musician. I have to admit, I wasn't a country fan when I met her—"

"I bet you are now," Emma Jean said with a wink and a beaming grin.

Shane swallowed the lump in her throat, wondering if the maid had seen them on the couch in the music room. The color began to drain from her face. She knew Haley had mentioned her duties, but she couldn't remember what she'd said.

"I best be on my way. What time does your bus leave in the morning?" she asked, looking at Haley.

"We should be gone by nine-thirty at the latest."

"I'll come tidy up after you've gone. You have fun and be careful," she said, pulling Haley into a hug. "I like her. Your momma and daddy would, too," she whispered.

"Uh huh," Haley mumbled.

"I'm glad you have her looking out for you," Emma Jean added before pulling away.

"Thank you for the food. You know you don't have to cook for me," Haley said, smiling like a little girl.

"I know that. I do what I want. Besides, you'd starve to death if it wasn't for me." She turned to Shane. "You keep her safe," she said, squeezing her hand. "It was so nice to meet you."

"I'll do my best. I'm sorry again for startling you," she said, keeping her composure as thoughts raced through her head.

"I'll be fine." Emma Jean smiled and walked out the door as quietly as she'd come in.

***

Haley and Shane sat side by side at the island, finishing the last of their dinner as the sun began to set.

"Why does she call you Haley Jo?" Shane asked.

"That's my first name. Jo is after my father, John. I dropped it and legally changed my name when I signed with my label, but my family still calls me Haley Jo."

"I see," Shane said, adding, "you seem excited about getting back on the road."

"Absolutely. Live performances are unlike anything else. I love the energy I get from the fans. It's a natural high."

"I'll take your word for it." Shane ate her last bite and got up with her plate to toss it in the trash. She wondered why Haley had cabinets full of beautiful dishes, but opted for disposable plates. "What does Emma Jean do when she's here?"

"What do you mean?"

"Does she go in and clean *all* of the rooms, or just specific ones?"

Haley looked at her with her face slightly distorted in an odd expression. "She cleans everything but my music room and den, and she only cleans my bedroom when I'm not home. Other than that, she pretty much keeps the rest of the house in order. Why?"

"I was just asking. She seems really nice," Shane said, sighing inwardly, knowing the older woman hadn't seen them together.

"She's sure smitten with you," Haley laughed. "You never told me that story about how you became a Deputy Marshal."

"I guess you never asked," Shane replied. "How did you wind up in music?"

"That would be my father's fault. He bought me the guitar, as Emma Jean told you. I taught myself to play it, and singing just came naturally to me. My mother had always been a big part of the church, singing in the choir and playing the piano. I actually learned piano first. She started teaching me when I was old enough to sit still. She used to play Loretta Lynn, Patsy Cline, Dolly Parton, and Juice Newton songs on the piano when we were the only ones in the church. Those were actually the first songs I learned to play. My father loved Johnny Cash, Elvis, the Beatles and pretty much all rock and roll from the seventies. As an only child, I got a good mix of the two of them. Anyway, when I was about fourteen, my father took me down to a local honky tonk called the Hillbilly. The bar owner thought my old man was nuts, but he shook his head and waved his hand at the stage. My knees knocked together as I walked across the room with my guitar, but as soon as my fingers touched the strings, I came to life. I sang Dolly Parton's *Jolene*, and blew him away. That was the start of my first steady gig. I played there twice a month on Saturday nights until I left for college. I still have an open invitation to play there anytime I want, and I usually do when I'm in town."

"Wow. Is that the reason you sing it now on tour?" Shane asked.

"Oh yeah. I've sang it on every one of my tours to pay tribute to how I got my start. Dolly loved it when I told her my story the night I met her at the CMAs, and she gave me the go ahead to record it. She's a hoot in person."

"I bet," Shane replied, tossing her plate in the trash. "I remember hearing it on one of your albums."

Haley looked at her slightly slack jawed. "You've listened to my albums?"

"Yeah, when I was first hired. You can tell a lot about a person by the songs they sing or books they write. Every artist puts a little piece of themselves in their work, no matter what form of art it is."

Taken aback, Haley merely nodded.

"Speaking of the tour, what's the rest of the schedule? Do you know?" Shane questioned, changing the subject.

"St. Louis, Chicago and Atlanta are the next three stops, I believe. There are ten more regular stops, plus the three I missed," Haley replied, tossing out her own plate.

Shane nodded, mentally calculating how much longer she'd be a part of the tour if she didn't put a stop to the letter writer.

"I have some work to do, so you'll hear music," Haley said, walking into the living room.

"I'll keep my distance. You know I'm not trying to cause a distraction," Shane said, grabbing her laptop.

"It's too late for that," Haley mumbled to herself as she headed to her music room.

***

Haley needed to get herself in the mindset for the tour, but the harder she worked, the more her thoughts slipped back to Shane, who was only a room away since she hadn't heard her go up the stairs. She'd played her piano, picked her acoustic guitar, and even played her Les Paul as she went through her set list for the show. There were no changes from the previous show since the band was literally playing the next night. She hadn't had time to go over anything with them. In fact, except for a brief phone call earlier in the day after she'd found out everything was back on, she hadn't spoken much to the band. They'd exchanged sentiments and hugs at the funeral, but other than that, everyone had pretty much kept to themselves. Realizing she'd done all she could do, and it still wasn't helping her focus, she turned out the lights and went up to her bed.

Shane had listened to Haley sing and play music from her position in the living room until she fell asleep on the couch. She finally woke around four in the morning and went up to the bed to be more comfortable. Thoughts of Haley and the tour clouded her mind as she drifted off once more.

Chapter 25

The bus arrived on time, driven by Ricky Swaffey, better known as Rico Suave to the crew and band. She quickly loaded her gear and told him to get on the road. She was glad Rich had chosen him to drive for her. Many of the road crew guys also worked as drivers, but only a couple were allowed to drive her bus when Fizzy was unavailable. Rico Suave had been one of them.

This one was a little smaller than the old bus, and had a slightly different layout. The living area had a couch, with a chair and table across from it. The open kitchen galley was next to the chair, and the dinette table with two chairs was beside the couch. A wall with a door in the center, separated the sleeping quarters from the living space. Through the door was a short hallway with the washer and dryer on the left side, and a single bunk room on the right. It was set up nearly identical to the one Shane had slept in on the old bus. The other side of the hallway had another wall and doorway that led to the bathroom. The toilet and a small sink were on the left with a door to give the area privacy, and the shower and larger vanity were across from it. Another doorway led into the master bedroom, where a queen-sized bed was located, along with various closet cabinets, including one with a six drawer, built-in dresser.

"This is ridiculous," Haley mumbled, noticing that she once again had to share a bathroom with Shane, and this time she also had to walk through it to get in and out of her room, giving her even less personal space. "Damn it, Rich. It's a good thing you're just leasing this bus for the tour. I might have strangled you!" she growled, making her way into her own room to put her clothes away.

Shane heard the grumbling, and assumed Haley wasn't happy with the bathroom location, as she unpacked her suitcase and placed her clothes in the single closet cabinet and built-in two drawer dresser. She laid her laptop on the bed, and put her gun and holster in the nightstand next to it. Then, she flopped down on the bed with her phone and pushed the call button next to Dennis's number. It rang a few times before he finally picked up.

"I'm back on the road," she said before he could answer.

"Already?"

"Yep," she sighed. "We're headed to St. Louis, I believe."

"Wow. That was fast. Okay. So, how is everything going?"

"As to be expected. Haley is fit to be tied about something, as usual. I have to say, she is quite different at home."

"Hopefully, this will all be over soon. Have you given anymore thought to my suggestion?"

"Yeah. Using her as bait isn't the problem. She's plenty visible. We have to wait for him to come to her."

"Do you think he will?"

"To be honest with you, I figured he would've already done so by now. Maybe he's just a lonely loser with nothing better to do than write threatening letters based on fake promises."

"That would be a good thing."

"Yes, but then again, she'll have to deal with the threats for however long he decides to write them, or until we catch him. Did you get that magazine subscription information?"

"I sent it a little bit ago, actually."

"I don't have the Wi-Fi password for the bus," Shane exhaled heavily. "I'll probably have to wait until we arrive at the arena to look at it on the computer. I'll see if I can pull it up on my phone. I'll touch base with you tomorrow."

"Sounds good. Oh, and Jeremy tracked down the person who stole Lee Edmond's identity. His name is Julio Valero, and he's in Puerto Rico."

"That's great. I know he'll be happy. That guy has nearly bankrupted him twice now."

"I know," Dennis said before hanging up.

Shane set her phone on the nightstand and opened her laptop. The bus name and logo popped up, but she had no idea what the password was. "Great," she mumbled, walking out of her room after trying a few different codes, including the old one, none of which worked. She knocked on the closed bathroom door and opened it when she didn't get an answer. "Haley," she called, standing in front of the other closed door in the bathroom, that led to Haley's room. "Do you have the Wi-Fi password for the bus?"

"What?" Haley growled, pulling the door open.

"Did Rich give you the internet code? I tried—"

"Huh? No. I don't have any code. Ask Rico, or better yet, call Rich," she snapped.

And just like that, the bitch is back. Shane shook her head, humming the tune to Elton John's song as she went back to her room to call Rich.

***

Shane had nodded off on the couch in the living room during the drive, waking when she felt the bus come to a stop and settle into its lowered and parked position. She sat up, looking out the large windows at the arena as she stretched her muscles. "I need to get into the gym," she mumbled to herself. This case had turned into a full-blown assignment away from home, and she hadn't exercised since she'd arrived.

Knowing Haley would be itching to get to work, Shane went to her room to put on her shoes and shoulder holster for her gun. Then, she slipped her Glock in place and pulled a black, fleece jogging jacket that was light and zipped in the front before walking into the bathroom.

"I'm going to check things out and see if Rich is here yet. He has our two-way radios. Please don't get off the bus until I return. You have my cell number if you need me," she said to the closed door leading to Haley's room.

When she didn't hear a reply, she shrugged and went about her business. She needed to check with arena security and figure out what was going on with the rental security.

"Fancy meeting you here," Rich called as Shane entered the arena. "How was the drive?"

"Uneventful," she said.

"Let me guess, she's back to bitch mode."

Shane raised a brow.

"She turns into a whole different animal on tour. I think it's because she's such a perfectionist. She puts herself under so much pressure. When she's not on tour, she's as sweet as can be. Anyway." He smiled. "Here's your radio and another for Haley to use on the bus. I'll let you take it to her."

"Thanks," she muttered.

"The hired security should be here by four-thirty. The stage is already set up and ready to go. I know she's probably chomping at the bit to get inside. The band is already setting up, so you can go ahead and take her in."

"Okay. Let me know when the rental cops arrive. We need to keep things tight."

"Got it," he said as his phone began to ring. "It's the insurance company. We've been arguing all day about the bus settlement," he added as he moved away to answer it.

Shane walked around the backstage area, which was set up pretty much the same as all of the other shows. Then, she headed back out to the buses. The door to Haley's bus was open. She was still inside, but standing on the bottom step with her arms crossed, leaning against the doorframe.

"I was wondering if you forgot about your hostage," she said sarcastically.

"Nope." Shane shook her head. It was hard to pull her eyes away from the white t-shirt with Pink Floyd's logo stretched across Haley's breasts, and the naturally tanned skin peeking through the rips along the thighs of her jeans. "This is your walkie-talkie," she said, handing it to her. She'd already attached her own to the waistband of her jeans and ran the wire for the earpiece up under her jacket. It was loose from her ear and lying over her shoulder.

Haley rolled her eyes as she clipped the walkie-talkie to her pocket. "Can we go now? I *do* have work to do."

"By all means," Shane said, backing away and bowing slightly with her arm stretched out like she was curtseying.

Haley shook her head and stepped off the bus with Shane quickly falling instep next to her.

***

For the next hour and a half, Haley and the band went back and forth, working on their set list while trying to get back in the groove. They were having issues with timing, which was to be expected since they'd been away from each other for a week.

Shane stayed backstage for a little while longer, then went outside to see if any early concert goers had arrived to get a sneak peek at the headliner. When she went back in to escort Haley to the bus to get ready for the show, she heard a single guitar playing. Cocking her head to the side, Shane snuck up the back of the stage and leaned against one of the metal supports. The rest of the band had already left, and the arena staff was busy getting everything ready for the doors to open. A few of their security personnel was walking around the floor, so Haley wasn't completely alone.

***

Haley strummed a slow melody on her guitar as she hummed. She needed to call Shane so she could go back to the bus, but that meant she'd have to see her again. At least in her house, she could hide away for hours, nearly forgetting the charismatic woman was even there. But on the bus, they were once again closed up in a tight space and she had no place to escape to when her thoughts ran wild.

She looked around at the fully lit arena. Rows of empty seats filled the floor and thousands surrounded them in the lower and upper decks. A shutter ran down her spine when she realized the letter writer could easily be sitting in any one of them, watching…waiting to hurt her, if that was really his plan.

Haley sighed and set the guitar back in the stand. *I think you would've tried by now if you really wanted to harm me, so the hell with you. I have a show to do.* She straightened her back and turned to walk off stage. That's when she saw Shane, and immediately shrieked, sounding like the screaming goat video everyone was sharing on YouTube.

Shane bit her lower lip almost hard enough to make it bleed to keep from laughing. She'd never heard Haley make that sound before.

"Fuck you!" Haley growled.

"Are you okay?" she asked, still struggling to keep it together.

"I'm fine!" Haley snapped, walking past her and exiting the stage.

"I'm sorry. I really didn't mean to startle you. I was looking for you to see if you were ready and heard the guitar," Shane said, falling in step with her.

"What is it with you and hearing music. It's like some kind of trance that makes you seek me out. It's actually a little creepy."

"What?"

"Nothing," Haley grumbled, boarding her bus. "Tell Rich to find some damn food. This bus has nothing in the fridge."

"Okaaaay," Shane said, blowing a deep breath out through her pursed lips. She quickly called Rich, telling him Haley demanded that he stock the bus during the show. He said a few choice words then hung up. She had an hour before the start of the show, and an hour before Haley's performance began. The last thing she wanted to do was get on that bus with her, but all of the security measures were in place, and so far, there was no fanfare near the bus area.

"The hell with her," she said aloud, then grabbed the door handle.

Haley was in her room, so at least she didn't have to deal with her right away. She went into her room and turned her laptop on. Rich didn't have any idea what the password was for Wi-Fi when she'd talked to him earlier in the day. He was supposedly trying to find out, but he hadn't mentioned it again. However, the venue had a good signal, so she was able to jump on their connection and open the email from Dennis with the magazine subscription files. She uploaded them into Excel, hoping to be able to easily sort them.

Chapter 26

Shane needed to be working on the case, but she couldn't miss an opportunity to watch Haley perform, so she stood on the side backstage, watching the exceptional woman sing her heart out as the crowd cheered and sang the words to every song. She had no idea what that felt like, but was sure it was an adrenaline high unlike any other. Shane didn't care for Haley's attitude, but she respected her immensely as an artist and entertainer.

Towards the end of the show, Haley switched from her acoustic guitar to her custom Telecaster guitar, and stepped up to the mic. "Most of you probably know we recently lost a dear friend who was like a family member to us."

The big screen behind the band flashed to a picture of Fizzy with his birth and death dates written on it.

"I sang this at his funeral at the request of his beloved wife and mother, and vowed to honor him by singing it at the rest of our shows. However, there's been one minor change. Fizzy loved to listen to me play this thing. So, I'm going to do this song the way he would've wanted to hear it," she said, then her guitar came alive as she played the first chord. "It's been seven hours and fifteen days...since you took your love away," she sang.

The big screen began scrolling through various pictures of Fizzy on the different tours.

Shane knew Haley had planned to play it at all of the shows, but figured she'd hop on the keyboard, not play her electric guitar. She had to agree with what she'd said about Fizzy. She liked this version better too, not that there was anything wrong with the piano, but the bluesy sound coming from that guitar, mixed with her smoky twanging voice was as smooth as a hot knife cutting through butter.

The ambiance was breathtaking as the crowd softly sang along while holding up their cell phones with the flashlights on. The dark arena looked light the night sky filled with thousands of bright stars.

"This is what she lives for. Look at that crowd eating out of the palm of her hand," Rich said, stepping up next to Shane. "Some artists have it and some don't. I'm pretty sure she was born with it."

"What's that?" She asked.

"Charisma."

Shane didn't have to say anything. She knew exactly what he was talking about. She'd been drawn to Haley since before she ever met her. There was something about the look in her eyes in the case file photograph that made Shane unable to say no. Despite the massive battles they'd had over the course of their time together, Shane still felt like this was right where she needed to be. Otherwise, she was pretty sure she would've left a long time ago. "I'm going to go check the mob outside. Radio me when she's done," she said.

***

"That was a great crowd!" Haley said, flopping down on the couch in the bus. Her throat was a little sore from having not performed in a week, but other than that, which she'd fix with some warm tea and honey, she felt really good. "What'd you think?" she asked, tapping Shane's thigh with her boot as she walked by. "Or did you not see the show?"

"I didn't think my opinion mattered," she said, stopping and turning around. "They loved you, as always. And, yes, I saw the show. I'm never far away."

"I know," Haley muttered, watching her walk into her room.

"Dinner should be here any minute. I ordered Chinese," Rich said from the chair across the room as he ended the call he was on. He'd missed the playful little banter between them. "The show was fantastic," he added. "You're going on the Good Morning Chi-Town radio show tomorrow morning. I'll pick you up around seven-thirty. Their office isn't far from the arena."

"Sounds good. Hey, we're going back through Nashville on the way to Atlanta after Chicago, right?"

"Yeah. Why? Do you need something from home?"

"No. I want to stop and play at the Hillbilly."

"Are you sure that's a good idea?"

"No one knows I'll be there. I'll make sure Earl doesn't announce it."

"Okay," Rich said, scratching his goatee in thought. "Shane's going with you. I'll meet the bus and drive you to the bar. Afterwards, you can both fly with me down to Atlanta. That way, the convoy can keep going. You don't want the band with you?"

"No. Just me and my guitar like old times."

"I know that's where you like to try out new music. You have something new you're working on?"

"I don't know, maybe. I just want to clear my headspace, you know?"

He nodded.

"Thanks," she said, getting up to hug him bye.

As soon as his SUV was out of the parking lot, headed to the airport, the Chinese restaurant driver showed up with all of the food. The road crew manager divvied it up, and knocked on Haley's bus door with their bags.

Hearing the loud knock, Shane jumped up from the bed, where she'd been sitting, going through the file on her laptop. She took off out of the small room, shoeless, but still wearing her t-shirt and jeans, and her gun was still strapped under her arm. She held her hand on the grip, ready to snatch it out of the holster as she side-stepped Haley to get to the door first. She grabbed the bags of food and closed the door.

"You don't have to get so excited when someone knocks on the door," Haley chided, going through the bags when Shane set them on the counter in the galley.

"How do you know the person on the other side of that door isn't the letter writer...or even some other crazy fan?"

"I seriously doubt he works as a Chinese food delivery driver," she replied sarcastically.

"In all seriousness, what would you do if someone snatched the door open and tried to get on the bus?"

Haley shrugged as she evenly distributed the food from the containers. "That's why I have you, Barney Fife."

"I won't always be here," Shane replied.

"Thank God," Haley uttered.

"Maybe you should take a self-defense course."

Haley laughed hysterically. "You're not serious? I constantly have security around me, whether you are here or not. I was fine before you got here, and I'll be perfectly fine when you're gone.

"Okay," Shane said, dropping the subject as Haley walked away with her food, obviously not wanting to share a meal with her.

Later on that evening as the buses pulled out of the parking lot on their way to the next venue, Haley grabbed her guitar and notepad and walked out to the living area. Shane was passed out on the couch with one leg dangling over the side and her foot touching the floor, still dressed in her t-shirt, jeans, and socks.

Haley set her guitar down on the floor and sat in the chair across from the slumbering woman. "Why are you able to get to me like you do?" she whispered. *I've never had anyone get under my skin so easily, yet turn my head like a cat in heat.*

She thought about waking her, but it wouldn't matter. She grabbed her guitar off the floor and headed back to her room.

***

The bus hit a pothole on the highway, causing it to bounce a little, but it was just enough to wake Shane. She sat up, stretching her back. "I have to stop doing this," she mumbled as she got up and walked down the short hallway her room, but stopped when she heard Haley's voice. It sounded almost like she was in distress. Hesitating momentarily, she went into the bathroom to get a better listen behind the door to her room. As soon as she heard the soft cries of a nightmare, she turned the knob and stepped inside. She'd never been in the master suite of the bus, but it was more than twice the size of her room, with a queen-sized bed. She heard Haley crying and wrestling around with the covers, but barely saw her in the dimly lit space.

"Haley," she called, moving closer to the bed. "Haley, it's Shane. Listen to my voice."

A couple of seconds later, Haley stopped thrashing and opened her eyes.

Shane forgot where she was for a split second as her eyes met Haley's. She felt herself leaning closer as Haley's lips parted.

"Shane?" she murmured, her bare chest rising and falling heavily under the comforter.

"You were having a nightmare," Shane said, pulling herself out of the fog that had taken over her head. *You don't want this. She doesn't want this.* She backed away slightly. "I heard you."

"I was dreaming about the bus crash," Haley said, coming down from the adrenaline rush.

"That's to be expected."

"I'm fine now."

Shane nodded. "Goodnight...or morning, I should say. The sun will be rising soon."

"I should get up anyway. I have that radio show soon."

"What radio show?"

"Chicago Morning, or something like that."

"Thanks for telling me," Shane said bitterly.

"I figured Rich would. He's the one who set it up. He's picking me...*us*, up at seven-thirty."

Shane shook her head. "You can talk to me, you know. It would be a good idea to keep me informed. I'm not one of these damn rental cops."

"It's all the same to me."

"You're so..." she growled, biting back the words before she let loose on her.

"I'm what? Say it," Haley snapped as Shane moved to leave the room.

"Stubborn. You're so goddamn stubborn!" Shane said angrily.

Haley wanted to smack her and run after her at the same time. "Fuck!" she yelled, tossing her pillow at the door. Then, she flung the blanket and sheet off her heated, naked body.

Shane didn't hear the pillow smack the wall. She was already in the living area, pacing the floor like a caged animal. She wished they were stopped so she could get off the bus…get away from Haley. If the windows on the side rolled down, she would've stuck her head out like a dog. Anything to get some air and cool herself down. *I can't take much more of this. I'm either going to strangle her, or do something even dumber.* She opened the door to the driver compartment, which was also the way to the buses exit door. "How much further?" she asked.

"Morning," Rico said with a smile. "We'll be pulling into the venue in about thirty minutes."

"Great. Thanks," she said, closing the door. When that bus rolled to a stop, she was getting as far away from Haley Nielsen as possible…at least until Rich showed up.

Chapter 27

"Good Morning Chi-Town!" the radio DJ said into the microphone. "This is Johnny Five. I'm alive and here with a special guest. She's playing at the Allstate Arena tonight. It's none other than country music superstar, Haley Nielsen! Welcome, Haley."

"Thank you," she said, leaning a bit closer to the large microphone on her side of the table. "It's great to be back in Illinois. I haven't played here since my first tour."

"Rebel Sweetheart is the name of your new album, which is phenomenal by the way. Tell me more about it."

"Well, Johnny, I think this album shows my growth as a musician and artist. I've evolved over the last six or eight years, and my music has as well."

"I'd say," he laughed. "Rebel Sweetheart is almost like a rebellion against the norms of country music. Would you agree?"

"I think country music itself is changing with the times. I'll always be a country music singer, but I love a little blues and rock and roll too. I guess this album is a little rebellious, but it's a little more of me being me...sort of in a take it or leave it way. Johnny Cash was frowned upon when he sounded different from everyone else on the radio. I think everyone has their own sound and their own style. That's what makes us unique."

"I certainly agree with that. Now, on another topic, you were seen recently at the CMT Awards with a mysterious guest, who also happened to be on your bus when it crashed. By the way, we are all so heartbroken with the loss of your driver," he said, then continued. "This same person accompanied you to his funeral, as well. I believe she's a former U.S. Marshal named Shane Crowley. Is that correct?"

"Yes, she's the head of our security and my bodyguard, if you want to call her that."

"Is there any more to it?"

"I'm not sure what you're getting at, but Ms. Crowley is employed by my manager, Rich Bergman."

"Why would you need a personal guard? I mean to the extreme that she has been…on your bus, at your house, beside you at an awards show."

Haley's jaw tightened. She knew he was trying to get a rise out of her by creating some kind of scandal story. "Actually, I've had some threats made on my life recently. As you said, Rebel Sweetheart isn't quite the norm of country music, and some think I shouldn't have recorded this album. They don't scare me, and they never will. However, my manager is a little overprotective. He hired Ms. Crowley for the tour. It's not a big deal, and it's certainly not some juicy scandal story. I'd say I'm sorry to disappoint, but honestly my private and personal life is no one's business."

"There you have it folks. I hate hearing about the threats, Haley."

"Thanks," she replied, still angry, but doing her best to keep a smile plastered on her face.

"Anything you want to tell us about Tucker Miller? I heard a rumor you two might be headlining a couple of your tour dates together."

"That is most definitely not true. I'm not sure who is feeding you all of this false information, but I'd think about using a different source," she stated. "Tucker and I share a label. That is all. My tour is exactly that, *my* tour. There was some talk of him maybe playing a few of my dates while we handled the loss of my driver and bus. However, my manager was able to get us another bus quickly and here we are, back on the road, ready to rock the roof off the Allstate Arena tonight."

"Sounds great. I know I'll certainly be there. Thank you for stopping by to talk with us this morning."

"Thank you for having me," she said.

"Haley Nielsen, playing at Allstate Arena tonight at seven."

As soon as the light came on, indicating the show had gone to commercial, Haley ripped her headphones off. "What the hell was that all about? Thanks for blindsiding me!"

"I'm so sorry. My producer wanted me to question the relationship with your bodyguard. He's a homophobe and a racist."

"Lovely," she spat.

"Honestly, I think people should love whomever they fall in love with. The hell with what anyone thinks. That's probably my wife's doing though, she's the most free-spirited person I've ever met. I'm pretty sure she'd burn her bra in the street if that movement ever came back around," he joked. "I really do love your music, so does she, and my daughter. They'll all be with me tonight. I'd love for them to meet you."

"Thank you for being truthful with me. I'll see what I can do." She smiled.

"I really hate that you're getting threats. Some people in this world don't belong here," he said, shaking his head.

Haley nodded in agreement, before shaking his hand and leaving the booth.

"What the hell was that all about?" Rich questioned when they got into the SUV.

"His homophobic, bigot boss thinks she and I are sleeping together," she said through clenched teeth.

"Oh, for fuck's sake. It's almost 2020. People need to move on with their damn lives," he growled.

"Great, so you do too!"

"Haley, I don't give a shit who you are sleeping with. It could be that old housekeeper of yours for all I care. My point is, it's none of anyone's business. If you wanted them to know, you'd tell them. There are thousands of outlets you could use."

"I am certainly not sleeping with Emma Jean," Haley laughed. "I'm not in a relationship with anyone. You know that," she said to him. "I'm married to my music. I don't have time for romance and all of that other crap. It just pisses me off when people speculate about something they know nothing about." She looked over at Shane. "And why are you so quiet? Do you think it's okay for them to start stupid gossip rumors involving you?"

Shane shrugged and sighed. "I'll never see these people again, so honestly, I don't care what they think of me or say about me."

"Wonderful," Haley muttered, crossing her arms.

"Look, it's one radio show in one city. The tour is two-thirds of the way finished. This only came to light because she's been seen with you outside of the tour. People speculated. You could've been seen with Tucker Miller like the label wanted, and the same thing would've happened. It didn't matter who you were with or what you were doing…it's the fact someone was with you. People don't usually see anyone with you, so it stirred some gossip."

"I didn't want her here in the first place," she replied furiously.

"You needed her here. It's not safe."

"Oh, not again with this letter writer bullshit. I think if we go another week with nothing new, she can work remotely. There's no need to have her right beside me twenty-four/seven."

"I disagree," Shane said.

Haley sighed angrily as she looked out the window. She'd never wished for a tour to be over, but this time, she was done. She wanted to go home and forget about the letter writer, the accident, losing Fizzy, and ever meeting Shane Crowley.

***

Shane was standing nearby when Haley stepped off her bus wearing jeans and a tight-fitting green and black flannel shirt. The top three buttons were open and dangerously close to allowing her breasts to spill out. She was in rare form, still fuming from the morning radio show. She knew the band and entire road crew had listened live. They were unaware of the death threats until now, and she was dreading facing them. She regretted ever doing the show to begin with.

"Can I go to rehearsal now?" she said, crossing her arms, looking at Shane.

"I don't know. I'm just a rental cop that isn't needed."

"Oh, for fuck's sake." Haley shook her head and began walking into the arena. Shane fell instep next to her, but a little back so she wasn't in her line of sight.

The band was waiting on stage when Haley entered.

"I wish you would've told us about the threats, Haley," Vince said when she walked up the stairs. "We're not just acquaintances, we're your damn band. We've been with you since the beginning. And as the band leader, I feel a little pissed about being completely left in the dark."

"I know. You all have a right to be pissed. We were trying to keep this is as quiet as possible. It's not a huge deal. There's no need to be concerned. I told Rich to keep it quiet."

"We knew he said he was beefing up security, which was why Shane joined the tour, but I'm mad too. Damn it, Haley. We would do anything for you. You're our sister from another mister," Joey said. "We should kick his ass after the show tonight."

"Personally, if you *were* a lesbian, I think that would be cool as shit. Country music would flip their damn lids!" Stiles laughed. "I mean, I know there have been a few others, but no one as popular as you. Shane's not a bad catch either."

Haley shook her head and sighed. "Come on, we have work to do."

Vince smacked him in the back of the head like a father scolding a child. Stiles shrugged and picked up his guitar.

***

Halfway through rehearsal, Haley needed a breather. She couldn't get focused. Her mind kept playing the radio interview. She was waiting for Rich to come to her with the label's harsh words any minute, and every time she saw Shane, it just made it worse.

"I know you're out there," she growled into the mic. "Can I please have an hour without you up my ass?"

"Is she talking to me or you?" Rich whispered, looking at Shane.

"That would be me," she mumbled, getting up from her seat.

"She can't possibly see you."

"She doesn't have to," she added. "Make sure someone calls me when she's done. I'll be around."

Rich nodded. He felt bad for her. He'd been on the sharp end of Haley's lashings more times than he could count. He simply couldn't understand why Shane's mere presence was enough to set Haley off. *If they're not sleeping together, maybe they should be*, he thought as he continued watching the rehearsal while texting and emailing on his phone.

***

If Shane was a smoker, she would've inhaled an entire pack while waiting for Haley to finish. She was finished with the back and forth confrontation. Haley Nielsen was literally making her crazy "She's either going to move on, or I'm out of here. Someone else can deal with her," she mumbled to herself.

When rehearsal finally ended, Shane walked Haley to the bus and stayed outside, hovering around the arena and the stage, anything to avoid seeing her until the start of the show when she'd have to walk her back again. No words were spoken between them. In fact, neither woman looked at the other at all.

"The rattlesnake's back," Rich said, stepping up behind Shane, who was outside of the arena, staring at the bus.

"I have a feeling it may strike tonight," Shane replied slowly, her voice sounding a little deeper than its usual tone.

Rich felt like he was standing in a landmine, waiting for one of them to explode.

"I take it you haven't told her about the insurance company," Shane said.

"No." He shook his head. "I was going to today, but the radio show blew that for me."

"Has there been any word from her label?"

"Oh, hell yeah. They aren't happy, not with the radio show, not with her, and certainly not with me. They're pissed they were kept in the dark about the threats, and they demanded to know if she's gay," he sighed. "I have a feeling they will drop her if they find out."

"Wait…" Shane cocked her head to the side. "You know?"

"I had a feeling. I wasn't certain until you came along."

"Whoa. Wait a minute. There is nothing going on between her and I."

"There doesn't have to be. You have chemistry. I've never seen her like this with anyone."

"Like what?"

"So…I don't know…back and forth, I guess. It's almost like love and hate. I'm not saying she *is* gay, but I wouldn't be surprised. That's all."

"I don't know and don't care. She's never mentioned it to me. Hell, we've barely talked about anything."

"Come on. She's almost finished," Rich said, nodding towards the arena door.

Shane hadn't missed a show yet, but this time, she'd chosen to stay outside. She looked over at the mingling people who were slowly turning into a crowd, before following him inside.

***

Haley was playing her Telecaster guitar and singing *Finish What Ya Started* by Van Halen, when Rich and Shane walked up to the back of the stage. The rest of the band played with her and sang backup vocals.

As soon as the song was over, the audience continued cheering loudly as Haley traded guitars, going back to her acoustic one. She strummed the first bars of her next song as she stepped up to the mic. "Jolene, Jolene, Jolene, Jolene!" she began singing. "I'm begging of you please don't take my man."

After a few more lines, the band slowly joined in. The arena hummed as if everyone in there was singing. Chills ran down Haley's spine. She loved it when the crowd sang along. She strummed her guitar harder, playing louder and dragging out the lyrics as she lost herself in the music. It was the last song of the night, and she was going to make it a good one.

***

As soon as she was finished, Haley walked off the back of the stage, glaring at Shane as she pranced past her, and straight down the hallway towards the exit. The air was heavy and thick between the two of them. Rich raised a

191

brow in Shane's direction. He sure as hell wasn't going after her. Shane's sigh sounded more like a growl as she took off in Haley's direction, reaching her just as she was opening the door.

"Try not to stand in one place too long. Keep moving down the line," Shane said as Haley began signing autographs and taking selfies with the people outside.

Haley ignored her.

"Are you finished?" Shane asked sarcastically after giving her all of five minutes, which was way too long in her mind.

"The warden says I have to go," Haley said to the crowd, then turned her gorgeous eyes on Shane.

Once they were both on the bus, Shane slammed and locked the door. Haley had disappeared to her room. "Oh, no you don't!" she yelled. "Come out here! We need to talk!"

"What's your problem?" Haley snapped, opening her door and stepping out into the hallway. She'd removed her boots and socks, and exchanged her jeans for cutoff shorts.

"You!" Shane squeezed her fists to keep from touching her. "I've had enough with being treated like a piece of shit! I've done nothing but try my best to keep you safe. What the hell happened when you boarded this bus? You were…normal at your house. Now, you're back to being…" Shane clenched her teeth together. "You're a bitch!"

"Fuck you! You have no right to talk to me like that!"

"You have no right to treat me like that either! I'm tired of apologizing and tiptoeing around you! You're a grown damn woman. It's time you act like it!"

"You're fired!" Haley shouted.

"You've tried that, remember?! I'm not some dumb rental cop or a stupid radio disc jockey. Look at me damn it!"

Shane's eyes were at least two shades darker when Haley looked into them. Blood raced through her veins and her heart thumped in her chest as Shane moved closer. She'd never been so turned on and angry at the same time.

"You make me crazy," Shane murmured in a low tone.

Haley swallowed the lump in her throat as her back touched the wall.

"I went out of my way to take you to Graceland. I saved your life when the bus crashed. I comforted you when you were in need. I've done nothing...NOTHING, but be respectful to you. All the while, you stomp around barking orders, acting as if you can't stand me. Now, what is it, Haley? Do you hate me that much? Am I that much of a burden on you? What the fuck is your problem?" Shane snarled, her face inches from Haley's.

"You! Goddamn it, you're my problem!" Haley replied angrily, staring back into her eyes. "You think I make you crazy," she sneered. "You have no idea what you do to me. Everywhere I go, everywhere I turn, you're there. I can't get away from you. I can't work. I can't sleep. You want to know the truth? Fine. I hate you, Shane. I hate the minute you walked into my life and turned it upside down! I hate the fact that I want you so bad I can't think straight anymore!" she growled, twisting her hand in the front of Shane's shirt and pulling her close as their mouths came together roughly in a blazing hot kiss.

Shane nipped at her lips, tasting a hint of tequila and lime on Haley's tongue as she licked it. Haley moaned, pushing her mouth harder into Shane's before they both pulled away to get air into their lungs.

Shane grabbed Haley's hands and held them up above her shoulders, pinning her to the wall as she pressed their hips together. "Is this really what you want?" she asked, her tone still low and demanding. Her eyes traced a burning path down Haley's neck to the soft skin between the top of her breasts, watching her chest lift and fall with each rapid breath, before moving back up to the glassy eyes staring back at her.

"I want you. I want to feel you...touching me...inside of me...everywhere," Haley breathed.

Shane let go of her wrists and ran her hand over her shoulders, moving down her chest to cup her breasts. Haley moaned, tilting her head back to offer more of herself. Shane grabbed the open sides of her shirt and pulled them apart, ripping the buttons in one swift motion, revealing a lacy black bra. She pressed her lips to Haley's once more in a fierce kiss that laid claim to her mouth, before pulling away and running her lips from the delicate skin under Haley's ear, down to the baby smooth skin of her breasts. She still had her bra on, but Shane kissed all the way down to the lace, dragging her tongue across to the other side as her hands slid down to Haley's abdomen. She spread her hands on either side of her belly button, feeling the taut muscles jump with every panting breath.

Haley could do nothing but surrender herself to the hands working their way lower, and oh how she wanted them lower. She'd dreamed about giving herself to Shane so many times, she almost already knew what it would feel like when Shane took her. Her knees knocked together in anticipation as Shane unbuttoned her cutoffs, tucking her thumbs inside the waistband at her sides. She pushed them over her hips, drawing her panties down with them as they fell to her ankles. Shane's breath tickled her sensitive skin as she moved to her knees, dragging her lips over her stomach.

In one swift motion, Shane pushed her legs apart and licked her swollen wet center with her flattened tongue. Haley bit down on her lower lip, tasting the metallic tinge of blood as she cried out. Shane kept her tongue moving over and over, suckling every fold as she teased her opening with the tip. Then, keeping her mouth on Haley's body, she slowly moved back up, standing as she reached her breasts, then her neck...all the way to her mouth. Her hands followed, sliding up the top of Haley's thighs, resting on her hipbones.

It drove Haley wild tasting her own salty sweet aroma on Shane's tongue. She was so close, Shane's demanding kiss was liable to push her over the edge, but her body hummed with arousal. She wanted more, and she was going to get it as Shane's hand began to move down her thigh.

Haley whimpered through their kiss as Shane pushed two fingers inside of her and teased her clit with her thumb. Her body was pinned to the wall by Shane's, otherwise, her shaky legs may have dropped her to the floor.

Shane kept her mouth on Haley, moving from her lips to her neck and upper chest, then back again. All the while, her fingers slid in and out of her slippery, hot center, working in a circular motion and pounding deeper with each thrust. With her free hand, she reached down, lifting Haley's thigh up to her waist to give her more leverage. She continued sliding in and out of her until the warm muscles surrounding her fingers squeezed painfully tight, stilling them deep inside.

Haley pulled her mouth away, crying out like a wild animal owning the night as she gasped for air. Her body writhing between Shane and the wall as the powerful orgasm building inside of her finally exploded.

Shane waited until Haley came down from the intoxicating high, then she slowly released her fingers and put her leg down. She ran the knuckles of her clean hand up Haley's torso, lifting her chin when she reached it, so that they were eye to eye. Then, she leaned in, kissing her softly.

"Consider this my resignation," she sighed, pulling away. "I'll stay on through Atlanta, then I'm out," she added before going into her room and closing the door.

Haley felt completely raw as she rearranged her clothes and walked into the bathroom. This was it. Shane had given her exactly what she'd wanted. She should've been anything other than lost, which was what she truly was as she turned on the shower and stepped under the hot spray. A single tear ran down her cheek. She casually wiped it away, unsure of why it was even there. She wasn't hurt, not physically, not mentally…not at all. She felt like a drug addict who had just come down from the high of a lifetime. In a way, she had experienced that…to a certain extent at least, as the euphoria of the most powerful orgasm she'd ever had slowly faded away.

When she'd finished going through the repetitive motion of washing her body and shampooing her hair, she stepped out and toweled off. She avoided the mirror, knowing her own eyes would give way to the things she didn't want to think about right now. Entering her room, she dried her hair as much as possible with the towel, then crawled under the covers of her bed as naked on the inside as she was on the outside.

For the first time in nearly a month, her mind was blank. She closed her eyes, allowing herself to fall sleep.

***

Shane contemplated taking a shower when she heard the water stop, but the last thing she wanted to do was see Haley. It was over. They'd both given and taken what they'd wanted from the other. There would be no more fighting; no more treading softly; no more anything…really. In forty-eight hours, she'd be gone. The thought of never seeing Haley again stung a little, but they were both better off. Rich would get someone new to track down the letter writer. She'd give him or her all of her notes. Haley would be able to go on and finish her tour, and she could get back to her life and her regular work. Following some star around wasn't exactly her idea of fun to begin with. She was happy to get back to the peace and quiet of her apartment, and the silly nonsense of working low key cases with a bunch of guys who told dirty jokes all day.

As she slowly drifted off to sleep, she thought about her old cases, wondering how many were still open.

Chapter 28

Haley pulled the covers over her head when the early morning sun peeked through the blinds, sending slivers of orange right into her face, because she'd forgotten to close her blackout curtains when she went to bed. She could tell they were still on the road, which meant she couldn't escape the confines of the bus. What she really wanted was a hot cup of tea with honey, but decided to go back to sleep instead.

In the other room, Shane tossed and turned until she finally just lay awake, staring at the ceiling. Her stomach growled like a grizzly bear, reminding her that she hadn't eaten since lunchtime the day before. Checking her watch, she knew they still had several hours to go because the buses didn't pull out until just before dawn. "The hell with it," she muttered to herself, slinging the comforter off. She dressed in a pair of sweatpants and a t-shirt before leaving her room in search of something to eat so her body would stop acting like it was starving to death.

In the galley, she found the refrigerator and cabinets somewhat filled with groceries. She had no idea when that had happened, but was thankful for Rich for coming through. She went to work making the coffee she'd found, using the one cup machine. Then, she grabbed a box of cereal from the cabinet, with some kind of marshmallows and corn flakes in it and poured it into a medium-sized bowl. She dumped enough milk to make it float, grabbed a spoon, and began to chow down while she waited for her coffee to finish.

As soon as the brew was done, Shane took the remainder of her cereal and her coffee to her room and turned her laptop on. If she couldn't sleep, she might as well work. She was more than halfway through with the Christian magazine subscriptions for residents of Nashville and the surrounding area. Nearly fifty percent of the subscriptions were in the names of churches, hospitals, and businesses, and the other half was women's names. "He could've gotten this magazine anywhere!" she huffed, nearly spilling her cereal in her lap. She quickly grabbed her phone.

"Shane? It's the crack of dawn," Dennis said, answering his phone.

"I know you're awake and in the office."

"Of course, I am. I figured you slept in these days since you worked late into the night."

"I'm fine. Listen, I've been over your list a dozen times. The guy could've picked this magazine up from anywhere. Half of the subscriptions are for churches and businesses. The rest are all women. Mind you, he could be married and just snagged his wife's magazine."

"Okay? What's your angle from here?"

"I don't have one," she said.

"Why'd you call, then?"

"I resigned my position last night. I'm coming home day after tomorrow."

"What?"

"If you want to work something out with Rich and send someone else so we keep the paycheck, that's fine. I'm not doing this anymore. I'll keep working to figure out who is behind all of this until I'm gone."

"Okay," he sighed. "I'm honestly surprised you lasted this long."

"You and me both."

"If anything changes, let me know."

"I will, but I doubt that'll happen. Hey, one thing I noticed with the list…the church near Haley's house was on it, and I believe her maid might be on there too. I doubt her family is doing this to her, and the church could just be a coincidence since all of the churches in Nashville and the surrounding areas seem to be on there too," she said between bites of cereal.

"What is that crunching sound? We must have a bad connection. Where are you?"

"More than likely still in Illinois. We haven't been on the road long. Anyway, it's probably this sugar-filled cereal I'm eating."

"That's a new development," he laughed.

"I woke up starving. Someone stocked the bus, but I guarantee it wasn't Rich. Haley is going to be pissed when she wakes up. Rich probably sent Rico Suave shopping."

"Excuse me?"

"Rico. That's our new driver. He's part of the road crew and was Fizzy's back up driver for Haley's bus. Anyway, I'll call you from Nashville. I'll have to fly back there to get my car from her house."

"Sounds good," Dennis said, before ending the call.

***

Shane was asleep on the couch when Haley gave into her hunger and came out of her room in search something to eat. "Do you always sleep out here?" she said, shaking her head.

"Not intentionally," Shane replied. "I wouldn't bother if I were you," she added when Haley began opening the fridge and cabinets.

"What the hell? Who did the shopping? A ten-year-old?" Haley grumbled.

"Told you." Shane shrugged. "The cereal isn't half bad, although it may give you diabetes."

"Wonderful," she muttered, microwaving water for her tea. "I'll just grab something when we stop in Nashville."

"Wait. What?" Shane sat up. "I thought we were headed to Georgia."

"We are...well, the road crew and band are. Since the show in Atlanta is tomorrow night, and we have to go through Nashville, I'm stopping to play at the Hillbilly tonight by myself. Rich is picking you and I up when the cavalry stops to change shifts."

"You could've told me ahead of time."

"I was a little preoccupied...don't you think?" Haley deadpanned.

Shane shrugged and stood up.

Haley's eyes shifted to the bare skin showing above the waistband of Shane's jeans where her t-shirt had rose up in her sleep. Following her line of sight, Shane quickly pulled it back down and walked away. She was barely in her room when her phone began ringing. Seeing that it was Dennis, she reached for it.

"Thank you for calling Hell. Press one to save my soul," she answered.

"What the fuck?" Dennis laughed. "Shane?"

"Yep, that's me. I'm still here. There's nowhere else to go, bud."

"Stop eating that sugary shit. It's making you crazy."

"I'm afraid it's not the cereal," she sighed. "Anyway, what's up? Oh, and apparently, Haley is playing by herself at some Honkytonk tonight in Nashville while the rest of the group goes on to Georgia. She and I are flying down with Rich afterwards. I wish I'd known. I would've made plans to leave tonight…in my car, instead of staying on for another venue."

"That's great."

Shane pulled the phone from her ear and looked down at it. "Great? What's so damn great about it?"

"Listen, I'm calling because that guy you told me to send all of the letters to, he just called. The paper is the same printer paper you can buy at any store, like all the others. The first few letters had no finger prints or DNA, and this didn't either…but, this last one did have an imprint. You know where someone writes something on a piece of paper on top of it and it makes an indentation?"

"Yes, Dennis. I was a Deputy Marshal. I know what the hell an imprint is. What did it say? I knew he was rushing with this letter. That's because he found out at the last minute."

"I agree. It's not much to go on though. It said: DEA EETIN URDAY."

Shane slammed the nightstand drawer open and closed, looking for a notepad and pen. Once she finally found what she was looking for, she quickly wrote the letters down in the order that he read them. "The last word is Saturday."

"I thought the same thing. Any idea what the rest is?"

"No. Let me play around with it. I'll call you back. This could be the big break." As soon as she hung up her phone, she went into the Google search screen. The first thing that popped up to correct the spelling was Deacon

Meeting. "Son of a bitch!" she yelled, slamming her fist on the nightstand. "I knew it!" She quickly dialed Dennis back.

"That was quick," he answered.

"It's Deacon Meeting Saturday," she exclaimed.

"What? how did you come up with that?"

"Google. Anyway, it's someone in a fucking church," she said, shaking her head. "I had a feeling, but was hoping I was wrong."

"What now?"

"We need to cross reference churches with deacons who are in the Nashville area, and who also have subscriptions to that magazine."

"I'm on it. There are probably a hundred or so," Dennis said.

"Try more like four-hundred."

"Are you serious?" he squeaked.

"Didn't you look at the list you sent me? I guarantee you thirty percent of them, if not more, have subscriptions to that magazine," she sighed. "This is a lead, but not a very good one. Anyone coming or going from the clerical area of at least three hundred churches could have grabbed the paper...as well as the magazine. It's not a lot to go on."

"I'll still work on it. If I can help you eliminate some of them, that may help."

"Dennis, he was really sloppy this time. He could make a move on her soon. I don't like it."

"I know. I agree. I thought you quit, though."

"I did. I'm still done after tomorrow night's show, but at least I'll have a place for the person to start. Maybe a fresh set of eyes is what's needed. I'll touch base with you tomorrow." She ended the call and tossed the phone on the bed to keep from smashing it into the wall. She grabbed the pencil and notepad, flinging them instead.

"What's going on in there? It sounds like you're in a wrestling match," Haley called from outside the galley, near the hallway as her eyes scanned the wall from the night before.

"I'm fine," Shane replied, opening her door. "Who knows about you performing at that bar tonight?"

"No one but the owner. Why?"

"Just checking. I have a lead on your letter writer, but it's a long stretch."

"What do you mean?"

"It could be one of thousands of people living in or near Nashville, who attend a church with deacons."

Haley raised a brow. "Most of Tennessee goes to church, it's like a family tradition in the south. I'm also pretty sure they all have deacons."

Shane nodded and held her palms up. "Long stretch."

"Wonderful," Haley muttered, walking past her to get her guitar. "Are you hiding in there all day?" she asked, turning back to face her before entering the bathroom to get to her room.

"I don't know."

"Well, I'd like to work…therefore, I kind of need to know."

"I thought you can't work around me?"

"I can't, but I'm going stir crazy on this bus."

"Are we going to talk about last night?" Shane asked.

"Why bother?"

Shane nodded her head. "I have some calls to make. I'm sure Rich will want to get started as soon possible with my replacement. I also have to book my flight back to

Nashville to get my car. Can you please make sure Emma Jean will be there?"

"Fine."

"In the meantime, I need to shower, so…"

Haley rolled her eyes and walked through the bathroom to her room, returning a few minutes later with her notepad, pencil, and guitar. Shane watched her step into the living room and get settled before going to take her shower. At the moment, all she wanted to do was wash off the remnants of last night.

Chapter 29

Afternoon had come and gone by the time the entourage pulled into a truck stop to refuel and shift change the drivers. This was the longest leg in the tour so far, but it had only happened this way because of the couple of missed shows. Most of their drives were no more than eight hours at a time, and the drivers were allowed a maximum of ten hours.

Shane was sitting in the living room, dressed in jeans and a black t-shirt with a black button-down shirt over it to hide her gun, watching out the window. As soon as the dark SUV turned into the parking lot, she got off the bus.

"Is Haley ready to go?" Rich asked through the open window as he came to a stop.

"I'm sure she is. Have you talked to her today?"

He shook his head. "Is she still in rare form? I figured she'd be happy about tonight. She loves playing at the Hillbilly, where people don't seem to care who she is. They just love listening to music."

"I left you a voicemail earlier."

"I never even checked my phone. I've been nonstop with the label all day. What's going on?"

"I resigned last night."

"You did what?" he squawked like an angry bird. "Why? What happened?"

"It's been a long time coming. She and I are like oil and water. It's just not…healthy," she said, choosing her words carefully. "I'm staying on through tomorrow night. When she's back on the bus after the show, I'm out."

"Wow…" he muttered. "I don't know what to say."

"I have some contacts I'll give you, so hopefully you'll have someone ready to go. Also, I have a solid lead, but it's a pretty long stretch. I'll leave all of my notes, so hopefully the new person can pick up where I'm leaving off."

Rich shook his head and chuckled. "You know, she told me she'd give this a month. Then, you were out of here. It's funny how she outlasted you. I swear that woman is something else. She can charm the skin off an alligator and bite you like a cobra at the same time."

"She's something…alright," Shane sighed.

"Well, you should enjoy tonight at least. It'll be a lot smaller crowd. Hell, Emma Jean and Marvin may even be there."

Shane nodded, then turned her head when she heard the bus door open. Haley was wearing her usual threadbare jeans with a wide black leather belt and large silver buckle. Pointed toe boots were on her feet, and a tight back Johnny Cash t-shirt with a deep V cut in the collar, was hugging her breasts. Her long blonde hair cascaded around her shoulders and down her back in spiral waves. "I hear that train a coming," Shane muttered in a fake southern drawl.

Rich laughed. "If she wasn't like a daughter to me, my wife would skin me alive for hanging around a woman that beautiful," Rich said. "Should be outlawed."

"I'm pretty sure she is an outlaw," Shane replied, stepping away and glancing around the parking lot for anything suspicious as Haley walked over and got into the SUV.

"Can you have one of the roadies get my Tele? I want to take it with me," she said to Rich, as she slid across the seat.

"Sure. Anything else?"

"Nope, but you're stopping for some real food. Whoever stocked the bus is still in elementary school," she said sarcastically.

"Okay," he uttered as he got out of the vehicle.

Shane slid into the front passenger seat.

"You're not riding back here with me?"

"Do I need to?"

"Nope."

Shane stared out the window, watching one of the roadies get Haley's guitar for Rich. A minute later, he walked back to the SUV with the hard, black case.

***

The Hillbilly was just as it seemed, a hole in the wall honkytonk that smelled like stale beer. It was a fairly decent sized room with vaulted ceilings. There were stools all along the bar that ran halfway down one wall, and various high-top tables were in the back. Regular round tables were staggered along the sides of the dance floor. The stage was three feet off the ground and had old whisky barrels and potato sacks sitting on both front corners. A microphone, a couple of amps, and an old console piano were sitting on it. Autographed pictures of country artists and album posters littered the walls, all the way up to the ceiling.

"Well, God put an angel in front of me. I see it with my own two eyes!" an old heavyset man said as he waddled up to Haley, wrapping her in a big hug.

"Aww, you're so sweet," Haley gushed.

"Here she is, all the way from her big city tour," he added. "It's been too long."

"I know." Haley shook her head. "The road's been hell this time around. I needed to feel my roots, even for just a couple of hours."

"You're welcome here any time your pretty little heart desires," the big man said with a grin. "I'm surprised your caretakers aren't in here."

"I was home recently, but I didn't tell them I was passing back through."

"Yeah, I'm sorry to hear about your bus driver. It sounded like an awful accident."

"It certainly was. We were lucky to make it out alive," she replied, looking at Shane. "Anyway, I'm not here for sappy stories." She smiled brightly.

"It's always a good time when Haley Nielsen comes to visit," the big man said.

"Big Earl, you remember my manager, Rich Bergman," Haley said. "And this is Shane Crowley. She's working security for me."

The man nodded, recognizing Rich, who was always with her when she played.

"This is Big Earl Smidley."

Shane smiled politely and shook his hand.

"I gave this pretty little lady her first gig when she was just a baby. Her old man brought her in one night with her guitar and said, 'Earl, you gotta hear this kid sing.' I thought he was off his rocker, but I let her give it a try. Lord almighty, the place came alive. Her voice blew everyone away. I knew she was going to take over country music one day."

"You should see her play in front of a packed arena," Shane said.

"Oh, I have…a few times actually, and when she played the Opry. But, I love it when she comes in here to let her hair down. She could sing her ABC's and I wouldn't care. I just like to hear her sing and play music."

Shane grinned at Rich, who just laughed.

"Enough with the chitchat," Haley said with a big smile. "I came to play music."

"Well, alright, then. Get to it. What are you drinking? It's on the house tonight."

"Nothing for me," Shane said.

"Me either," Rich added.

"I'll have two shots of JD, one for each of them," Haley said, pointing her thumb over her shoulder to Shane and Rich.

Big Earl went behind the bar and poured two iced shot glasses full of Jack Daniels and slid them over to her. Haley winked at him. Then, she walked over to the stage and set them on the piano before opening her guitar case.

"I'm not sure if you know who I am...and that's fine with me. I came in here tonight to see some old friends and play a little music. Is that okay with you guys?" she said into the microphone as she adjusted it for her shorter height.

The place was packed by this point and several people were already cheering.

Haley put the strap of her guitar around her neck and plugged the amp cord into it. Then, she adjusted the knobs to give the sound a little more country tone. "This was the very first song I played here, and as Big Earl likes to say...I was just a baby, at the ripe old age of fourteen." She grabbed one of the shot glasses and held it up towards the bar. "This one's for you, Earl!" she yelled, chugging it, and setting the empty glass back down. Then, she walked back to the microphone, strummed a few chords, and went right into singing *Jolene*. She started the song slow, using the full range of her voice as it picked up pace.

The fifty or so people in the bar cheered loudly, holding their beer bottles and cocktail glasses up in the air as she finished the song. One woman yelled, "We love you, Haley."

She smiled, strumming the guitar a few times. "I think you need to be seasoned to sing this next one. I mean…you have to have lived through some shit, man." She played a short intro on the guitar, then stopped. "I also think you have to know what the hell Tennessee Whiskey tastes like!" she added, walking over and grabbing the other shot glass, which she lifted in the air to the crowd, then chugged, getting another round of cheers. Then, she set the glass down and began singing Chris Stapleton's hit song *Tennessee Whiskey*. She usually didn't make eye contact with anyone when she sang, but her eyes wandered over to the side of the stage where Shane was leaning against the wall beside Rich.

When the song was over, she set her guitar down and walked over to the piano, turning the microphone on and adjusting it a little bit. "Have you ever searched for words, but couldn't quite find them? Well, to me, the right song sometimes has a way of helping out with that situation." She played a few keys and paused. "As I was lying in my bed early this morning, staring at the ceiling as we rolled down the highway. By the way, I came all the way from Chicago on my bus to play here tonight, and I'm headed down to Georgia on a plane as soon as I leave here. Anyway, this song came to mind. To me, it's definitely the right one." She glanced over at Shane before playing the beginning bars of Air Supply's *Making Love Out of Nothing at All*. "I know just how to whisper and I know just

211

how to cry. I know where to find the answers and I know just how to lie," she sang.

The hair on the back of Shane's neck stood on end as a tingle ran down her spine. The harder Haley played the notes on the piano, the more Shane was glued to her. Haley's voice carried throughout the bar as she sang her heart out. Several people in the crowd sang along with their drinks held high in the air, and a good amount of them had their phones in the air.

You're going to be irreplaceable, Rich thought, looking at Shane. He'd never seen this side of Haley. Sure, she connected with her audience as a hell-raising, country-spitfire...but this softer, more passionate music was not something she usually played. He'd tried to get her to add a few of those songs to her last two albums and she'd refused, not that it had mattered much, they were still gold and platinum with chart-topping hits. Nevertheless, she seemed to be showing more of her true self on and off the stage recently, and he was pretty sure Shane Crowley was the reason for it.

When she finished the song, Haley got up and grabbed her guitar once again. "I've always loved this woman. She is a true badass. Those of you who know me...you know I like to rock out, so...Hillbilly, let's do a little Joan Jett, *I love Rock and Roll*," she said as she adjusted the tone of the guitar and started the intro to the song. Recognizing it, the crowd began to clap along. "I saw him dancing there by the record machine...I knew he must've been about seventeen," she sang while jamming on her guitar. Everyone in the bar was singing with her and a lot of people were dancing.

Shane couldn't help tapping her foot. She was a big fan of Joan Jett as well, and Haley's smoky, twanging voice added a little texture to the song. Not to mention her phenomenal guitar playing. She'd never seen Haley perform anywhere except her tour, which was predominantly country music.

"Sing it, girl! Woo hoo!" one lady yelled as she danced in front of the stage, causing Shane to chuckle.

Haley finished the song and waited for the loud crowd to die down. "When I look around the walls, I see all of the history in the place. So many names have passed through here. This bar is so special. I know it's where I first started, but it doesn't matter if you're Backwoods Barbie, trying to make a little cash or a Country Music Superstar looking to get away from the tourists and just play music. In here, you're all the same. Anyway, I have one more to do for you, then I'm going to get my butt out of the way for the band that's being paid to be here tonight," she laughed. "Thank you again to Big Earl for letting me pop in every now and then and have a little fun." She played a little riff on the guitar, then stopped to change the tone once more. "This is a brand new one. In fact, I just finished writing it recently, so don't shoot me down. It's called: *Remember, A New Day*." She smiled and started a soft intro on the guitar. Then, she began singing the slow melody, glancing periodically at Shane as the words rolled off her tongue.

I always remember the passion
we share at night in my dreams
But like any good love affair
It ends when a new day begins

Midnight in Amarillo,
closed my eyes and you were there
the taste of your lips

Sydney Canyon

your fingers in my hair

I always remember the passion
we share at night in my dreams
But like any good love affair
It ends when a new day begins

Two a.m. in Tulsa
you're the reason I can't sleep
We toss and turn, tearing at the sheets
the fire burns
between you and me

I always remember the passion
we share at night in my dreams
But like any good love affair
It ends when a new day begins

Another sleepless night in Topeka
when you lie down next to me
the feel of your skin on mine
that dreamy look in your eye

I always remember the passion
we share at night in my dreams
But like any good love affair
It ends when a new day begins

"Well, that's certainly different," Rich said, scratching his goatee.

"Yeah," Shane mumbled.

"Alright, Hillbilly. Y'all were so good to me. Until next time…" Haley said, blowing kisses in the air before removing her guitar and walking off the stage.

"Is that going on your next album?" Rich asked.

"Oh, I don't know," she said, setting her guitar in the case. "It's just something I wrote on the road. I thought I'd try it out."

Big Earl squeezed into their little corner. "Haley…woman, you have one hell of a voice," he said, shaking his head. "And the way you play that guitar and the piano…you blew my mind."

"Thanks," she replied with a smile. "You know, I played my first Telecaster right there on that stage."

"I remember that," Big Earl said. "You were with Bonnie Raitt…am I right? You both stayed after we'd closed that night."

Haley nodded and smiled. "You're right. I stayed to watch her play after me and she said, 'Little girl, give this a try.' She pulled her guitar out of the case and handed it to me. I nearly peed my pants, but I strapped that sucker on and went to town." Haley laughed. "She tried to show me how to play the slide, but I worked the frets like magic. She said, 'Girl, you have a gift, don't ever change the way you play.'"

Big Earl grinned and shook his head. "Boy was she ever right."

"I saved up and bought my first Tele not long after that. It's hanging on the wall in my music room, along with other guitars I've collected over the years."

"I wish you had more time to play," he said.

"Me too," she replied, watching the band set up. Earl had pushed them back an hour when she'd called, saying she was passing through and wanted to stop in and play a few songs.

"Who are these guys?" she asked.

"They're not half bad. They call themselves The Wrecking Crew. I believe they all work construction together."

Haley chuckled. "We'll hang around and listen to a couple, then we have to get to the airport to catch up with my tour. We're playing Atlanta tomorrow night."

"Sounds like fun. Ya'll drink whatever you want, and stay as long as you can."

"Thank you," she said, giving him a hug. "And thank you so much for always letting me come in and play, which is usually at the last second."

"We always love having you here. You know you're welcome anytime."

"I know you two aren't drinking, and I'm not interested in getting drunk, so let's listen to these boys for a few minutes, then head out," she said after he walked away.

"That's fine. We don't have to be at the airport for a couple of hours," Rich replied.

***

The Wrecking Crew wasn't bad. Haley could tell music wasn't their day job, but she enjoyed the couple of songs she'd heard anyway. When Rich leaned over, tapping his watch in front of her, she nodded and stood up. He grabbed her guitar case and followed along as they made their way through the crowd. A few people shook Haley's hand and a couple of inebriated women hugged her neck. One guy reached out for her, but Shane blocked his path.

216

"That was fun. I need to play here more often. I seem to spend more time on the road than I do anywhere, anymore," she muttered.

"You don't have to tour with every album, you know," Rich said, still behind her. Shane was beside her as they crossed the parking lot.

Haley turned her head, about to say something sarcastic to Rich, when she heard a noise.

"Haley!" a guy called as he stepped out between two cars, lunging towards her.

He'd appeared so quickly, Shane had no time to react and grab her gun. She saw a sliver of shiny metal reflect in the parking lot lights as she dove in front of Haley. Then, a searing pain tore through her chest.

"Nooooo!" Haley screamed as Shane's body slammed back against her, nearly knocking her down as she began to collapse. "Shane!"

Sor...ry," Shane slurred, coughing up bright red blood that spewed from her mouth before her eyes closed.

Rich dropped the guitar case and ran after the guy, but he'd disappeared like a ghost. He turned around, running back to Haley, who was on her knees, holding Shane's limp body against her.

"No. No. No. Shane, please. Open your eyes. Please!" Haley cried.

Rich was already on the phone with 9-1-1 by the time he noticed the knife sticking out of Shane's chest and the pool of blood at her side.

Someone who happened to be leaving the bar saw them and quickly ran inside to get help. Big Earl ran out with the patrons.

"Rich, please help her," Haley wailed as tears streamed down her cheeks, dripping onto Shane's body.

"They're on the way, honey. I'm sorry," he said, squatting down next to her, all the while peering around for the man who'd fled, hoping he didn't return.

Big Earl and the others searched the parking lot, but they didn't see anyone.

***

"Please tell me she's still alive," Haley said through her tears as the paramedics arrived and quickly went to work on Shane.

"She is for now, ma'am, but if we don't get her to the hospital soon, she won't be," he replied.

Rich pulled Haley away, holding onto her as they loaded Shane into the ambulance. "What hospital are you taking her to?" he asked.

"We're going up the road to meet the medivac. I believe they are flying her to Nashville General," he said, before slamming the doors and running around to drive the rig.

The ambulance left in a hurry with the lights and sirens going.

"Come on, we have to get out of here," Rich said, ushering her into his SUV.

"We need to get a statement," one of the police officers said.

"I'll drive her to your nearest station. She's not safe out here," Rich said.

"The woman who was stabbed, do either of you know her?" the officer questioned.

"Yes. This is Haley Nielsen, and that was Shane Crowley, her bodyguard."

The officer nodded. "Follow me."

"I want to go to the hospital, Rich. Damn it!" she said when he got into the SUV.

"We will, but we have to give our statements to the police. It won't take long," he said, taking off after the police car.

"She can't die," Haley mumbled, still crying. "Why would somebody do this?"

"I don't know."

"Was it him? Was that the letter writer?"

"I don't know."

"God damn it! What *do* you know?"

"You're alive. Shane was alive when they left." He shook his head. His heart was pounding so hard, he was sure he was going to have a heart attack...or perhaps a stroke. "Look, there she goes," he said, pointing out the window at the helicopter flying away in the distance.

"I should be with her. The hell with the police. They can come to the hospital to get my statement."

"We're almost there. He said the substation was only a few miles away."

Chapter 30

Rich and Haley sat in a small room with a table and two chairs that was normally used as an interrogation room. However, being that she was celebrity, they were trying to keep her out of site.

"I'm Detective James Kenny," a middle-aged man said as he walked in with another, younger man and sat down across from them. "This is Roddy Hill. He'll be taking the lead on this investigation. I'll be here to assist him if need be."

"I'm Richard Bergman, and this is Haley Nielsen."

"I understand your bodyguard was attacked outside of the Hillbilly, am I correct?" Detective Hill asked.

"Yes," Haley muttered.

"Did you see the person?"

"No. I'd turned my head to say something to Rich. He was walking behind us. Shane was beside me. I don't even know what happened. She jumped in front of me and fell back against me. Then, we sunk to the ground."

"I didn't get a good look, either. It was a man, maybe five-foot nine or ten. He had on jeans and a dark jacket with a hood. I only saw him from behind as he was running away."

"Any idea where he came from?"

"No. He just appeared."

"I remember hearing my name," Haley said.

"Yeah, he yelled her name, and then it was over. It happened so fast."

"Any idea who it might have been? Does Shane Crowley have any enemies that you know of?"

"She's a former U.S. Marshal, so she could have," Haley said. "But..." She looked at Rich.

"Haley's had a stalker for the past few months. He's written a handful of threatening letters," Rich sighed. "That's why we hired Shane. She's been working to track down who it is."

"Do you think this letter writer is the attacker?"

Haley shrugged. "All I know is, he had to have been trying to stab me, not her. She jumped in the way."

"Do you still have the letters?" he asked.

"Shane sent everything to labs she has contact with. There was nothing on them. She and Dennis Williams, the owner of the company she works for, were working together on the case. I don't know if they currently have anything or not. I can give you his number. In fact, I need to call him right now. If you'll excuse me," Rich said, stepping out of the room and into the hallway to call Dennis, who was listed as Shane's next of kin and emergency contact.

"I'm sorry, Ms. Nielsen. We'll do everything we can to catch this person."

"Thank you. Am I free to go?" she asked.

"Yes. We have your information. We'll be in touch if we need anything further."

"Did you check with Big...Earl Smidley? The Hillbilly might have cameras outside."

"Yes, ma'am. We're in the process of getting that footage right now."

Haley nodded and walked out of the room. Rich was just ending his call.

"Dennis is on the way. I told him to book a private jet. We'll cover the expense."

"We're done here. If you don't take me to the hospital, Rich, I'm calling a fucking Uber," she said through clenched teeth, afraid she may start crying again. "I don't know if she's dead...alive...anything."

"It's not safe, Haley. Please let me take you to a hotel. Once Dennis gets here, I'll feel safer with you out in plain sight."

"You're fired," she spat, walking away.

"Wait! What?" he caught up to her quickly.

"You heard me, Rich. I'm going to the god damn hospital with or without you!"

"Fuck," he grumbled. He had no one to call. The road crew and buses were several hours away and more than likely getting close to Atlanta by this point. "Fine. But, we're doing this my way."

Haley nodded.

"Ms. Nielsen, I was just coming to speak with you before you left. I'm Daniel Easton, the captain of this district. I wanted to assure you that we will be doing everything in our power to catch the person who did this. We have our best detectives on the case."

"Thank you," she replied.

"We came in through a back entrance. Would it be possible to be escorted back out as discreetly?" Rich said.

"We really need to get to the hospital," Haley said, wiping away a few tears.

"Are you a good driver?" the captain asked, looking at Rich.

"Yes. Haven't had a ticket since I was in my twenties."

"What hospital?"

"Nashville General."

"Come on." He motioned, leading them down a hallway. "Mathis," he said, stopping an officer who was passing by. "I need them escorted to Nashville General…code 8."

"Yes, sir," the officer said.

"And stay close to her. This is country star, Haley Nielsen. Her bodyguard was just stabbed while saving her life."

"I'm sorry," he said, looking at her.

Haley tried to form a smile but nothing happened.

"I'll have someone replace you as soon as I can. Until then, you're all the security she has."

The officer nodded. "I suggest you stay close, but keep at least a car length between us," he said to Rich.

"No problem," Rich replied, walking beside Haley as the officer led them down a hallway.

***

Shane was taken directly to surgery when the helicopter arrived. She had a collapsed lung, and blood was accumulating in the cavity between the chest wall and lung. The doctors quickly went to work, stabilizing her blood pressure. Then, she was taken to surgery for the VATS procedure to remove the knife, close the wound, and remove the excess blood so that they could get the lung working correctly. She coded once on the table when her blood pressure dipped, but they were able to get everything under control.

By the time Haley and Rich had arrived with Officer Mathis, Shane was out of surgery and moved to ICU, where she was on heavy pain medication and sleeping comfortably.

"So, as I told you in the hallway, we were able to get her stable and close the wound," the doctor said. "She has a drain tube right here," he added, pointing to the clear hose with bloody fluid coming out from under the blanket and going into a machine beside the bed. "This just helps suck out any excess blood while it heals. She'll have this in for about three days. We'll reevaluate her at that point. She's in great health, so I expect her to go home after that."

"Okay," Haley said, unsure of what questions to ask. Shane looked so pale and weak with wires and tubes from various machines connected to her that were monitoring her oxygen level, heart rate, blood pressure, and fluid level from the drain.

"She should be awake in a few hours once the meds start to wear off. She'll be in a lot of pain, though. If you have any questions, the nurse can page me."

"Thank you," Rich said.

Haley moved to Shane's side and grabbed her hand. "I'm sorry," she began to cry. "I should've listened to you."

"Don't beat yourself up over this," Rich murmured, placing his hand on her shoulder. "She protected you. That was her job."

"I know it was her god damn job! But, she almost died, Rich! This shouldn't have happened."

He sighed inwardly. "Dennis should be here soon. I got a text saying he was in the air."

Haley ignored him as she sat on the stool, holding Shane's hand and running her other hand up and down her arm.

"When he gets here, why don't you let him take you home?"

"I'm not leaving her side," she growled through clenched teeth.

"Excuse me?" a nurse said, popping into the room. "I thought you might want her things," she added, handing a plastic hospital bag to Rich that contained all of Shane's clothing, as well as her watch and gun holster with her Glock still snapped inside of it. "The knife was given to the police."

"Thank you," he replied, setting the bag on the floor in the corner before taking a seat in the chair. "I need to make a few calls. I'll be right outside the door."

Haley nodded.

As soon as he was gone, she brought Shane's hand up to her cheek. "I'm so sorry. It should be me lying there," she murmured, mostly to herself since Shane was on heavy medication.

***

The entire right side of Shane's torso ached with pain that throbbed to the beat of her heart. She felt like she'd been beaten to within a fraction of her life by a baseball bat. She tried to adjust her position, but that only escalated the piercing pain. It was so dark and cold. She wasn't sure where she was, or what had happened to her, but she felt alone and helpless. She began calling out Haley's name, hoping she wasn't in danger.

***

Haley had fallen asleep with her head on the bed next to Shane while still sitting on the stool and holding her hand. A soft moaning sound caused her to stir. She sat up, feeling the stiffness in her sore muscles from the awkward position she'd been in.

"What time is it?" she asked, looking at Dennis in the dimly lit room.

He was sitting at the foot of the bed in the chair. He'd arrived earlier, allowing Rich to leave and handle his part of the situation. "Around three a.m., I think."

Haley nodded and yawned. She was about to lay her head back down when she heard Shane whispering her name.

"I'm here," she said, squeezing her hand. "Shane? Can you hear me? I'm right here. Open your eyes."

***

Shane fought to see in the dark, thick fog surrounding her, but she heard Haley's voice in the distance. *Where are you? How do I get to you? I'm lost.* Haley's voice rang in her ears again, telling her to open her eyes. Shane searched and searched for the direction of the sound, but couldn't figure it out. It was almost like she was floating through space, with no sense of direction.

***

"Dennis, get the nurse," Haley said nervously. "Something's wrong."

Shane was squeezing her hand and wincing in pain. She still hadn't opened her eyes.

He opened the door and called down to the nurses' station. The police officer had left once Dennis had arrived and explained that he was trained to handle the situation and would be resuming Haley's security detail in Shane's place.

226

A few seconds later, a tall, dark-skinned nurse came into the room and flipped the switch, fully lighting the room. Dennis and Haley both flinched from the brightness.

"What's going on?" she asked, walking over and checking the machines, as well as the drain.

"She's moving and grimacing. I also felt her squeeze my hand a few times," Haley said.

The nurse smiled. "She's coming off those meds and waking up. Those things put you in the Twilight Zone." She shook her head. "She needs to wake up so we can see what her pain level is before we give her something new." She made sure everything looked fine on the machines. Then, she ran her hand up and down Shane's left arm. "Shane...come on, darling. You have people here waiting for you to wake up. I know it hurts, but I can't take it away until you open your eyes for me."

Haley squeezed Shane's hand, then ran her fingers through her short, dark hair. "Please wake up," she whispered in her ear before kissing her cheek.

Shane began to stir once more.

"Can you dim the lights for me?" she asked, looking back at Dennis. "I don't want to blind the poor woman."

Dennis quickly lowered the lights, and Shane's lids started fluttering.

"Haley," she mumbled.

"I'm right here," she said, squeezing her hand. "It's okay."

Slowly, Shane's eyes began to open, starting with slits. She blinked a few times, then fully opened them.

"Well, hello there," the nurse said.

"Shane?" Haley whispered.

Shane rolled her head towards Haley's voice, holding her breath as the beautiful woman came into view.

"Wh…at happ…" she struggled to speak. Then cried out in pain as she cleared her throat.

"Hold on," the nurse said, reaching for the melted ice chips in the plastic bucket. "Here, take a tiny sip of water, honey. Your throat is dry as a bone from the breathing tube."

Shane did as she was told, feeling the cool liquid soothe her throat as she swallowed.

"Now, that should be better. I'm Felicia, your nurse for tonight. You're at Nashville General Hospital. You had to have a little surgery, but you're fine."

"Haley?" Shane croaked.

"I'm right here. Everything's okay."

"On a scale of one to ten, where is your pain at right now?" the nurse asked.

"Everything…hurts," she winced.

"Okay. I'm going to give you some medicine in your IV. This one won't make you as sleepy as the other one."

Haley watched her put the syringe into the IV line and push the plunger down. "I'll come back in to check on you in a little bit. Right now, all you need to do is rest. That's the best thing for you." She looked at Haley and Dennis. "It's probably best if she sleeps the rest of the night. She'll be a little more awake in the morning."

"Thank you," Haley said.

"Honey, your back will never be the same if you spend all night on that stool."

"I tried to give her my chair," Dennis said.

"I'll have another one brought in." She winked in Haley's direction.

***

228

The rest of the night went by in a blur. Haley tried to nap in the chair with her feet propped up on the bed, but Shane groaned in pain every time she moved in her sleep, instantly waking her. Dennis found it nearly impossible to sleep in the chair he was in, and wound up on the floor, propped up in the corner of the wall.

As soon as the sun rose the next morning, slivers of orange rays peeked through the blinds. Haley looked over at Shane, gasping when she saw gray eyes staring back at her. "Hi. Are you in pain? Do you want me to get the nurse?"

"Water," Shane said hoarsely.

Haley grabbed the water cup and held the straw so she could take a sip.

"Well, good morning," the night nurse said as she walked into the room. "Oh, lord. Don't tell me you spent the night on that cold, hard floor," she said, looking at Dennis.

"I did," he said, groaning like an old man as he got up and stretched out.

"One of the morning nurses brought coffee, bagels, and donuts for you both," she said, handing him the bag and cup carrier. "How's your pain level this morning, honey?" she asked, checking the machines and the amount of fluid in the drain.

"Hurts like hell to even breathe," Shane replied.

"That's because your lung had a hole, and the doctor had to go in and sew you up." The nurse patted Haley's shoulder. "We're all big fans of you, Ms. Nielsen, and we're so sorry this happened. It's been all over the news."

"Thanks," Haley sighed.

"I just wanted to check on our patient one more time," she added as she opened the blinds a little more to let some natural light into the room. "Today is my Friday, so you'll probably be gone by the time I come back in." She patted Shane's arm near her wrist. "It's time for your pain medicine, so I'll go ahead and give it to you now." She pulled the syringe from the computer cart she pushed around from room to room, scanned the ID bracelet on Shane's wrist, then scanned the medicine code. "This should kick in soon," she said, pushing the medicine into the IV line.

Haley watched her put the syringe into the orange BIO HAZARD box on the wall and grab the handle for her cart.

"You'll have a good nurse tonight. I'll tell her to see what she can do to get you better sleeping arrangements," she said with a smile as she exited the room.

"She's the nicest nurse I've ever encountered," Dennis muttered, still stretching his sore muscles as he took a sip of coffee.

"Did he shoot me?" Shane asked, grimacing in pain as she adjusted her position.

"No. You were stabbed in the chest." Dennis said. "Right here," he added, pointing to the same spot on himself.

"He got away, didn't he?"

Haley nodded.

"I'm sorry."

Haley shook her head and grabbed Shane's hand. She wiped away a tear that slid down her cheek with her other hand. "No. Don't you ever say that to me again. He was coming for me, Shane," she cried. "You jumped in front of me, and he stabbed you."

"Don't cry," Shane whispered.

"I'm sorry. I should've listened to you." Haley grabbed a tissue from the bedside table to dry her face.

"Don't be sorry."

"You got stabbed, Shane. Why did you jump in front of me?"

"I was just doing my job," she mumbled as the pain meds began to take effect. They didn't knock her out, but they did make her somewhat groggy.

"How is she?" Rich asked, walking into the room.

Shane was already back to sleep.

"In pain," Haley sighed.

"I just got off the phone with the label. The tour is postponed until further notice." He looked over at Haley, who was sitting in the chair, staring out the window. "The story is all over the news."

"Yeah, the nurse told us," Dennis said between bites of bagel. "Have you spoken to the detective?"

"I did. Just a little bit ago, actually. They have the knife. It's some kind of antique blade thing. There were fingerprints on it, but they are not in the system."

"Dennis, we need those prints and that knife," Shane croaked.

All eyes turned to her.

"I thought you were asleep," Haley said.

"Just resting."

"Send the prints to my contact with the marshals, and have him match them with the others. If the police won't give you the knife, get a picture of it at least," Shane said. Her face was all scrunched up, clearly showing the pain she was fighting against.

"I'm on it. Get some rest," Dennis replied. "Are you going to be here for a while?" he asked, looking at Rich.

"I was going to take her home to shower and change clothes," Rich answered, nodding towards Haley as he grabbed a donut from the bag.

"There is a shower here. Just bring me some clothes," she said. "I'm not leaving."

"Go," Shane mumbled. "I'm okay."

Haley shrugged.

"So stubborn," Shane muttered.

"Alright," Haley sighed. "I could use a shower. I'll be back in two hours."

"Dennis, don't leave her side," Shane said.

"I won't," he replied.

"The band and road crew are on their way back to Nashville. I have business to take care of downtown. I'll check back in a little later. Let me know if anyone needs anything," Rich said.

"Leave me the detective's name and number. We'll swing by the police station and see what we can squeeze out of him," Dennis said.

Rich nodded and handed him the detective's card before grabbing another donut and leaving the room.

"I'm ready if you are." Dennis looked over at Haley.

"I'll be back," she said, squeezing Shane's hand.

"Do you want this coffee or anything?" he asked.

Haley shook her head. She didn't drink coffee, and wasn't in the mood to eat.

Chapter 31

Later that afternoon, Haley was sitting in the chair with her feet up on the bed, nearly asleep, when the doctor came into the room. Dennis had been pacing around the hall outside of the room, on and off the phone with the detective, as well as Shane's contact with the U.S. Marshal Service.

"You look a little better than you did last night," the doctor said, checking at the machines. "I'm Dr. Thomas Mercer. I was your surgeon. You came in with a knife sticking out of your chest. Do you remember any of that?"

"I remember something happening to me, but I didn't know what it was until they told me," Shane replied.

"It was touch and go there for a quick minute. Your blood pressure dropped, and we had to shock you. But, once you were stable, we went in with a procedure called VATS. We basically used tiny tools and a tiny camera to go in and fix the damage to your lung so that it could re-inflate. VATS allows us to do everything without cracking your chest open. The good news is, you don't have much fluid draining anymore, so I'll probably take it out tonight. If that happens, and we get you up and moving around tomorrow, walking and so on, you'll get to go home. You'll be on a strict regimen for the next few days, but after a week, maybe two, you should be back to normal. You're in overall great health, so you should heal quickly."

"That's good," she said, still grimacing with discomfort.

"That tube is what's causing most of your pain. A day or so after it comes out, you'll see a huge difference." He pressed the button to elevate the head of the bed a little more. "Here, this should help you take deeper breaths and keep that lung full of air."

"Will she need help at home?"

"She shouldn't be left alone, at least for the first few days. She needs to get up and walk around, but nothing strenuous and no stairs. She'll also need help dressing her wounds. Make an appointment with my office in about a week to have the stitches removed."

"Can I fly?" Shane asked. "I live in Memphis."

The doctor shook his head. "No, not for at least three weeks. The pressurization could cause your lung to collapse again in the air. Anyway, I'll come back in this evening and take the drain out."

"You didn't happen to take a picture of the knife, did you?" Shane asked.

"Yeah. We do that for the file when someone comes in with an impalement or anything like that."

"Can we get a copy of it?"

"Sure. We gave the knife to the police last night. It was quite unusual, and very sharp. Whoever stabbed you, they were intending to do a lot more damage."

Haley looked away, shaking her head. Her sadness was slowly turning to anger at the person who did this.

"I'll have the nurse bring you the picture. It was taken with the knife lying on the surgical table after it was removed."

"That'll work. Thanks," she said.

"I guess I won't be needing access to the knife, after all," Dennis said to the detective on the phone. Then, he ended the call as the doctor left the room.

"You're staying at my house while you recover," Haley said. "There's plenty of room for the two of you."

"What about the tour?"

"It's over at the moment."

"I think it's a good idea," Dennis said. "I'll be able to keep her safe, and you can work on the case while you heal."

"I quit, remember?" Shane said, staring into Haley's eyes.

"You said after Atlanta. We never made it there, so... it looks like you're still working for me." Haley smirked.

Shane sighed.

"Emma Jean would love to have someone to coddle besides me. Let me help you, Shane," Haley said seriously.

"Okay."

***

The doctor removed the drain tube and stitched the hole closed later that evening, and the next morning, Shane was discharged. Rich put Shane and Haley in his SUV and Dennis followed them in his rental car. The drive from Nashville out to Brentwood wasn't too long, but by the time they arrived at Haley's house, Shane was already worn out.

When they walked inside, the mouth-watering aroma of home-cooked food filled Shane's nose, making her almost forget about the pain in her chest and side. Her stomach growled in anticipation.

"Emma Jean made you a snack," Haley laughed, hearing the rumble. "This way," she said, opening the door to the den. "I know you can't go up the stairs, and the formal living room is stuffy. I figured you'd be more comfortable in here."

Shane had never been in this room of the house. It definitely looked more lived in than the rest of the rooms.

There were two comfortable-looking couches forming an L-shape, with a square, oak wood coffee table in front. A fireplace was on the wall across from the table, and a large TV hung over the mantel.

"Thanks," Shane said, taking a seat on one of the couches.

"I have plenty of blankets and pillows down here, so we'll make you a bed when you're ready to lie down. There's a bathroom through that door over there," she pointed. "And this one leads to the dining room and the kitchen from there."

"I remember the layout. I've just never been in this room."

"This den is my cozy place. If I'm not in the music room, this is usually where I am. Anyway, Dennis, come on. I'll show you around. You'll be in one of the guest rooms upstairs."

"Oh, I can just take the other couch down here. There's no need to fix up a room or anything."

"They're guestrooms, so they're already fixed up."

"Go on. You'll be more comfortable," Shane said.

Dennis nodded and followed Haley as she gave him a tour of her house and left him to choose a room to sleep in. Back downstairs, she found Shane in the kitchen.

"What the hell do you think you're doing?" she said, raising a brow like a mother scolding a child.

"Looking for that food I keep smelling."

"Emma Jean cooked for an army, so you'll have to be more specific…and you don't need to be up walking around. I can get it."

"Haley, you don't have to wait on me hand and foot. The doctor said it was good to move around."

"He also said don't exert yourself," she huffed, crossing her arms.

"Oh, for crying out loud. Are we going to start fighting again already?"

"Nope. You're going to stop being stubborn and go sit your butt on the couch while I heat up some lunch for you." Haley made a shooing motion with her hand.

Shane shook her head and gave in as she walked slowly back to the den. Walking wasn't really the hard part, it was getting up and down that made her feel like her right side was tearing in two. She yelped as she eased herself down onto the couch.

Hearing her, Haley rushed in to help. "See, you shouldn't be getting up and down."

Shane ignored her as she reached for the TV remote, but it was too far away.

Haley stood in front of her with her hands on her hips and a smirk on her face.

Shane exhaled loudly. "Can you please hand me the controller?"

"See, you needed my help. How hard was that?" Haley said, getting it for her before going back into the kitchen.

"Is she always like this?" Dennis whispered, coming into the den and sitting down. "So...demanding?"

"Yes...but this is different," Shane said. She'd never seen Haley care about anything other than herself, and what was next on her agenda. She had noticed a softer, more relaxed side of her when they were staying at the house during the funeral and when they were waiting for a new bus, but it was nothing like what she was seeing now.

Dennis simply nodded.

"Let me see that picture," Shane said.

"Are you sure you want to get into that right now? You just got out of the hospital—"

"He's going to get away if we don't get moving on this. You have to be my legs on the ground, but I can do the rest remotely from here."

"Okay," he said, getting up to go get the picture from his room.

"Bring your laptop, too!" she called.

"What do you need that for?" Haley asked, coming into the den from the dining room.

"I have work to do."

"You need to eat and rest."

"I'll be fine," Shane stated, locking eyes with her. Before Haley could say anything, she continued. "He didn't get to you. It's not over."

Why are you so hardheaded? Haley felt like smacking the wall, but she kept her temper in check as she changed the subject. "Do you want to eat in here? I have tray tables."

"I can come to the kitchen. Is the island okay?"

"Are you sure you can get on and off a stool? Will that be comfortable for you?"

"I'll manage."

"I'll bring it in here," Haley said, getting the tray tables out of the closet.

Shane shook her head. There was simply no reasoning with Haley when she had her mind set on something.

***

By the time Dennis had come back downstairs, Haley had all of their plates on the trays, with their lunch ready to be eaten. He and Shane had completely forgotten about the knife. It was long after she'd finished, that she fell asleep. Dennis sat in the formal living room, scrolling around on his computer, trying to figure out anything he could about the knife.

"She's not going to rest until this is over, is she?" Haley murmured, walking across the room over to the French doors leading out to the pool deck. The sun had set long ago, and the sky was littered with tiny little stars as she looked out through the open blinds. She was so tired. She felt like she was carrying the weight of another person on her back.

"I'm afraid not," he said. "Shane is cut from a different cloth. She's either all in, or not at all with everything she does."

Haley nodded.

"Did you know she flat-out refused this assignment when I first gave it to her?"

"No," she said. "But, I can see why. We've done nothing but butt heads since she got here."

"That wasn't the reason."

"You mean the Marshal Service?"

"Uh huh. My company does private investigation and protective service. Until now, she's only worked in investigation."

"She told me why she left."

"Really?" He cocked his head to the side with surprise.

"Yes."

"I've seen so much change in her this past month." He shook his head.

"Why did you give her this assignment if you knew she didn't want it?"

"Because she is the best there is. I knew your situation could mean trouble, and I knew she could handle it."

"She got stabbed…nearly to death, forty-eight hours ago."

"But, she did her job, Haley. She protected you. You didn't get stabbed."

"I don't understand," Haley sighed. "What makes a person literally put your life above theirs?"

"It's not that simple. She's trained to do a job. It's ingrained in her. It's not about one life over another…however, it became that way in the Marshal Service. It was no longer about the job, it was about the person. That scared her. When the girl died, it tore her apart because she felt like she'd failed. That's why she left. She blamed herself. That's also why I knew she was the best for this job and wouldn't turn it down once she saw…" He trailed off.

"Saw what?"

"You," he said, looking her in the eyes.

"Huh?"

"When she put a face to the case, it made it very real for her. Sure, in the beginning she probably thought it would be any easy babysitting job, but somewhere along the line, it became a hell of a lot more for her. When I say she's not going to stop, you bet your ass she will turn over every rock from here to Arkansas looking for him. He's not going to get a second chance to try and hurt you. She won't let it happen."

"All of this is because of the Marshal Service?"

Dennis half-grinned and shook his head. "No. All of this is because of *you*. She's not going to fail *you*."

"Did you know she quit?"

240

"She mentioned it, but that's not like her."

"The night before she got stabbed, she told me she'd work until Atlanta, which was the next stop, then she was done."

"Do you know why?"

"This whole arrangement has been miserable. I hated her being here, and she hated being here just as much."

"I think there's a lot more to it than that."

Haley shrugged.

"Do you know she still has clearance as a Deputy Marshal?"

"I thought she quit?"

"That's just it…Shane doesn't quit *anything*."

"Why isn't she working with them, then?"

"Because she asked for time off to get her head right after the psych evaluation cleared her for duty. She didn't feel ready. When she didn't go back, they put her on an unpaid sabbatical. Although, she is eligible to be reinstated at any time. They call every other month asking her to come back."

"Are you serious?"

"Yes. I didn't know any of that until yesterday when her contact, who had been helping us out, found out what happened to her. He told me everything."

"I wonder why she won't go back," she said.

"Because I got tired of putting my life on the line for people who didn't deserve it, while the ones who did…sat back and called the shots…literally," Shane said from the doorway.

Dennis wasn't sure what to do. He had no idea how much of the conversation she'd heard.

"Do you need me to get you anything?" Haley asked, walking over to her.

"I'm fine. I need to use the restroom."

"Here," Haley said, turning on the light and opening the door so she could get in and out easier.

"It's true…what he said. Every word."

Haley met her eyes, but didn't say anything as she pulled the door closed.

Chapter 32

Haley had trouble sleeping, and it wasn't because of the couch. She'd fallen asleep in the den and stayed there the entire night many times. No, it was because her mind wouldn't shutdown. She kept trying to process her conversation with Dennis. She and Shane had spent so many weeks fighting against one another, she never took the chance to learn anything about the person who was literally at her side around the clock for almost a month. *You hated her because you wanted to push her away. You* had *to push her away. Otherwise—*

Haley's inner thoughts were interrupted when Shane began moving around in her sleep, causing her to cry out in pain.

"No!" she exclaimed, thrashing around.

"Shane," Haley whispered, rushing to her side. "It's just a dream. Wake up." She ran her hand through her hair, realizing she was drenched in sweat. "I'm right here." She took Shane's hand and put it on her face.

Finally, she stopped flailing around and began to open her eyes.

"You okay? That was a nasty dream," Haley said, still holding Shane's hand to her face while her other hand slowly moved through her hair.

"I..." Shane grimaced as she sat up a little bit, pulling her hand away. "He was...right there. It was so...real."

"Did you see him?"

"Not his face. Just a dark hood and...the shiny blade."

"It's just a nightmare. However, you're covered in sweat, and I'm afraid you stink." Haley wrinkled her nose.

"What time is it?"

Haley looked at the clock on the wall. "Four."

Shane lied back down. "I don't have the energy to take a shower right now."

"That's fine. We'll do it in the morning. Try to get some sleep. I'll stay right here."

"Are you protecting *me* now?" Shane looked up at Haley's bluish green eyes.

"Something like that." Haley smiled.

***

The next morning, Shane stood in the bathroom with Haley just outside the door as the hot water ran in the shower.

"I'll be fine. I feel better today," Shane said, trying to remove her clothes by herself.

"You can't even take your shirt off. How are you going to shower?" Haley huffed. "Your stitches can't get wet, and you have them in two places!"

"I'll manage," Shane mumbled.

"Why are you so damn stubborn?" Haley growled. "Just let me help you. You'll be in and out."

"Damn it, Haley. I can do it myself!"

Dennis could hear them yelling as he headed down the stairs in search of something to eat for breakfast. Unsure of what to do, he just stood in the foyer. He had no clue as to what stage of dress Shane was in, and didn't want to impede on her privacy, yet at the same time, it sounded like they were having a huge argument.

Before he could make up his mind, Rich pulled up outside. He quickly opened the front door, allowing him to step inside.

"I don't need to be babysat!" Shane yelled.

"Is that what you think I'm doing?" Haley growled back. "You have no idea what that's like, trust me. I've been dealing with it for a month!"

"I didn't hold your hand when you went pee, or wipe your ass!" Shane snapped. "I'm just trying to take a fucking shower!"

"Well, I'm just trying to assist you so you don't mess up your stitches, smart ass!"

"I don't know what to do," Dennis said. "They've been at it for at least ten minutes. The water has to be cold by now."

"They always act like they want to scratch each other's eyes out," Rich said with a shrug as he walked into the kitchen. "I think they should just have sex and get it over with."

Dennis's jaw dropped as he followed behind him. He knew Shane was a lesbian, but he had absolutely no clue about Haley. "Really? You think that's what it is?"

"Sure. You can cut the sexual tension between them with a knife," Rich replied, shaking his head. "They'll either figure it out or kill each other."

Neither man had noticed the silence in the house.

Haley and Shane stared at each other, obviously having overheard the conversation in the kitchen a few feet away.

"I'll...uh...wait out here," Haley said. "Yell if you need help or anything."

"I can't get this stupid shirt off," Shane mumbled.

"Come here." Haley reached out, pulling the t-shirt up and over Shane's head, revealing her naked torso. There was a half inch long line of black stitches on her right side of her chest above her breast, and another, slightly longer row of stitches on her side just below her breast. Her entire right side was still a little swollen around her stitches, but the bruising from the surgery was nearly gone. Haley's eyes raked over Shane's breasts and down to the twitching muscles of her flat stomach, before finding her eyes. She quickly cleared her throat and turned to walk away.

Shane watched her go, then she closed the door and finished undressing. Rich's words played in her mind as she washed her hair and body, but trying not to get her stitches wet was nearly impossible. *What would he think if he knew we'd already had sex…twice?* "It definitely didn't solve our problem," she muttered to herself.

***

Haley sat on the edge of the couch, still holding Shane's t-shirt in her hand. *What the hell has gotten into me?* She shook her head, setting the shirt to the side. Her ears perked up when she heard the water stop. She waited in anticipation for Shane to call for help, but she never did. A few minutes later, the door opened and Shane appeared, clean and freshly dressed.

"Listen, I'm sorry," Haley started as she stood up.

"It's okay. I know you are just trying to help," Shane replied, walking over to her.

"I just…it's my fault this happened to you."

"Haley, it's over. I'm fine. A little sore still, but I'm getting better. In fact, the stitches look like they will be able to come out soon."

"The doctor said to make an appointment with him in a week."

"I'll just take them out myself in a couple more days."

"What?!"

"It's actually not difficult at all, and it doesn't hurt."

"Don't go all Roadhouse on me," Haley laughed, shaking her head. "I know you're a badass, but taking out your own stitches is a little much."

Shane grinned. "Thanks for thinking of me as a badass, but Patrick Swayze, I am certainly not. However, this isn't my first go around with stitches. There's really nothing to it."

"Somehow, I'm not surprised."

"Why is that?" Shane's brow furrowed.

"Let me guess, you got cut or shot or something when you were a deputy marshal."

Shane shook her head. "Nope. I was ten and fell off my bike trying to jump my friends skateboard ramp. I had a gash in my leg that needed six stitches. I was the talk of the neighborhood for weeks."

Haley smiled and chuckled. "Did you take out your own stitches then?"

"Yep. Well, the doctor started it, and then showed me how. I've also had them two other times…both of which I removed myself."

"See…Roadhouse…a real badass," Haley teased.

Shane shrugged. "I was thinking more like Ghost. Do you happen to have a pottery wheel?"

"Go find yourself some breakfast. You make me crazy!" Haley muttered with a smile.

"So, you've said," Shane replied, walking away.

Rich and Dennis nearly fell over each other trying to pretend to be busy with breakfast. Shane eyed them suspiciously. Then, to the stove to see what was in the pans covered with foil. "Emma Jean was here?" she yelled.

"Yeah, early this morning," Haley replied, coming into the kitchen. "You were sound asleep."

"You should've woken me."

"Next time, I'll beat two pots together when she arrives, sort of like a dinner bell," Haley said, her voice full of playful sarcasm.

Shane rolled her eyes. "Dennis, Emma Jean is Haley's maid, but honestly, she's more like her caretaker. You'll probably see her coming and going. She's super sweet, and an excellent cook. If you waited for Backwoods Barbie, you'd starve to death."

"Nice," Haley muttered.

"Now...now, ladies. Let's place nice today," Rich said.

"Don't get me started. I know why you're here, looking bright-eyed and bushy-tailed," Haley grumbled. "I'm not doing it."

"Doing what?" Dennis asked.

"Good Morning America wants to interview me about the new album, but really, they just want the scoop on all of the shit that's been going on for the past two months with the letters."

"I think it's great publicity, especially with us postponing the tour right now," Rich pleaded. "Besides, the label is all for it."

"I'm done kissing their asses, Rich. I'm not doing it. It's not happening. If I didn't go on Nashville Morning News, why the hell would I fly to New York City? I don't care about the album. I don't care about the label. Right now, all I care about is..." She trailed off. "He hasn't even been caught! I'm not traipsing all over creation," she snapped, grabbing her breakfast plate and walking away.

Shane shook her head. "You had to go and piss her off, didn't you?"

Rich finished his breakfast and tossed the plate in the trash. "I'll call you later," he yelled on his way out the front door.

"I won't answer!" she replied loudly from the den.

Dennis just sat on his stool, staring at the food on his plate.

"Welcome to my world, buddy. Eat up,"

Shane said, plopping down next to him

with her plate.

Chapter 33

"May I come in?" Shane asked from the doorway of the music room. Haley had disappeared in there later in the day.

"Sure. How are you feeling? Do you need anything?" Haley asked. She was sitting on the old leather sofa where they'd first slept together.

Shane paused for a second, wondering just how many people had actually had sex on that couch. She grimaced thinking about it. "I'm fine...you know that song you sang at the Hillbilly?"

"Which one?"

"*Your* song."

"What about it?"

"I thought it was really good. Can I hear it again?" Shane asked.

Haley shrugged. "Only if you sit down."

Shane nodded and took a seat on the other end of the same couch.

"I'm not sure I'll remember all the words. That's the only time I ever sang it anywhere. It's just something I wrote while on the road," Haley said as she grabbed her acoustic guitar from the nearby stand and strummed a few chords.

Shane stayed silent as she watched her pick the strings, and listened to her sing the melody. She was pretty sure Haley Nielsen could play a banjo with one string and sing bible verses and still sound amazing. She was by far the most talented person Shane had ever met, and working as a deputy marshal, she'd met presidents and dignitaries from all over the world, including some of the most mastermind criminals. But, nothing and no one compared to the woman sitting next to her.

Haley finished the song and kept her guitar in her lap. Her pretty, bluish-green eyes danced as she looked at Shane.

"I hate to interrupt," Dennis said from the doorway, sounding a little frantic. "But, there's a horse in your backyard…on the pool deck, to be exact."

Haley laughed. "Oh, that's Wilson. Marvin will be over to get him once he realizes he's gone. Wilson comes to visit quite a bit. He's too old for us to ride him anymore, but Marvin lets him out to run the pasture. He knows how to open the gate with his muzzle, so you have to keep an eye on him."

Dennis looked at Shane, who simply shrugged.

Haley set her guitar back on the stand. "Come on. I'll introduce you."

"To Wilson?" Dennis questioned.

"Marvin, Emma Jean's husband," she laughed. "They live in the house on the other end of the property," she explained as they walked through the living room. "All of this used to be my grandparents beef cattle ranch when I was a kid. This was their house. It was a couple thousand square feet smaller back then. Anyway, they struggled with the economy and the bank took everything from them when I was a senior in high school. After college, I signed my first record deal and bought the property back from the new owners. The bank had split it and the person who bought that side, built a house. I made them an offer they couldn't refuse, and gave the house to my parents. Emma Jean and Marvin were their best friends, and when my parents passed, they sort of took over looking out for me, I guess. Anyhow, I gave them the house a few years back. Marvin keeps up with the outside of everything, and Emma Jean handles the inside. She's also a pillar at the local church, just like my momma was."

"It's a beautiful home," Dennis said.

"Thank you," Haley replied. "Oh, here comes Marvin now," she said, seeing the tractor. "He must've been out mowing and Wilson snuck off."

Dennis and Shane followed her out of the patio and onto the pool deck, where a large grayish white gelding stood. It had a beautiful white mane and tail.

"Wilson, I haven't planted anymore flowers since you ate the last ones," Haley said with a laugh as she walked up, petting him.

A large green tractor came to a stop ten or so yards away, and a man wearing faded jeans, an old denim shirt, worn boots, and a tan cowboy hat, climbed down.

"That damn horse is going to drive me crazy," he said. "Hey, kiddo," he added, coming up and giving her a hug. "Emma Jean said you're doing okay after that mess a few days ago. Did they find the guy that attacked your friend?"

Haley shook her head and smiled. "No, not yet. Here she is actually," she said, taking a step back. "This is Shane Crowley. She's the one who was stabbed, and that's her boss, Dennis. This is Marvin Blackburn."

Shane and Dennis both shook his hand.

"I hear you've been taking good care of our girl on the road," Marvin said.

"Yes sir." Shane nodded.

"She can be a downright handful, but she's worth every penny. She's every bit as much of her momma as she is her old man." He beamed. "Anyway, thank you for looking out for her. I'm glad to see that you're okay. Emma

Jean has taken a liking to you like a shiny new quarter, so you must be alright."

Shane smiled.

"Come on, horse. I've about had enough of you," he said, smacking Wilson on his hind quarter to get him moving in the right direction. "Take some time to smell the roses, kiddo," he said with a wink in Haley's direction. "Before you know it, you'll be an old timer and wonder where the hell your youth went." He started walking away, then turned back around. "I thought you had flowers out here."

"I do," she laughed. "Wilson ate them all!"

"Well, I'll plant you some more!" he called as got back up on the tractor and started it up.

The horse began slowly trotting back towards the pasture gate on the other side of the property. The tractor putting along behind it.

"That was interesting," Dennis said.

"You city folks don't go around us country folks that often, do you?" Hayley chuckled.

"Memphis has its country side, don't let anyone fool you," Dennis said with a grin. "I've just never had a horse come visit me before. Have you, Shane?"

"I'm from Arizona. It's like a different planet compared to Tennessee altogether. I've told you that."

"Yeah," Dennis nodded. "On more than one occasion."

"You feel like taking a walk? I can show you around a little bit," Haley said.

"Fresh air is great for the healing process," Dennis said, looking at Shane. "I need to get back to my computer. Your contact with the marshals is supposed to be sending me some information."

"I guess it's just us." Shane shrugged as he walked away. "So, how big is your property?" she asked, falling in step next to Haley.

"Oh, it used to be about a hundred acres at one time. My grandparents sold off some of it to help when money was tight, but the bank split it up pretty good after they got a hold of it. As things are now, I own about thirty-five acres. I gave ten acres to Marvin and Emma Jean when I gave them the house. That's how it was parceled. It's all rolling hills full of thick grass and scattered oak trees, some of which are quite old. In fact, this one right here is probably over a hundred years old. It's the largest tree on the property."

"Really?" Shane looked at the large tree. It had willowing branches that spread wide and hung low.

"Yeah. I got married under this tree…a long time ago," Haley said, sounding nostalgic.

"I never knew you were married."

"Only four people ever knew about it: me, Junior, Billy Jack, and Anna Leigh. See, I was twelve, and the second oldest of the group by about three months."

Shane smiled.

"Junior and I were married right here. Billy Jack did the ceremony, and Anna Leigh was my maid of honor." She smiled, placing her hand on the tree. "That silly day was also my first kiss. Although, it was more like being kissed by a seal, as Junior had no idea what to do other than stick his tongue out and squish our lips together."

Shane laughed.

"It was awful," Haley giggled. "What about you? How was your first kiss?"

"It certainly wasn't as eventful, and I definitely didn't get married," Shane said. "I was about fourteen.

Anyway, I was outside, hanging out with my friend Maeve. "I asked her if she knew what it was like to kiss someone. She said no. I said, 'Well, maybe we should try it out so we know.'" She shrugged. "We went behind the bushes and locked lips. I remember it being wet and weird."

Haley laughed.

"It took us a couple more tries and by the end of the summer, we'd gone all the way."

"No shit?!"

"Yep." Shane nodded.

"Wow. So, did you actually go steady or date when you got older?"

Shane shook her head. "Her father was in the Air Force. They moved away after the next school year. I looked her up once when I first became a deputy marshal. She was living in California, with a husband and two kids."

"Wow," Hayley exclaimed. "That's interesting."

"Not really. We were just kids ourselves, experimenting on each other one summer." Shane shrugged. "I learned a lot that year."

"It sounds like it." Haley smiled as her eyes landed on Shane's.

"Do you want to make a new memory for your tree?" Shane murmured.

"Are you asking me to get married, Deputy Crowley?" Haley grinned.

"I'm proposing…" Shane said, still locked onto her eyes. "You have a real kiss under your beautiful tree."

"I definitely know you do *not* kiss like a wet seal," Haley replied, moving closer.

"Is that a yes?" Shane asked, inches away from her.

"Kiss me, Shane," she whispered.

Closing the distance, Shane pressed her lips softly to Haley's. She parted them slowly, and gently touched their tongues together, before pulling away, leaving them both breathless.

"That was definitely better than my first go around at this tree," Haley murmured.

Shane smiled. "We should probably get back to see if Dennis has heard anything."

"Yeah," Haley agreed, clearing her throat. She glanced over her shoulder, looking back at the tree as they walked away.

***

"Are you sure?" Shane said into the phone, shaking her head.

"I'm positive," the man replied. "Listen, Shane. My offer still stands. What happened to you doesn't change anything."

"Now…is just not the time, Paul," she sighed.

"I can't hold the door open forever."

"I know," she said, ending the call.

"Was that your contact with the U.S. Marshals?" Dennis asked, walking into the den. Shane had her laptop open with several different pages up on the screen.

"Yeah, Paul Rutledge. He's a good friend. We went through the academy together," she said. "Funny, he'd be my superior now. He was promoted four months ago."

"Is that why he's trying to get you to go back?"

Her gray eyes met Dennis's questioning brown ones. She nodded, and changed the subject. "The fingerprints match the letter writer, which I knew.

However, the knife is a war relic. It was issued to certain regiments of soldiers during the Vietnam War."

"No shit?" he uttered, looking at the picture she'd pulled up on the screen. It matched perfectly with the one the doctor had taken of the knife he'd removed from her chest.

"I need you to start checking military antique dealers in and around the Nashville area. See if any of them have sold one in the past six months, or come in contact with someone wanting to sell one."

"I'm on it," he said, getting up to go get his computer and his phone.

"Hey...how are things in the office? I'm okay here, if you need to get back."

"Everything's good, and right now, you need me here. You can't protect her, and you can't do all of this legwork yourself. The office will be fine," he reassured her before walking away. What he'd failed to mention was, this was the only life-threatening case his firm had ever dealt with. That was the main reason he'd assigned it to her. She was the only person with enough experience to take it on. He had no idea it would ever go this far, though.

Hearing the piano brought a smile to Shane's face. She wanted to go see what Haley was doing, but decided against it. She was back to playing music on her own. That's what mattered. With Dennis working on the antique stores, Shane started compiling a list of Vietnam Veterans. Using several sites she found on Google, she was able to find the information for the platoons that came out of the Nashville area, as well as surviving Vietnam Vets who currently lived in the area.

"Holy hell," she said, realizing there were several thousand names listed. *This is like trying to find a needle in a damn haystack.*

***

Haley hadn't intended on playing any music. She was more focused on writing. The tour was postponed, but it hadn't been canceled. When all was said and done, she'd have to go back on the road and finish the last leg. There was no way the label was going to forfeit the millions of dollars they were scheduled to make off those venues.

She'd sat at the piano, messing around with a few tunes, before picking up her acoustic guitar. With her eyes closed, and a smile on her face, she let herself forget what was going on around her as her fingers strummed and picked chord after chord. It felt good to hear music in her ears and feel the strings under her finger tips.

After the kiss with Shane under the shady branches of the old oak tree, Haley couldn't get her off her mind. The entire day had gone by, yet she could still feel the tender touch of her soft lips.

Her fingers worked the frets while her other hand strummed the strings with a pick and her barefoot tapped the floor. The guitar chords came together, forming the melody of *Smoke* by A Thousand Horses, a song that had reminded her of Shane for some time now. "She comes rolling right off the tip of my tongue so easy," she began the lyrics, playing and singing a slower, acoustic version of the normally upbeat song. "She'll be the first damn thing I want when I start drinking," she continued.

Chapter 34

Bright orange rays of sun slowly rose up over the ranch, cascading light through the blinds and curtains covering the windows of the large house. Shane was lounging on the couch in the den, watching the slivers of light dance on the wall, when she heard the back door open. The area she'd been stabbed in a week ago was still a little tender, but it had healed nicely. She got up without so much as a grimace and walked through the dining room.

"Good heavens!" Emma Jean gasped, holding her hand to her chest. "You scared the dickens out of me."

"My apologies. I heard the door and—"

"Out of instinct, you went into security mode." She smiled. "I only wish that one upstairs cared half as much about herself as you do. I keep telling her anyone off the street could come in here and she'd have no clue."

"You have the code to get into the house, and you live next door, so you cut through the pasture without using the gate at the street," Haley yawned.

Emma Jean and Shane both turned to see her leaning against the entrance wall.

"Besides, I always know it's you when you come in," she added, walking towards the stove to start the kettle for her tea.

"I can do all of that," Emma Jean said, shuffling both of them out of the kitchen. "Breakfast will be ready in thirty minutes."

"You really don't have to cook for me, Ms. Emma Jean," Shane replied.

"Well, no…I don't. I have to breathe, and one day I have to die, but I like cooking and I most certainly have to keep this one fed," she said, flicking her thumb in Haley's direction. "You're here, so you're included. Now, leave this old woman alone and let her work."

Haley stood with her arms crossed and a brow raised at Shane.

"What?"

Haley shook her head. "I told you to leave her be. She's never going to let you win that argument."

"I see that," Shane sighed. She moved into the formal living room, across from the open kitchen. "Hey, do you have any small, sharp scissors? You know, like the ones used to trim facial hair?"

Haley eyed her suspiciously. "Why? Are you growing a beard?"

"Funny," Shane deadpanned. "I need tweezers, too."

"Now I'm really curious."

"It's nothing exciting. I'm just taking my stitches out."

"The hell you are!" Haley exclaimed. "The doctor said to call in a week to make an appointment."

"I don't need the doctor. It's easy to do, and I told you I've done it a few times."

"What if it's not healed? No, Shane. I'm calling your doctor."

"Haley, for God's sake. There's no need to call the doctor! It's just stitches. You cut them and pull them out!"

"Excuse me, would you two please take that nonsense somewhere else? I'm trying to work in here," Emma Jean chided.

"Well, do you have them or not?" Shane asked, bringing her voice back to a normal tone.

"Of course."

"May I borrow them?"

"Fine. If you hurt yourself worse, I'm not taking you to the doctor," Haley snapped and walked away.

"I do have my car here, so no worries!" Shane yelled after her. "She's as stubborn as an old donkey," she muttered.

"People don't call them jackasses for nothing," Emma Jean said.

Shane spun around, surprised she'd heard her with all the noise she was making with her cooking prep.

"I might be getting up there, but this ol' girl still has a set of dog ears!" she laughed.

Shane shook her head and smiled.

***

"I can't believe you're just clipping the threads and plucking them out of your skin like that," Haley said, watching Shane remove her stitches. Her stomach rolled into knots, threatening to spew the breakfast she hadn't yet consumed. She'd forgotten all about looking at Shane's body as she stood in front of her in a sports bra.

"It's really not a big deal. It doesn't hurt at all," Shane replied as she removed another one and delicately placed the small black thread onto a paper towel that was lying on the coffee table in the den.

"What if it starts bleeding?"

"Do you trust me?" Shane asked, stopping her progress to look into the bluish green eyes staring back at her.

"Yes," Haley whispered.

"Then, believe me when I say it will be fine."

Haley shrugged and sighed heavily. She continued watching in silence while Shane removed the last couple of

261

stitches and revealed the two healed wounds. The skin was pink and the scar lines were raised, but there was no more bruising in either area.

Shane wrapped the paper towel up in a ball, then handed the tweezers and scissors to Haley. "Pour a little rubbing alcohol on them for disinfecting," she said as she pulled her t-shirt back over her head.

"Breakfast is on the warming burner for whenever you two are finished bickering," Emma Jean said from the doorway.

Haley walked over, giving her a hug and a kiss on the cheek. "What would I do without you?"

"Cook your own meals," Emma Jean laughed.

Haley chuckled and shook her head. "She's too damn good to me," she muttered when Emma Jean left. "They both are, really. They're as close to having parents as if mine were still alive."

Shane nodded.

***

After breakfast, Haley disappeared into her music room when the band arrived, leaving Shane alone until Dennis came down.

"How are you feeling?" he asked, walking into the den.

"I took my stitches out this morning." She grinned. "All healed up."

Dennis smiled and shook his head. "These are the names I was able to get from the antique stores and military surplus shops within thirty miles," he said, handing her the paper he was holding. "I just got off the phone with the last one."

Shane scanned the list of a dozen names. "This isn't much. You won't believe how many Vietnam vets and families live in the area. We'll be here until next year if we have to sift through that list. Let's cross reference your names with the magazine subscriptions. Maybe we'll get lucky."

"Sounds good. I need to check in with the office. I have a voicemail from Anthony," he said, pulling out his phone. "I'll catch up to you in a minute."

"Anything I can help with?" she asked. Anthony mostly handled cheating spouse cases, which she wasn't familiar with.

"He's working on a new case and needs a little guidance. No big deal."

Shane nodded as she went into the den, leaving Dennis to his phone call. She immediately opened her laptop and pulled up the spreadsheets she'd made with the magazine subscriptions and began cross referencing them.

***

"Good morning," Haley said, running into Dennis in the foyer.

"Whatever you're working on sounds good," he replied.

"Oh, we're just messing around with a little jam session, but thank you." She smiled. "Did you have breakfast?"

"No, not yet. I was just talking with Shane."

"Did she tell you she took her stitches out?"

"Yeah," he laughed.

"I wanted to smack some sense into her. She refused to let me call the doctor."

263

"I can hear you!" Shane yelled from inside the den.

"Good!" Haley replied. "She's stubborn as hell."

"I believe you carry that title," Shane said, leaning against the doorway.

"Speak of a pain in the ass, and one shall appear," Haley said, rolling her eyes as she walked away, heading to the kitchen to get the charger for her cell phone. On her way back, she contemplated stepping into the den, but thought better of it. She needed to clear her head, and listening to them talk about the letter writer only made her angry.

The band was playing around, picking the tune to an old Nitty Gritty Dirt Band song, *Fishing in the Dark*. Haley recognized the melody as soon as she walked in and quickly picked up her acoustic guitar. "Lazy yellow moon coming up tonight, shining through the trees," she sang with a big smile on her face.

By the time they got to the end of the song, the band was harmonizing with her smoky drawl leading the charge, and their guitars were humming together like a bunch of hillbilly banjo players out in the woods.

Everyone smiled and laughed when they finished.

"Man, I haven't played an old one like that in forever," Haley said. "What made you guys start that up?"

"Oh, I don't know. Nostalgia, I guess," Joey answered, looking around. "I love this damn room."

"We've written some damn good songs sitting right here," she added.

"Hell yeah we have," the other guys said in unison.

"Do you think we'll finish the tour?" Joey asked, setting his guitar in the stand.

"It won't get canceled. The label isn't going to lose millions of dollars," she replied.

"That's bullshit. What about the attempt on your life? Or the fact that your security guard nearly died saving you?" Stiles growled.

"Look, I love what we do, but it's not safe out there for you, Haley," Vince said.

"I agree," Eddie added. "Shane's good, but…"

Haley held up her hand. "We're not going anywhere until this guy is caught. The label agrees with me for a change. I just meant, at some point, we will pick up where we left off. There's no need to get your Levi's in a twist, boys." She grinned. "Now, let's have some fun. We have nothing better to do than make music!"

***

On the other end of the house, Shane scanned the list of magazine subscriptions, searching for the names of the people Dennis had from the antique shops. "I only see one," she said, looking at him. "See if you can find a picture of Randall Oliver Thomas of Nashville."

He typed the name in the internet search box on his computer and began scrolling through the selections that came up.

"Looks like he's a seventy-year-old black man."

"Damn." Shane shook her head. "That's certainly not the guy who attacked me." She picked up the paper with the list of names.

"Are you certain he's affiliated with a church?" Dennis asked.

"Yes, well religion in general, not necessarily one church. He got his hands on that magazine somehow."

"What about a janitor?"

"For a church?"

"Yeah, or religious based hospital maybe."

"Could be. I'm going to email this list to Paul Rutledge and see what he can find out. In the meantime, let's internet search each one and see if anything religious comes up."

Dennis nodded. "I'll take the top half, you take the bottom."

***

Shane emailed the names, then dialed Paul's number. He answered on the second ring.

"You do know that it's six a.m. here, right?"

"Yes, and I also know you're already in the office."

Paul chuckled. "Are you looking for a hard search on these guys?"

"No, that'll take too long. See what comes up on a soft search. Also, I need a favor, Paul."

"Isn't this a favor?"

"A bigger one."

"Name it."

"I need you to leak information to the local news that the authorities have a suspect in my attack."

"What? Why would you do that?"

"I have a feeling he may get spooked. He's some kind of religious nut. If he believes they know who he is, he could turn himself in."

"He could come after her again."

"I'm aware of that."

"This is a lot bigger than running a restricted search. I'm going to need some collateral."

Shane pinched the bridge of her nose and sighed. "Fine. I'll think about your offer."

"You'll do more than that. When this is all over, you'll get on a plane and meet with me face to face in my office."

"Okay," she said, reluctantly agreeing.

"You know the brass is going to catch wind at some point. When they find out you've been on an unpaid sabbatical for the past year, they're going to be pissed. The only reason they are not investigating this case is because they think you're off the books."

"I turned my badge into Ingram. He refused to accept it. The extended time off was his idea, not mine."

"I know that. I'm merely pointing out, you need be ready to go back to work, or sign your separation papers when you see me."

"Understood," she said before hanging up.

***

The news story broke before lunchtime. It was brief, but filled with enough information to let the suspect know they were on to him. Shane only hoped her plan to spook him actually worked.

"What is that all about? We need to call the police department and see who they are looking at," Dennis said.

"Don't bother. It's all fluff."

"What do you mean?"

"I had Paul Rutledge leak false information."

Dennis furrowed his brow in confusion.

"Everyone has been calling me a former deputy marshal, but the story broke that I am actually a current deputy marshal, so now it is a federal crime. He's looking at life in prison versus a simple assault case that comes with

267

a sentence of a few years. I'm hoping this scares him into turning himself in."

Dennis nodded.

Shane's computer chimed with a new email. She quickly opened the message from Paul, and began looking closely at each of the men, narrowing down the list by removing those who were too old.

"Do you recognize him in any of them?"

"I don't know," she said, shaking her head. "He was wearing a damn hoodie and never showed his face. For all intents and purposes, it could've been you. I can guess height and weight, but it happened so fast, I wouldn't be certain."

"I have three names on my section of the list that are affiliated with local churches," he said.

Shane scrolled back through the pictures, looking closely at the three men Dennis named. "It has to be one of these three. This is the best lead we have. The only way to know for sure is to track them down and rule them out one by one."

"First of all, you're not a hundred percent. Second, we're not cops, and I'm pretty sure your Deputy Marshal status will only get you so far."

"I know." Shane sighed. "See if you can find the number to that junior detective who is handling my case."

Chapter 35

Haley walked with the guys to the front door as they were leaving. The morning jam session had gone better than expected, and they were all itching to get back in the studio to lay down some new tracks. They still had the remainder of the tour to take care of but, after that, they were all looking for a little down time, which included studio work.

"Hey, I didn't know they found the guy," Joey said, looking at the breaking news on his phone from the local station's social media page.

"What?" Haley asked, reading the brief report.

"That's great. As soon as he's locked up, we can get back to work," Vince added.

"Yeah…" She nodded, smiling and hugging them bye. As soon as they were off the front porch, she stormed into the den. "What the hell is going on? Nashville PD has caught him? Why didn't we hear about this?" she said angrily.

"That's because he hasn't—"

The doorbell cut Shane off.

"One of the guys probably left something," Haley muttered, turning to go to the door.

"No…that's probably the detective."

"What the hell is going on, Shane?" she demanded.

"I need you to trust me. I'll fill you in as soon as he is gone."

"I don't like being kept in the dark!"

"I know," she replied as the doorbell rang again.

"Someone needs to answer it," Dennis said.

"I've got it. It's my house," Haley snapped, then plastered a smile on her face as she pulled the door open.

"Ms. Nielsen, it's nice to see you again," he stammered.

"Likewise, Detective…"

"Hill…Roddy Hill, and this is James Kenny, he's helping me on the case."

"Yes, I remember. Please, come in," she said, waving her hand for them to step inside. Then, she led them to the formal living room on the back of the house. Dennis and Shane were sitting on the couch.

"I contacted the news about their report. They won't give up their source, but they're saying you're an active deputy marshal. Is that correct?" Detective Kenny asked sternly.

Shane nodded. "It's complicated."

"Not really. You either are, or you aren't."

Not wanting to get into a pissing contest, Shane bit back the remark she was about to say and gave him a simple answer. "I still have my badge, but I am currently on unpaid leave."

"What a cluster fuck," he mumbled.

"That makes this a federal case, and out of our jurisdiction," Detective Hill said.

"Not necessarily, and not yet anyway. It'll take a couple of days for the Marshal Service to catch on and start their own investigation, which is why you have to act now," Shane replied.

"We don't really have a suspect. That report wasn't true," Detective Hill stated.

"I know that. I have three suspects for you, tied up in a neat little bow. All you have to do is go have a chat with each of them," she said.

"How do you know they are suspects?" Detective Kenny asked, looking at the three pieces of paper she handed him. Each one had a suspect's picture, last known address, employer, and date of birth.

"I'm still a U.S. Marshal. I have connections. Listen," she sighed. "I'm not trying to step on anyone's toes. I just want this mess to end. Whoever wrote the letters was using pages from a religious magazine. The knife he used, which I'm sure you know, is a Vietnam Era relic that was given to soldiers in certain regiments. Those three men on that list are affiliated with churches who have subscriptions to that magazine, and have either purchased, sold, or tried to sell military antiques locally within the last six months."

"You did all of this from right here?" Detective Hill questioned, sounding dumbfounded.

"I *am* a federal investigator," Shane deadpanned.

"Why are you just now giving us this information?"

"Like I said, I'm not trying to step on toes. I just think you should pay each of these guys a visit. See where they were that night. I could be completely wrong, but if you do something now, you have a chance to potentially catch this guy, instead of waiting for the feds to do your job for you."

"We'll check them out," Detective Hill said, looking at his partner.

"Thank you. That's all I was asking for," Shane said, eyeing the other detective.

Haley walked them to the front door and happily shut it behind them as they left.

Shane flopped down on the couch in the den. "For fuck's sake. How hard is it to go talk to three people and ask where they were a week ago?"

Dennis chuckled. "Apparently, it's quite a task for Nashville PD."

271

"No kidding," Haley added. "Now, about the loop you kept me out of…" she said, pinning Shane with a stare.

"I'm going to go grab some lunch. Anyone want anything?"

"Nope," they said in unison.

"Okay," Dennis said, dragging out the word as he grabbed the keys to his rental SUV.

Once he was out of earshot, Haley opened her mouth to speak. Shane quickly cut her off.

"Look, all of this came to light this morning while you were in there with the band. I wasn't a hundred percent, and I'm still not, but I called them to go check these guys out because I can't do it. I was the person attacked, and even if I wasn't, it's not a federal case at the moment. I'd have no jurisdiction."

"I understand that. What pisses me off is, you could've told me. I don't like having things sprung on me."

"Oh, that I know," Shane said sarcastically.

"Are we really going to argue over this?" Haley crossed her arms, still standing in front of her.

"I'd prefer not to. I apologize. I was trying not to bother you."

"I'm pretty sure finding out who stabbed you and wrote hate mail to me wouldn't be bothering me. And, while we're at it, why do the police know nothing about the news report that says they have a suspect?"

"Because they didn't have one…until now."

"What?"

"It was a false report for about two hours. Now, it's true."

"Let me guess, you're behind that, too."

Shane pursed her lips, but didn't say anything.

Haley shook her head. "How does he put up with you?"

"Funny, I asked Rich the same thing about you."

Haley rolled her eyes and laughed as she walked out of the room. "Oh, for god's sake. I'm going to shoot that old horse one day!" she yelled.

Shane got up and followed her path, finding Haley in the middle of the living room, watching Wilson eat the flowers that were growing in the pot on the pool deck. She couldn't help laughing.

"Come on, let's take him back over to the pasture," Haley said, grabbing a carrot from the kitchen and walking towards the back door.

Shane followed reluctantly.

"Wilson, you're a pain in the ass, you know that?" Haley called, walking out of the screened patio and onto the pool deck.

Spying the carrot, the large horse moseyed over to her and neighed loudly.

"Oh, you want this? Stop eating my damn flowers!"

"I'm not a horse whisperer, but I think you might want to try a different approach," Shane muttered.

Haley looked at her with a raised brow, then she stepped onto the patio table, called the horse closer, enticing him with the carrot, before climbing onto his bare back. "You want to go for a ride?"

"Um…don't you need a saddle?"

"He's a hundred years old. I doubt he can walk fast enough, much less run. Come on, climb up behind me."

"What will I hold on to?"

"Me, silly," Haley laughed.

Great. I'm going to die. Shane sighed and mimicked the way Haley had gotten onto the horse.

"Come on, Wilson. Let's go home!" Haley said, clicking her mouth and giving him a light kick with her heels. She grabbed his mane to steady herself and steer him as he began a slow trot back across the field.

Shane held onto Haley with one hand on either side of her waist. It felt good to be close to her, but at the same time, it was hell. They were sitting so close, their legs were touching, and her crotch was against Haley's butt. She hadn't meant to sit up against her, but the natural curvature of the animal's back had put them in that position.

***

Haley wanted to wrap those warms arms completely around her waist and lean back into the body behind her as they rode slowly towards the large red barn. However, she knew better. With the case hopefully nearing its end, Shane would be leaving soon. There was no sense in complicating things any further. In fact, she was looking forward to getting her life back on track. With the threats gone, she could go back to normalcy. It was hard to remember what that even was anymore, the last couple of months had been such a hiatus.

"Wilson, you ol' fool. I wondered where you'd gotten off to," Marvin said, shaking his head. "Haley Jo, what in the world are you doing up there?" he snickered.

"I figured it serves him right for eating my flowers again."

"I don't reckon he's learned his lesson. All he wants is that carrot you're toting." Marvin opened the door to the barn and led the horse over to a ladder. "Come on, Wilson. They have to get down."

Shane climbed down first, then Haley followed.

"Deputy, it's good to see you again," he said, tipping his hat.

"You as well," she replied.

Haley gave him a big hug.

"You might as well go see Emma Jean since you're over here. She just finished a green apple pie. Believe me when I say you'll want a slice." He grinned.

Chapter 36

Shane's fork grazed lightly against Haley's as she went for another bite of their shared slice of pie. A thin grin spread across her face as Haley raised a brow in challenge over the last little bit. Emma Jean leaned against the counter, wiping her hands on a dishtowel with roosters printed on the front of it, while silently watching the exchange.

Intimacy was foreign to Haley, so witnessing how much she'd let Shane into her life, warmed Emma Jean's heart. She wasn't overly religious, but believed enough to say a silent prayer for God to keep Shane in Haley's life.

Haley got up from the table and took their empty plate and forks to the sink as Shane's cell phone rang. The curtains were open to a large window, allowing a full view of the acreage shared between the properties.

"You look like your momma with that sunlight on your face," Emma Jean said, squeezing her hand. She'd seen her smile fade the moment Shane answered the call.

"I miss them both so much."

"I know you do, honey."

"We need to get back to your house. The detectives are back," Shane said, standing and pushing her chair in. "Ms. Emma Jean, that was the best apple pie I've ever had," she added with a smile.

"I believe you're gonna make me swoon," Emma Jean teased. "She's a keeper," she whispered to Haley as she hugged her.

Haley laughed softly.

***

"I didn't expect to see you back so soon," Shane said, stepping into the living room.

Both of the detectives sat on one couch, and Dennis was across from them on the other.

"Do either you know this man?" Detective Kenny asked, showing Shane and Haley a picture of a white male in his late fifties.

"He looks familiar. Was he on the list I gave you?" Shane asked.

"I don't know," Haley said, shaking her head. "I've signed thousands of autographs."

"His name is Roger Dowell. He was the pastor at Lord and Savior Church, not far from here."

Haley's shoulders sank. "I know that church…and him," she mumbled as memories of her mother's passing came flooding back to her.

"I'm afraid he was found dead this morning of an apparent suicide," Detective Hill stated.

"Oh my God, that's horrible," Haley gasped.

"There's more," Detective Kenny added. "He was hanging above the altar with his bible opened to James Chapter 4. Two lines were underlined in red. 'So whoever knows the right thing to do and fails to do it, for him it is sin,' and 'Submit yourselves therefore to God. Resist the devil, and he will flee from you.' We also found other evidence that I am not at liberty to discuss because it is still an open investigation, but it appears Mr. Dowell was your letter writer. I'm fairly sure he was your attacker as well," he added, looking at Shane.

"I…" Haley held her hand to her chest. "I don't know what to say. Excuse me."

Shane watched her wipe away tears as she left the room.

"You're certain this was him?" Shane asked.

Detective Kenny nodded.

"Coward," she muttered, shaking her head.

"We should have our investigation completed by the end of the week at the latest. I may need to speak with you again. Will you be here…or?"

"Uh…no. Since he's…I guess my work here is done." She looked at Dennis and cleared her throat. "I'll be heading back to Memphis."

"Okay, well we have your contact information. Like I said, it's pretty cut and dry. I'll send you a final report once the case is closed."

"Thank you," she said, walking him out. "It's over," she mumbled to Dennis after shutting the door.

"Yep," he sighed. "Do you want me to book you on a flight with me?"

"No. My car is here. I'll need to drive it back."

"We can ship it if you want."

Shane shook her head. "I'll be fine. It's not that bad of a drive."

"Okay."

"You know, you can ride back with me, if you want."

"I'm going to try to leave tonight. I need to get back to the office."

She nodded. "I'll be on the road first thing in the morning."

"You did a lot of good here. This case…"

"It was something else," she said.

"Yeah it was." He held out his hand, which she shook. "I guess I owe you a bonus now."

"Big…huge…break the bank," she replied with a grin.

He laughed as he started up the stairs.

"Hey, Dennis. I'm driving back to Memphis, but I have to catch a flight to Phoenix right after."

"I figured." He nodded. "Are you coming back?"

"I honestly don't know."

"Fair enough," he said, continuing up to his room.

***

Haley came out of her room to say goodbye to Dennis when he left two hours later. She thanked him for everything and gave him a genuine hug, promising to give him tickets if she ever played in Memphis. Then, she walked into the den.

"My mother was the piano player for Lord and Savior," she began as she sat down on the comfortably worn couch.

Shane sat beside her.

"She spent every morning there, rehearsing with choir, or just playing music. She went to service on Wednesday evenings, then was back again on Sunday. The church made her feel at peace. She loved my father with everything she had, and called me her gift from God. She often told him God was the only other man she'd ever let into her heart," she said as she began to lose a few tears. "He wasn't a religious man, but we went with her on Sundays, at least when I was little. He stopped going when work on the cattle ranch became too much for him to take off. When he stopped, so did I. He said, 'You're old enough to decide on your own.' I was maybe ten. I still went with her in the mornings that I didn't have school, once my chores were done, of course. That's when we sat and played the piano together for hours. By then, Deacon Randy had become Pastor Randy. I remember him always being around when we were there, sort of hovering nearby, pretending to be working. I'm pretty sure he was in love with her. He may have even told her so, because she cut back to just working with the choir when I became a teenager."

Haley paused, staring off into space like she was in another place. Shane moved to grab her hand, but refrained herself as she continued.

"I remember walking in on them arguing one Wednesday evening. He was going on and on about my singing at the Hillbilly. I was probably thirteen at the time. Anyway, a year and a half later, she got sick with cancer and died six months later."

"I'm so sorry," Shane said.

"Thank you. My father and I didn't know what to do. He began working sun up to sun down seven days a week. I turned to the church, in particular, Pastor Randy, for help with my grief. That place was such a huge part of her life, I thought if I let it surround me, I might feel closer to her. But, after a week of going there every day, I told Pastor Randy that I thought I might be gay. I should've just went to my dad, but he was so lost, I wasn't sure how he'd take it. Pastor Randy preached at me for over an hour about how much of an abomination I was and so on. I knew my mother would not have felt that way. Instead of helping me grieve and find myself, so to speak, he pushed me away from the only thing I had left of her. The light that my mother shined on that place went dark that day. I never went back," Haley sighed and shook her head as she wiped the wet tears from her cheek. "My father had a pulmonary embolism while out on the ranch a year later. He'd had minor surgery on his knee two weeks before and wasn't supposed to be working.

We were able to get him to the hospital, but it had been serious enough to cause cardiac arrest, and he'd gone several minutes without blood or oxygen to his brain. After he'd been in a coma for a week, I begged Emma Jean and Marvin to pull the plug. I was about to turn sixteen, but still too young to make the decision on his life. I knew my father wouldn't want to live that way. He was better off going to my mother. I knew that's where he wanted to be. He loved me with everything he had, but she was his soul mate. Anyway, I held his hand while they turned off the machine, the same way he and I held hers as she took her last breath. Emma Jean and Marvin got me through the rest of high school and then college. I don't know what I'd do without them."

Shane gave in and grabbed her hand. Words weren't enough in that moment, even if she could find the ones she was searching for. She had no idea what that kind of grief was like. Both of her parents were alive and well, and probably sitting at the country club in that exact moment. Her heart broke for Haley and everything she'd been through. The fact that the very same pastor who adored her mother, shunned her, then tried to kill her, simply blew Shane's mind.

"I'm sorry. I didn't mean to dump all of that on you." Her eyes met Shane's sincerely as her lips formed a thin smile that quickly faded away.

"It's okay."

"I'm still in shock," she muttered, shaking her head and squeezing her hand before letting go of it.

"I can't imagine how you must feel."

"Angry. People of the church are supposed to be the savior, the only true person you can trust, but time and time again they fail the world. It's sad, really. And, I'm angry that he had the audacity to come after me because he was a hypocritical, hateful piece of shit. If the coward wasn't already dead, I'm pretty sure I'd kill him myself!"

"I can't fault you there, and I don't think anyone else would either. He deserved a lot more than he got. That's for sure."

"If he didn't go to Hell, my father has a boot on his neck right about now. That, I can guarantee."

Shane watched her smile once more, a little more sincerely this time.

"Anyway, I guess you have some packing to do," Haley said, looking at her.

"Yeah." Shane nodded.

"I'm sure Rich will be calling with news from the label about the tour before the sun rises in the morning, if not sooner."

"No rest for the weary?" Shane mumbled.

"More like no rest for the wicked." Haley grinned and patted her knee as she stood up.

Shane watched her walk down the hall towards the music room, before heading up the stairs to pack her suitcase.

Chapter 37

Haley sat at her piano wearing a worn Aerosmith t-shirt and an old pair of jeans, her fingers barely touching the ivory keys as she stared motionless. Thoughts of Shane and their time together over the past two months, rolled around in her head. She remembered her body feeling like it was on fire when Shane's foggy gray eyes traced a lazy path from her feet up to her head. She'd wanted to kiss her and slap her at the same time in that moment, as well as many others as the days and weeks passed. They'd shared so little with each other, yet so much of each other.

As her finger began softly playing a familiar melody, Haley found herself drowning in the lyrics of *Hallelujah* as she casually sang. She had no idea why, but in that moment, those words were everything she felt. It was love. It was hate. It was sadness. It was…the end. And it hurt like hell.

Feeling a presence, Haley opened her eyes. Shane was standing next to the piano. Her fingers slipped off the keys, her hands landing in her lap. She'd been too enthralled in the emotional rollercoaster the song had sent her on, to notice the few tears that had streaked her cheek.

***

Shane didn't have to go down the stairs to hear Haley. The melody of the piano mixed with her sultry, twanging voice, filled the house. She set her fully packed bag on the floor next to the bed and padded quietly down to the first level, stopping just outside the open door to the music room. She'd never heard Haley sound so raw…almost vulnerable. It took her breath away. Realizing it was tears in her voice, Shane leaned against the wall and slid down to the floor. Her heart broke for the woman in the other room and the pain she kept buried deep inside. Shane couldn't help feeling responsible for some of it.

When the last hallelujah faded away to nothing but soft piano strokes, Shane rose to her feet and walked into the room.

"Come with me," she said, holding her hand out to Haley.

Haley cleared her throat and stood up, taking her hand. "Where are we going?"

"For a drive."

Unsure of what was going on, Haley simply nodded. She'd been on an emotional whirlwind for the past twenty-four hours. Getting out of the house and clearing her mind sounded like a wonderful idea.

***

Shane's classic Corvette purred like a caged tiger when she started the engine. She revved it a few times to clear out the carburetor since it had been sitting for a few weeks. Then, she shifted into reverse and eased it out of the garage.

With the top down, Haley was able to enjoy the late afternoon rays of sunlight warming her skin. She breathed in the fresh, woodland air as they drove down the driveway and out onto the main road.

It didn't take Shane long to open the throttle on the muscle car, sending them careening down the two-lane road as she shifted through the gears. She'd missed the roar of the engine and the wind on her face. She grinned when she caught a glimpse of Haley smiling from ear to ear like a little kid.

"This thing hauls ass," Haley said.

"What?" Shane questioned, turning down the rock n' roll song that was blaring on the radio.

"This thing hauls ass!" Haley exclaimed, just before she threw her arms up and screamed like she was on a rollercoaster ride.

Shane laughed.

Great White's song *Once Bitten Twice Shy* came on the radio and Haley reached over, turning the volume back up as she sang along.

Shane found it hard to concentrate on the road. She'd never seen Haley this happy, and all she wanted to do was watch her.

"Do you want to drive?" Shane found herself asking as she slowed for a stop sign at an intersection. She'd never let anyone drive her car, so she had no idea why she was offering all of a sudden.

"The only stick I've ever driven was my father's old farm truck, but it was three on the tree."

"Four on the floor isn't so bad. I'll show you, if you want."

"Hell yeah," Haley said with a huge grin.

Shane drove for another mile, then pulled off onto a side road that led to an open, empty parking lot. She turned the car off and looked over at Haley. "The gears are very simple. First is up; second is down; third is up and over to the right; fourth is straight down. They are tight, but as long as you're not hotrodding it, you'll be fine. The clutch is a little stiff, so be careful not to pop it."

Haley bit her lower lip, which made Shane want to kiss that tender spot when she opened her mouth to speak.

"Are you sure about this? I don't want to mess anything up."

"It's fine. Come on," Shane said, getting out to walk around the car.

Haley got out and stepped around to the driver's seat. She had to move it up two clicks to be able to push the clutch all the way down. After going through the gears with the car off, she pushed the clutch in one more time and fired up the engine. Feeling the power of the small block V8 engine was exhilarating and frightening at the same time. Shane waited patiently, watching her chest rise and fall with each nervous breath, until Haley confidently shifted into first gear and let off the clutch. The car lurched forward quicker than she'd expected, but she quickly got control as she shifted into second and raced around the outer lane of the parking lot. She didn't dare take it out onto the main road. She'd never handled anything like this, and as much fun as it was, she didn't trust herself to remember what to do with the gears and the pedals and everything else if something happened.

After a few minutes of joyriding, Haley brought the car to a stop in a parking space that Shane had pointed out to her. Then, she cut the engine off. "Holy shit," she mumbled.

Shane laughed. "Better than sex?"

"Maybe." Haley grinned and raised a brow, playfully biting her lower lip again.

"Come on," Shane said, getting out of the car.

Haley followed, handing her the keys as they started down a path that led into the woods. "Where are we going?"

"To watch the sunset. I read that Radnor Lake was one of the best places to see it."

"Oh, really. When did you look this up?"

"A week or so ago."

Haley nodded and continued down the quarter mile trail, which eventually opened up into a beautiful lake. "This is gorgeous," she whispered, walking down to the water.

Shane leaned against the side of a nearby picnic table and scanned their surroundings. She knew there was another parking lot on the opposite side, but no one was around. The sun was only a few minutes from setting, so they'd caught it with perfect timing. Bright orange, pink, and purple hues filled the sky.

"I feel so free," Haley called, holding her arms out to her sides. She lifted her face to the sun and closed her eyes. She hadn't realized how much weight she'd been carrying around until it was lifted away the minute she found out the letter writer was dead.

Opening her eyes, she walked up to Shane and wrapped her arms around her. "Thank you," she whispered. "For everything."

"I was only doing my job."

Haley shook her head. "You did a lot more, and we both know it." Letting go, she turned around and grabbed Shane's hands, wrapping her arms around her as she stepped back against her. "I'm going to miss you," she said softly, mostly to herself.

"I know. Me too," Shane murmured, placing her cheek against the side of Haley's head.

Together, they watched the sun paint the sky until it was no longer visible.

***

Headlights danced on the asphalt in the dark as the car drove along the back country roads. The top was still down, giving way to the diamonds of the night, sparking above them in the sky. The drive back to the house took a little longer with Shane obeying the rules of the road. The last thing she wanted to do was hit a deer or run off the road in the dark and total her car. Both women stayed silent, and the radio was off. Shane had turned on the radio, but Haley wanted to listen to what she referred to as the sounds of the night. Shane couldn't see her face well in the dark, but she assumed her smile had faded away. Her mind shifted to saying goodbye. When she'd first met Haley, she couldn't wait to end the case and be rid of her. Now, she had no idea how she was going to drive away in the morning and not turn the car around.

The iron gate swung open as they neared the house. Haley had obviously pushed the button on her keychain as soon as they were close enough. Shane pulled through the gate and continued up the long, winding driveway. Haley went to push the button to open the garage, but Shane stopped her.

"I'm leaving in the morning anyway. It'll be fine," she said as she pulled to a stop and turned off the engine.

Haley nodded, but didn't say anything as she got out.

Shane watched her walk away as she pulled the top up. Haley was difficult to read. However, she'd gotten pretty good at it over the past month and a half, and the look she saw was full of emotion.

Glancing up at the star-filled sky, Shane let out a deep breath. She wasn't sure what was going to happen when she entered that house. Part of her wanted to get back in the car and drive until she was back in Memphis. Part of her wanted to comfort Haley and take away her pain. No matter what she did, this was it. This was goodbye. For weeks on end Shane had wished and hoped to say goodbye and never look back. Now, she wasn't sure she could say the words at all.

***

Haley was leaning against the kitchen island, staring her way when Shane finally walked into the house. Shane swallowed the lump in her throat. *So, this is it. This is where we're parting ways.*

"I wasn't sure how early you were leaving," Haley said. "So...I figured I should probably say goodbye tonight," she added, pushing off the counter.

Shane nodded, holding her breath as she moved closer, slowly closing the distance between them.

"I wish I could forget the past month and a half and only remember you," she whispered, putting her arms around Shane's neck in a warm embrace.

"Me too," Shane murmured, wrapping her arms around Haley's waist as she inhaled the scent of her hair. Knowing this was the last time she would ever see Haley or be this close to her, Shane leaned back, locking eyes with her. A second passed before their lips came together in an agonizingly slow, but incredibly passionate kiss. They stared breathlessly at one another as their lips gradually pulled apart.

Haley ran her hands down Shane's arms as she stepped back, breaking the connection between their bodies. As her right hand came in contact with Shane's left, she grabbed a hold of it and turned, leading her by the hand as they walked across the house and up the stairs. Coming to a stop in her bedroom, Haley faced Shane once again. Letting go of her hand, she reached for the tail of Shane's shirt and pulled it up over her head, along with her soft cotton sports bra, revealing the strong upper body that was burned into her memory from taking care of Shane's wounds a week earlier.

Shane tried to speak, but words failed her as the back of Haley's fingers grazed her stomach when she unbuttoned her jeans. Knowing exactly what she was doing and forgetting all of the reasons why she should stop, Shane pulled Haley's t-shirt over her head, tossing it back behind her. A pair of perky round breasts bounced free when she released the clasp on the lacy nude-colored bra.

Light from the full moon poured in through the open vertical blinds, casting the room in a soft glow. Two shadows mimicked their every move on the wall behind them as each woman ran her hands over the smooth, naked skin of the other. They'd had sex before, but had never taken the time to *feel* each other...until now.

Haley's mouth watered as she took a half step back to look at Shane. She'd never seen anything sexier than the half-dressed woman standing in front of her in pale blue moonlight. She looked like a real-life Calvin Klein ad with her jeans open and the waistband of her underwear visible. Unable to resist the urge to touch her, Haley moved closer.

Shane held her breath and tilted her head back as Haley's lips and tongue grazed her chest, tracing a path between her breasts and up to her neck. She kept her hands on Haley's waist, more to steady herself than anything else.

Haley found her way to Shane's mouth, claiming her lips in a breathless kiss as Shane's hands moved beneath the waistband of her jeans, slowly inching them down. Haley followed, gradually sliding her hands down

Shane's body before pushing her jeans off her hips. Their lips parted long enough to remove the clothing hindering them, before coming back together in another heated kiss.

Shane wrapped her arms around Haley's waist, closing the gap between them as their nude bodies came together. Carefully, she walked her backwards until the back of her legs came in contact with the bed a few feet away. Haley got up onto the bed, lying on her back in the center. Shane followed, running her mouth languidly up one thigh, then starting over with the other, carefully skirting the one place she wanted to taste the most. Casually moving further up, she traced a path over Haley's flat stomach before suckling the erect pink nipples of her breasts...finally landing on her lips as she lay her body down on top of her.

Haley's legs parted, allowing Shane to settle between them as their lips locked in a heated kiss. She ran her hands through Shane's hair and raked her short nails down her back as her body hummed with energy fueled by desire.

Sensing Haley's need to be touched, Shane ran her hand down between them, settling her fingers on the warm wet folds of her center. Haley's breath hitched in her throat. She fought hard not to break the kiss as Shane's fingers began slow, steady circles around her clit, inching agonizingly closer to slipping inside of her with each lazy pass. Unable to hold back any longer, Haley broke the kiss and rolled Shane over. Then, she sat up and straddled her. Long blonde waves of curls swayed along her back with some strands falling forward over her shoulder.

Shane stared up at her as she ran her hands along her thighs, up to her waist. Haley was beautiful, but she was breathtaking in the moonlight. Sitting up, Shane put one arm around Haley and pulled her close, pressing their breasts together while her other hand slipped between them, finding Haley's warm wet clit once more.

Haley gasped and bit down on her lower lip as Shane's fingers pushed inside of her. She wrapped her arms around Shane's shoulders as their mouths came together in another searing kiss. Slowly, she began moving her hips up and down, sliding herself along Shane's fingers, nearly freeing them before burying them deep inside once more. She was so close, but it felt so good, she never wanted it to end. In the back of her mind, through the thick fog of euphoria, she knew the end meant *the end*, and she was in no hurry to get there.

Shane let Haley control the pace, and by the feeling of the warm, wet muscles clenching her fingers, she knew it wouldn't be long. She tried not to burn each second to memory, but it didn't matter. She already knew this night was going to haunt her dreams until she forgot every last detail.

Haley tangled her fingers in Shane's short hair, and Shane tilted her head back. The desire burning in Haley's wild eyes nearly took her breath away. Shane tightened the arm draped loosely around Haley's waist and rolled her to her back with Shane on top of her, and her fingers still buried deep inside of her. Haley gasped as Shane moved down her body, dragging her lips along her sensitive flesh until she settled between her legs. Shane's eyes met Haley's once more in the moonlight as her tongue snaked out, licking her swollen clit while her fingers thrust in and out of her.

A carnal cry escaped Haley's lips as her spine arched. She reached down, grabbing Shane's head and holding her mouth in place as she rode the wave of pleasure bursting from her body. The moonlit room faded to black as her eyes slammed shut and her body went limp from physical and mental overload. Shane waited half a minute before slowly freeing herself from the confines of Haley's grasp and sliding up beside her.

Haley took an extra minute to catch her breath and clear the fuzz from her mind. Her green eyes opened and closed for a few seconds before lazily landing on the woman lying next to her. Slowly, she shifted to her side and reached out, tracing her finger over Shane's cheekbone and along her jaw line, then back up to her lips before inching down her neck to her chest. Keeping her hand moving, she ran her finger between her breasts and over her taut stomach muscles, slowly taking in every inch of the amazing body next to her.

Shane's senses were heightened like never before. Her body buzzed like a hot electrical wire. Sensing her need, Haley traced her path lower, running her finger down one thigh before moving back up to her throbbing center. Warm wet folds spread open as she slid her fingers through them. A soft moan escaped Shane's lips, which Haley silenced with a kiss as she pushed her fingers inside. Shane's hips rose, meeting each agonizingly slow thrust. Her heart pounded like a bass drum and her skin tingled like an addict at the highest of highs. Feeling like she was literally going to fly apart at any moment, she gripped the sheet beneath her, searching for anything to ground her.

Haley wanted her mouth on her, but there was no time. Shane had been ready to release before she'd even touched her. She picked up the pace, giving her what she wanted as she placed the pad of her thumb against Shane's clit, rubbing it back and forth with each deep thrust of her fingers.

Shane's lungs gasped for air as a powerful climax tore through her like a freight train, leaving a panting, limp body in its wake. It took a minute for her senses to calm and breathing to even out. She felt completely exhausted.

Haley stayed in her arms, listening to the sound of Shane's heartbeat and soft, even breathing as she drifted off to sleep.

Chapter 38

The soft cotton sheet slipped loosely over her smooth, tan skin as Haley stretched in her sleep. Long blond curls cascaded over her naked back. The staccato sound of rain pelting the window pulled her away from the confines of a sweet dream she'd never remember. She reached out, rubbing the cool sheet beside her before opening her eyes. A piece of paper dropped into her hand when she bumped the pillow it had been lying on.

What did you expect? She sighed, finally lifting her lids to the empty room. Rain poured down outside, streaking the windows and blurring her vision. The sun had tried to rise two hours early, but was stuck behind the heavy clouds. She placed the paper back on the pillow and stared at the ceiling. In time, she'd read it, but at that moment, she didn't want to know what it said.

***

Shane downshifted and pumped the breaks as the traffic slowed to a crawl through the construction zone near her exit on the interstate. She'd been on the road for the last two and half hours, leaving the dark, dreary rain behind a while ago. She'd turn the radio on and off so many times in the last hour, she had a feeling she might break the knob. Every station was playing sappy sad songs, at least that's how she was interpreting them. She knew she was a coward for not waking Haley when she left, but what was she supposed to say to her? They were wrong for each other on so many levels. Hell, they'd spent the better part of eight weeks hating one another. There was no way one night would be enough to change that. That last two weeks had certainly eased the tension between them, but Shane wouldn't call it anything other than a working relationship. She couldn't...because if she did, it would be *real*. She didn't want it to be real. She wanted to forget all of it, especially the way Haley had looked, sleeping next to her as she gutlessly penned her a letter. That was an image her brain would more than likely keep forever to haunt her dreams like the beating of a dead horse. However, she didn't have to try hard for her mind to put her right back there, pen and paper in hand...even while driving down the interstate, she could see the words as she wrote them.

Haley,

Forgive me for leaving this letter. I couldn't say goodbye to you, and truth be told, I still can't. It didn't take me long to realize I'd met my match in you. We played an antagonistic, and sometimes seductive, game of chess with one another over the past six weeks. I have to admit, I'm sorry to see it end, but this was a game that neither of us was going to win. I did my job; the letter writer is no longer a threat, and now it's time to go back to our very different lives.

For last night...there are no words. At least, none that make sense to me in the moment. I'll never forget you, that I do know.

Always,
Shane

The drive through Memphis took about half an hour, and once she reached her condo on the river, Shane pushed the button for the garage and parked her car. It felt so good to be back. She couldn't really call it home. In fact, she hadn't called anywhere home for some time now.

The smell inside wasn't pungent or stale, but it definitely wasn't the fresh country air she'd gotten used to. Shane opened the French doors to the balcony, letting the faint breeze blow in from the river while she walked over to the liquor cabinet and poured two fingers of her favorite bourbon over ice. Then, she stepped outside, taking a seat in one of the two chairs. Ice clinked against the edge of the glass as she took a long swig of the golden liquor.

The sun was high in the sky, and a few runners were jogging along the path that wound along the river. A tug boat chugged along, pushing a barge through the muddy Mississippi, and a small boat was anchored outside of the channel with two men fishing in it.

Deep down, Shane knew what she'd left behind. She was just too gutless to be honest with herself. The sound of the tug's horn grabbed her attention. Shane turned her head to see a skiff cutting across in front of the barge. She shook her head and muttered, "Idiot." Pulling her glass back to her lips, she finished the last of her drink just as her cell phone beeped with a message. She hadn't heard it ring, but then again, she'd probably turned it off on purpose. Dennis knew she'd be back today, but he'd told her to take as much time as she needed.

Shane walked back inside, poured another two fingers worth of bourbon into her glass and reached for her phone.

Your plane leaves at seven a.m. your time. I emailed you the flight information. Looking forward to seeing you. Talk soon.

She deleted the voicemail and saved the email. Then, she tipped the glass back, emptying its contents in one long swallow before heading to her room for a long, hot shower.

***

"We can leave today if you want us to," Haley said.

"I thought you weren't ready to get back on the road. Why the eagerness all of a sudden?" Rich asked.

"Does the label want us back on tour or not?" she growled.

He knew Shane had left, and he also knew that was a sore subject. Clearing his throat, he said, "Alright. Your bus will be there before five this afternoon."

"Fine," she replied, hanging up. She tossed her phone into the jumbled bed sheets and turned away from the folded letter staring back at her as she headed into her closet to start packing. She didn't bother calling the band. Rich would make sure everyone was on the same page.

Chapter 39

The dry, Arizona heat sucked the breath right out of Shane's lungs when she walked out of the airport. She felt like she'd stepped out of the refrigerator and into the microwave. She adjusted the jacket of her black pantsuit, wishing she could take it off.

"Where to?" the taxi driver asked, holding the door open.

"Federal Building," she replied, checking her watch as she slid inside.

He simply nodded and rushed around to the driver's seat.

Shane watched the streets of her hometown whiz by through the window as he drove towards downtown Phoenix.

"Here on business?" he asked, attempting to make small talk.

"Something like that," she mumbled, feeling like she was a thousand miles away.

"Are you FBI?"

Shane shook her head.

"CIA?"

"I wouldn't be able to tell you even if I was," she answered.

The man peaked into the mirror, taking in her stark black suit and crisp white shirt. "Are you sure you're not FBI?"

"You ever heard of Men in Black?" she asked seriously.

The man swallowed heavily, causing his Adam's apple to bounce. Then, he gave a short nod and pulled alongside the curb, throwing the car in park, all while staring at her in the mirror.

Shane winked and got out. She looked up at the building and headed inside without looking back.

"I have an appointment," she said, flashing her badge at the reception desk. The young man nodded and pointed towards the elevator. She didn't need directions. This was the first office she'd ever worked out of. She knew her way around like the back of her hand. What she wasn't used to, was Paul Rutledge, *Supervisory Deputy United States Marshal* written on the frosted glass door in black letters.

Shane knocked briefly, then turned the knob and pushed the door open.

"You look well," Paul said, rushing over to hug her.

"Well for...someone who is on sabbatical, pending retirement...or someone who was stabbed nearly to death two weeks ago? Or...perhaps someone who is getting bullied by her old friend?"

"Ouch. I deserved that," he said. "Sit down. Let's talk."

"You go first because honestly, I'm not sure what I want to say right now."

"Okay. Have you been to see your parents?"

"What do they have to do with this meeting?" she questioned.

"Come on, Shane. It's me. I might have a title, but I wouldn't be in the marshal service if you hadn't gotten me through FLETC, and we both know that."

Shane nodded.

"If you hadn't..."

"Left? Ran out? Quit? Which is it?"

300

"This position was yours. You wanted the titles and the authority that came with them. Not me."

"Then, why are we here...in *your* Supervisory Deputy office, Paul?"

"Damn it, Shane," he sighed.

"I didn't come here to argue. I'm sorry."

"What do you want? Do you want back in? Do you want to retire? What are you doing here?"

"You made me come in, and I promised to listen to what you had to say," she answered.

"Alright. You're good, Shane. Damn good. Too good to hang it all up..."

"Over a girl?" she said, pinning him with a stare. "She wasn't just a girl, Paul. I messed up. I broke the cardinal rule of WITSEC. Then, I let her get killed."

"I know."

"How? It's not in my file. No one knew I was involved with her."

"They didn't have to. Deputies lose people they've protected. No system is perfect. You lost yourself when you lost her. *That* only happens for one reason."

"Time had gone by. She was married. It was long over."

"Doesn't matter. It cut you deep enough to nearly bleed out."

"Fuck me for caring," she growled. "I'm human. It's hard not to care for the good ones when all we protect is dirt bags."

"I agree a hundred percent, which is why I asked to have you assigned to me."

"What can you do for me that no one else can?"

"Save your career before you piss all over it," he said.

Shane didn't say anything.

"I helped you back in Tennessee when I didn't have to."

"Why'd you do it?"

"Come back into the field. No WITSEC. You can work the Major Case Fugitive Program. That's what you were doing when you left anyway."

"I'm not coming back to Arizona."

"I know you've been living in Memphis. Is that where you want to go?"

Shane thought for a minute, then heard herself saying, "Nashville."

"I can bring you back in here and arrange a transfer…under one condition."

"I knew there was a catch," she mumbled, shaking her head.

"Are you in love with her?"

"What?"

"Answer me."

"I'm not protecting her…or anyone else anymore, so why does it matter?"

"I want to make sure your head is clear. The next time you fall out of commission, the chief deputy is going to bury you."

"I'll take my chances."

He sighed and shook his head.

"I'm fine, Paul. Honestly. I wasn't even sure I wanted to come back at all."

"Why are you here, then?"

"I promised to come here you out."

He nodded. "I want you to volunteer for SOG."

"What? Special operations isn't really my thing," she balked.

"Yes or no?"

"Full reinstatement?"

"Yes, as if you were never gone."

"Can I think about it?"

"I have a meeting in fifteen minutes, so you have about thirteen to decide."

Shane knew as soon as she agreed to come talk to Paul that she'd be reinstated, otherwise, she could've had him handle her retirement paperwork remotely. What bothered her was why she'd said Nashville. She had twelve minutes left. She could change her location. Did she want to? She was in a standoff with her old friend who also happened to be her current boss, but she had leverage. She could go anywhere. Eleven minutes. Her mind raced with thoughts of MCFP. She'd loved working those cases. She was good at working those cases. Ten minutes.

"Take SOG off the table," she said.

"What?"

You heard me. I'm in, if you take SOG out of the equation."

"Why?"

"I'm not interested. I've done enough high-profile bullshit. I want the simple life, or at least as simple as it gets as a Deputy Marshal. I'll work MCFP cases all day every day, but no SOG."

Nine minutes.

"Shane…"

"Paul…"

He was silent for two full minutes.

Seven minutes.

"Why are you pushing this?" she questioned.

"Because I know you, Shane. You have the potential to go places I never imagined. I always thought you'd be the one going up the chain, taking all of the titles. Hell, we both know you should be behind this desk. But, it turned out the other way around. Apparently, I kiss ass pretty good and you…you're way better at taking names, my friend. I just want to see you do everything you can in the Marshal Service."

"It's off the table. Put me in Nashville, and you have a deal."

"Will you consider volunteering at a later date?"

"Nope."

He sighed. "Alright."

Shane watched him type on the computer for a second.

"The Supervisory Deputy for Nashville is Lawrence Burgess. As far as he knows, you've been out of WITSEC and working MCFP this entire time on a high-profile case. He won't ask questions. It's above his pay grade."

"How did you manage that?"

"I snuck in some stipulations of my own when I agreed to bring you back in. I wanted to make sure you were protected."

Shane nodded.

"Shit," he said, checking his watch. "I have to go. I'll be in touch with your transfer details."

Shane shook his hand and returned his hug. The word Nashville bounced around in her head for a minute. She knew going in that she was going back to Tennessee or nothing at all, but at the last second, her mind had switched from Memphis to Nashville. *What the hell are you doing?* "Pouring salt on an open wound," she muttered under her breath as she walked out of his office.

Chapter 40

"I forgot how stressful this was," Haley said, flopping down on the couch in her bus with a light beer in her hand. Rich was across from her, scrolling through emails on his phone.

"Since when do you drink beer?" he said, ignoring her comment.

"I don't, but that's what the guys had on their bus, and I was thirsty" she said, grimacing at the taste of the beer when she took a sip. "I don't know how anyone drinks this nasty shit," she added, getting up to find something else.

"The detectives in Nashville finally closed the case," he mumbled.

"What? How do you know that? I thought it *was* closed."

"I just got an email from Shane. Detective Kenny contacted her with the final details."

The bottle slipped from Haley's hand, smashing against the bottom of the empty trash can. Startled, Rich dropped his phone.

"You kept in contact with her?" she said, just above a whisper.

"Yeah. You didn't?"

Haley bit down on her lower lip and closed her eyes. It had been two weeks since she'd left. Haley's thoughts took her right back to that last night, and subsequently, the note left behind the next morning. She shook her head and sighed. She'd finally read it once she was back on the road. Then, she opened the window and let it fly free. Why bother keeping it when she had it memorized?

"You okay?" he asked.

"I'm fine. What were these *final* details?"

"Nothing."

"It had to be something if she contacted you."

"Just some pictures and stuff."

Haley stared like a bull about to run him down.

He sighed. "They found pictures of you with crosses drawn over them and the word abomination."

"That's it?" She shook her head. "You had me thinking he'd done some twisted sadistic shit."

"Shane said there may have been more, but the detectives weren't fully disclosing everything to her."

"It's over. He's dead. I've moved on and I suggest you do too. Now, I have work to do if the label wants me back in the studio when the tour ends."

Rich didn't need to be told to get off her bus. The tone of her voice was warning enough. She obviously wanted to be alone, and he had a flight to catch anyway. Without so much as a goodbye, he got up and left. He knew her well, which was why he saw right through the façade she was fronting on and off the stage. *She was good for you. I knew it from the start. And you haven't moved on,* he thought, shaking his head at the stubborn singer.

***

Haley strummed her acoustic guitar while waiting for the words to come to her, but they never did. Ever since the mention of Shane's name, she seemed to be in a fog. It was almost as if she were back on the bus, breaking her concentration with her mere presence.

"She's gone, damn it!" she yelled at herself and slammed the guitar in the stand. It was three a.m., and the bus was slowly lulling side to side as it trudged down the highway. She should've been asleep, but that wasn't much better. How many times could she relive one night in her dreams? It had been over a week since Rich had mentioned her.

After staring out the window at the darkness passing by for what seemed like several minutes, she grabbed her Les Paul from the stand. She was reluctant to take it when she headed back out on the road. She'd nearly lost it in the bus fire, but somehow it had been put on the crew bus instead of hers that night after the show. She plugged it into the small amp she kept on the bus and played around with a few licks before settling into Janis Joplin's *Piece of my Heart*, which she sang and played like she was on stage in front of thousands. When really, she was playing to an empty bus. Her driver was the only audience she had, and even then, he was in the driver's compartment and not her living quarters.

Chapter 41

"Are you settling in okay?" Dennis asked.

"Yeah," she replied, looking around the room at her small, one-bedroom apartment. It was similar to the condo she'd had in Memphis, and had come fully furnished. The only thing she was missing was the muddy river and odd smell that had come with it.

"Did they hit you with a full case load?"

"Something like that," she muttered. "Same shit, different town. I'm pretty sure nothing has changed in the last year, except my location." She thought about her small cubicle on the third floor of the federal building. It was the same, stuffy gray space she'd worked out of in Phoenix. "At least, I'm not working protective duty. That was part of my deal coming back in," she added.

"I kind of figured you'd had your fill of that with Haley Nielsen," he laughed.

"Yeah, no kidding."

"Have you seen her?" he asked cautiously.

"No."

"I saw that she's back on tour. I think it's wrapping up soon...in Nashville, actually."

"Tonight," she said, sitting on the couch and kicking her feet up on the coffee table next to two thick manila folders.

"You going?"

"I don't know."

She'd thought about it a hundred times. Truthfully, she wasn't even sure Haley would want to see her, and she'd had no idea what to say to her.

"I think you should."

"Why is that?"

"There's only one reason you're in Nashville, and it's not because the US Marshal Service posted you there," Dennis stated.

She knew he was right, and she couldn't be mad at him for seeing through her. She'd been pretty transparent lately, especially when she'd gone in person to resign from his firm and pack up the little bit of things she owned at the condo. He'd told her he expected her to go back to being a deputy marshal, that was where she belonged.

"Maybe I'm here because I like the music," she muttered.

"You hate country music."

Shane laughed.

"Go to the show. You'll regret it if you don't," he said, hanging up.

Shane set her phone down and picked up the folders containing the files on two of her cases. She'd been back on the job as a deputy marshal for a little over a week and needed to get caught up on her case load, which was why she'd brought work home. That, and she'd needed a distraction for the weekend.

"Damn it," she spat, slapping the folder closed after scanning the first two pages. *This is crazy,* she thought as she got up and snatched her keys off the kitchen counter.

Chapter 42

"Are you ready for this?" Rich asked, leaning against the kitchen counter inside Haley's bus.

"Are you kidding me?" she laughed. "I've been ready for this tour to be over for months. It's literally been Hell."

"I agree."

"I think I'm ready to be myself, Rich. I've lived in the spotlight for years, but kept my life in the shadows."

"I had a feeling this was coming, especially with the last three or four tour stops. You've pretty much said fuck you to the label," he chuckled.

"I honestly don't care. If they drop me…they drop me."

"I wanted to wait until all of this was over, but…I guess now is as good a time as any."

"Don't you quit on me. I'll skin you alive," she deadpanned.

"With as many times as you've fired me and I've stayed anyway, I'm pretty sure that's never going to happen. Your label didn't want *Rebellious* to even get made. They were against it from the start, as was a lot of radio and media, until it blew everyone out of the water. I think this is the perfect time for a buyout of your contract. Things are messy where you're concerned, and they don't like messy. Besides, once you…you know, be real…it's going to get even messier."

"You mean when I come out they're going to flip the fuck out, right?" she laughed. "I know that. Are they already talking about cutting me?"

"No, they haven't caught wind of what's going on…however, I've been promoting you to another label."

He held his hand up when she went to speak. "Let me finish. They're very interested, and they're very open to speaking with you."

Haley crossed her arms. "Did you out me, Rich?" she said in a low voice with one brow raised up.

"Hell no. That's not my place. I was fishing around, talking with friends in the industry and after speaking with one of them, an executive from this label went to your show in Atlanta. I had no idea until I got a call from him they next day."

"So, he thinks I'm gay after going to one show and wants to sign me to some other label?"

"Nope. He has no idea. You blew him away with your show and he wants to buyout your current contract."

"So, what does all of this have to do with me being *me*?"

"He's an openly gay man, and has no qualms about anyone else being openly gay."

"What does he know about country music?"

"Last year's vocalist of the year, is with this label. And, their artists have won several other awards within the last couple of years."

"Wait a second. Isn't that the label with the two young guys?"

"Yes. Clive and Arnie Tillman."

"One of them is gay?"

"Arnie is, and together, they co-own the label."

"Wow."

"It's a good deal. I don't have all of the details yet because Arnie is waiting to see if your current label cuts you first. That will save his company big bucks. Either way, he wants to meet with you. They are looking for a headliner, and I think that's you."

"So, you sold me like a beef cow to the highest bidder," she teased.

"You and your big, fancy label mix like oil and water, and they're going to cut you, it's a matter of time. I had a feeling this would happen when the album released. So, I put a plan in motion. You don't pay me to sit on my ass and be at your beck and call. I promoted you where I knew you would have a chance to be yourself as an artist. The fans adore you, radio loves you, it's time you had a label that did, too."

"This is why I let you win certain arguments. I trust you, Rich. You've never steered me wrong."

He hugged her. "I'm not old enough to be your father, but if I had a daughter, I would want her to be like you."

"Don't get all sappy on me. I have to go rock the roof off this joint!" she laughed. "Come on, we have one more show to do!"

Rich radioed the security team that Haley was heading into the venue.

***

Nearly twenty thousand screaming fans cheered as Haley worked through her regular set list, which ended with *Smoke* by A Thousand Horses, which reminded her of Shane. She'd added it to the tour as soon as they'd started back. As much as it hurt to sing it, the words were true and she'd let her heart bleed them out all over the stage every night.

As soon as she finished, Haley wiped a tear from her cheek and grabbed her Telecaster. "Who likes Joan Jett?" she yelled into the microphone before singing,

"Ahh." And playing the begging licks of *Crimson and Clover*. The crowd went wild, cheering and singing along as she started, "Now I don't hardly know her, but I think I could love her."

***

"Wow. When did she start singing this?" Shane said into Rich's ear.

"Oh my God!" he yelled, turning around and pulling her into a hug just as Haley slowed the music down.

"How are you?" she replied with a smile.

"Good. You? How'd you get back here?" he asked.

Shane showed her badge, then put it away. "I'm back with the marshal service."

"I had a feeling you'd do that."

"How is she?"

"Still kicking ass and taking names."

Shane laughed. "I see that," she said as she watched Haley singing and playing her guitar. "I didn't know if she'd even want to see me, but…"

"She'll be happy," Rich said, patting her on the shoulder.

They both watched as Haley ended the song. Her band left the stage and she started walking with them, but stopped and walked back out to the spotlight. The fans chanted her name as she grabbed her Les Paul and pulled a stool into the spotlight.

"This is my last show for this tour. I'm sure all of you know the ordeal I went through over the past few months," she said. "It was Hell, but not all of it was bad. Some very good things came out of that nightmare." She began strumming a few chords. "Anyway, here's to you,

313

wherever you are tonight," she said as she began singing her blues rendition of Elvis Presley's *Suspicious Minds*. "We're caught in a trap. I can't walk out, because I love you too much, baby."

The crowd quieted, hanging on every word she sang and every chord she played. The stage was dark, with only a single spotlight shining down where she sat...completely alone on the stage.

Slowing the song down in the middle, she took her hands off her guitar and let the fans sing along with her. Then, she started right back up, strumming her Les Paul like a lover as she went on with the song. When it ended, she got up and set her guitar in the stand. Then, she turned back to the crowd and smiled brightly before walking off the stage.

Her eyes searched in the dim lighting for Rich, but landed somewhere else instead. She paused, holding her breath. The roar of the crowd was loud, but the thumping of her heart in her chest was all her ears heard. "You're here," she mumbled, believing her mind was playing tricks on her.

"There's nowhere else I'd rather be," Shane said. "I love you, Haley. And whether or not you feel the same way, I had to be honest with myself."

Haley crossed the distance between them with a look in her eyes and a stomp in her feet that made everyone around them think she was going to punch her out, but when she reached her, Haley said, "You're like a very, very good bad habit," as she wrapped her arms around Shane's neck. "I'm pretty sure I fell in love with you a long time ago," she added, pulling her down into a sultry kiss that left them both breathless.

Rich, along with her band members and road crew, clapped, whistled and cheered with happiness.

"How long are you here?" Haley asked, as they started walking out of the arena.

"I went back to work with the marshal service…and moved here. I'm renting a small apartment in town," Shane replied as she held open the car door for her.

The two security officers were slack-jawed as they watched Haley kiss Shane before getting into the car. She grinned as she walked around to the driver's side.

"Move in with me," Haley blurted as Shane started the car and drove away.

"What?"

"I'm serious. I love you, Shane. I want to go to bed with you every night, but more importantly, I want to wake up next to you."

"I don't know what to say." Shane shifted gears and rolled to a stop at the light. The billboard sign had a huge picture of Haley's face with the announcement of her concert that night. "Are you sure you want to come out? Because you know at some point, it'll happen."

"I don't give a shit what anyone says. I love you. That's all that matters to me."

"Always the rebel," Shane laughed, then looked over at her. "I love you, and I'd love nothing more than to live with you."

Haley smiled and leaned over, meeting her lips for a heated kiss.

ABOUT THE AUTHOR

Sydney enjoys reading everything from magazines to historical books and boasts about her massive collection of paperbacks and hardbacks in her personal library. She's also a huge fan of multiple TV shows, which she says take up too much of her time. She enjoys writing novellas and is the author of the bestselling novellas: *One Night* and *Shadow's Eyes*, as well as the bestselling full length novel: *Second Chance*.

You can like her fan page at facebook.com/sydneycanyon

Other Titles Available From Triplicity Publishing

A tale of Spiders and Canned Soup by Kathy L. Salt. Living on your own can be hard, but even more so when you're dealing with haphephobia; the death of a twin sister; and a crush on your teacher. Mika is still in contact with her foster family who homes the loves of her life, three young children she would do anything for, when she begins attending University of Aberdeen and meets Pauline, an Australian that teaches Viking history. Neither woman is used to breaking the rules, and their way to each other is a hard one, especially when Mika vows to get custody of the children, whether she is ready to be a parent or not. *A story about growing up. A story about dealing with grief. A story about Mika and Pauline.*

A Night Claimed by Domina Alexandra. Bonnie Collins had plans. And being a werewolf wasn't one of them. Attacked by a rogue who was out to claim her, and facing what she now has no choice of becoming, Bonnie can't let go of her human life as a Paramedic. The last thing Bonnie needs is more challenges. However, Rikki, the Alpha of Mill City will be just that. Finding her to be possessive and ruling, Bonnie begins challenging the Alpha's every breath. Finding out her attack was no accident only makes her more angry at the situation. A group of rogues are out to get her. With no clue why, Bonnie has no choice but to seek help from the alluring Alpha and her pack, accepting the new world she was forced into.

Deadly Deception by Cade Brogan. Three die in a psychiatric hospital. A triple homicide. A contagion, deadly and mysterious, is the killer's weapon of choice. A dart flies. A woman dies in the shower, her neck punctured. A homicide, hours from Chicago. Poison, deadly and concocted, is the killer's weapon of choice. As her city teeters on the verge of panic, Detective Rylee Hayes is forced to divide her attention between two killers—one whose actions could result in a global pandemic and the other, an old nemesis, whose next target is her fiancée. And the clock ticks down…

Stunted by Breanna Hughes. Professional stuntwoman Jessie Knight takes her job very seriously and although she works in the entertainment industry, she has zero desire for fame or notoriety. She also has a very strict no-dating policy when it comes to coworkers. That is, until, she meets famous actress Elliot Chase on the set of her new film. The adrenaline rush of the stunts is nothing compared to the sparks that fly between them. After a passionate night together, a sex tape is leaked that sends Jessie and Elliot's private and professional lives into a spiral. Will the fallout be too much for them to last? Or will they find a way out of the mess together?

Mission Compromised by Graysen Morgen. Natalia Moreno is thrilled when she arrives in Fiji for a relaxing vacation. However, she soon discovers the overwater bungalow she's staying in has been double booked for the entire stay, and the resort is full. Annoyed and frustrated, she has no other choice but to share her hut with a stranger. Christian Garnier is sent to Fiji for what she refers to as a working vacation, until she finds out she has an ornery roommate for the next two weeks who is dead set on making her job twice as hard. Soon, all hell breaks loose and the two women are sent around the world on a wild goose chase.

Stargazing by Kathy L. Salt. Lissa stared open-mouthed at the GIF that played over and over on the screen in front of her. Heat flushed to her face, igniting her skin. Her heart started pounding in her chest. *Stupid internet, it should really come with a warning label.* She's never been interested in relationships or sex and as the years have gone by she has retreated more and more into her work. Everything changes when she meets Star, a porn actress with a heart of gold and a troubled childhood. *They say that opposites attract, but how much of that is true? What chance do they have when one of them is a virgin and the other one star in pornography?*

A New Beginning by KD Rye. There's a quietness, an empty space, that surrounds your life after losing someone you love. Autumn lives in that empty space, day after day, following the same routine, in unresolved angst. She doesn't know how to keep her head above water until the arrival of May, a mysterious dream-like girl who just moved in. Autumn finds refuge in their quickly defined friendship. As her mother falls deeper into depression, Autumn doesn't see a way out of her current situation, until May shows her that anything is possible. However, nothing is what it seems and Autumn has to decipher if the relationship she has built with May is real.

I Belong with Her by Domina Alexandra. Tajel Pierce loves the thrill of being a paramedic. Every call she goes on gives her a rush. She makes no time for a personal life. No one can ruin her love for her career. Then there is Arianna Castaldi, who just transferred to her new paramedic position in a whole new state. All she needs is a new start without any distractions. Arianna and Tajel's relationship doesn't start off perfect. Embarrassed of the one night stand Arianna believes she had with Tajel, she wants to pretend they never met and make their relationship strictly business. The only choice they have to keep from strangling each other is to go from denying their feelings to accepting them as they work through intense 911 calls.

Awakened by Fate by Lynn Lawler. Jackie is a woman living life according to her own rules. She's married, but it's the unspoken, open kind. She can have as many female lovers as she likes; she just can't talk about them. After a bizarre encounter turns her world upside down, things slowly begin to change. She finds herself in desperation as she searches for answers. What she discovers is nothing is delivered in a neatly wrapped box. Now that everything has been brought out into the open, she finds she can't run away from her truth anymore. With her new life, comes new responsibilities and a different outcome than what she was expecting. Jackie isn't alone in the story. She meets several new people who help her along her journey.

Nautical Delights by S. L. Gape. Lady Elizabeth Barrington has spent her entire life trying to please her family; constantly opting for a quiet life, she utilises her profession as a doctor to keep out of her families' clutches; bar the annual two-week Caribbean private cruise, where there is simply no budge. Confined to two weeks on board the Iconica super yacht, she intends on keeping her head down and enjoying as much of the holiday as she can, whilst keeping her family at arm's length. Until a crew member catches her eye.

Whispers of the Heart by KA Moll. Days after completing her fellowship in pediatric ophthalmology, thirty-five-year-old Aki Williams travels from her home in Los Angeles to a small town in Illinois, interviewing for a job that she doesn't want. What she does want is to meet her biological sister, Jack Camdon, a sister whom she didn't know existed until she dreamt of her. Three years ago on Sunday, forty-three-year-old professor of archaeology, Carsyn Lyndon, lost her parents and her wife in a tragic accident. Since then, she's suffered from PTSD and loneliness. She's kind-hearted and handsome but dates no one. When she meets Aki at her four-year-old Godson's birthday party, they're incredibly attracted to one another, and those feelings intensify during a family camping trip— a particularly interesting development for Aki since prior to that she'd never considered that she might be a lesbian.

Worlds Apart by S.L. Gape. Hollywood A-lister Heidi Spencer-Brady is everything you'd expect of an Idol. Loved by all, the British Beauty is graceful, talented, humble and so far removed from the 'typical' LA scene. When her husband's infidelity with his new 'leading lady' is leaked, Dawn, Heidi's best friend and manager, goes all out to protect her. She arranges for Heidi to go back to the UK and stay on her cousins farm they had visited as children, much to the disappointment of the animal fearing Heidi.

Castor Valley (Law & Order Series Book 2) by Graysen Morgen. Jessie Henry is torn when she reads about the capture of the Doyle brothers, two young men who were part of her old gang. Unable to let them hang for a crime she's sure they didn't commit, Jessie leaves her wife and the Town of Boone Creek behind, and sets out on a journey back to the one place she thought she'd never see again, *Castor Valley*. Ellie Henry watches the love of her life leave, not knowing if she will ever return. When she gets an odd telegram, nearly a week later, she fears Jessie is in trouble. With no other choice, she goes to the one person who can help her.

Close Enough to Touch by Cade Brogan. Joanna Grey injects the deadly poison into the chamber of the syringe—time after time. She's murdered before and she'll do it again. She's intelligent, educated, and beautiful. Rylee Hayes is a respected homicide detective. Her best friends are her grandparents, her coonhound, and her partner—in that order. Kenzie Bigham is the single mom of a thirteen-year-old, a church secretary, and a woman who's struggled much of her adult life with her own sexuality. Their paths will cross when Rylee's new investigation involves members of Kenzie's congregation. Will Rylee have what it takes to meet the challenge of a serial killer who's proven herself to be a more than worthy opponent?

Fight to the Top by S. L. Gape. Georgia is a forty year old, single, Area Director from Manchester, UK who is all work and definitely no play. Having no time to socialise or spend time with her family she prides herself on being fit and well-polished. Erika is an Area Director for the same company, but in the United States. Whilst she is

322

concentrating so heavily on the promotion she has been fighting for, she's starting to feel like her life outside of work is falling apart. The two women are exceptionally different, and worlds apart. Both of their lives are turned upside down when their jobs are snatched from under their noses, and they are suddenly faced with being thrown together by their bosses for one last major project...in Texas.

Boone Creek (Law & Order Series book 1) by Graysen Morgen. Jessie Henry is looking for a new life. She's unknown in the town of Boone Creek when she arrives, and wants to keep it that way. When she's offered the job of Town Marshal, she takes it, believing that protecting others and upholding the law is the penance for her past. Ellie Fray is a widowed, shopkeeper. She generally keeps to herself, but the mysterious new Town Marshal both intrigues and infuriates her. She believes the last thing the town needs is someone stirring up trouble with the outlaws who have taken over.

Witness by Joan L. Anderson. Becca and Kate have lived together for eight years, and have always spent their vacation in a tropical paradise, lying on a beach. This year, Becca wanted to try something different: a seven day, 65-mile hike in the beautiful Cascade Mountains of Washington state. Their peaceful vacation turns to horror when they stumble upon a brutal murder taking place in the back country.

Too Soon by S.L. Gape. Brooke is a twenty-nine year old detective from Oxford, who has her life pretty much planned out until her boss and partner of nine years,

Maria, tells her their relationship is over. When Brooke finds out the truth, that Maria cheated on her with their best friend Paula, she decides to get her life back on track by getting away for six weeks in Anglesey, North Wales. Chloe, a thirty three year old artist and art director, owns a log cabin on Anglesey where she spends each weekend painting and surfing. After returning from a surf, she stumbles upon the somewhat uptight and enigmatic Brooke.

Blue Ice Landing by KA Moll. Coy is a beautiful blonde with a southern accent and a successful practice as a physician assistant. She has a comfortable home, good friends, and a loving family. She's also a widow, carrying a burden of responsibility for her wife's untimely death. Coby is a woman with secrets. She's estranged from her family, a recovering alcoholic, and alone because she's convinced that she's unlovable. When she loses her job as a heavy equipment operator, she'll accept one that'll force her to step way outside her comfort zone. When Coy quits her job to accept a position in Antarctica, her path will cross with Coby's. Their attraction to one another will be immediate, and despite their differences, it won't be long before they fall in love. But for these two, with all their baggage, will love be enough?

Never Quit (Never Series book 2) by Graysen Morgen. Two years after stepping away from the action as a Coast Guard Rescue Swimmer to become an instructor, Finley finds herself in charge of the most difficult class of cadets she's ever faced, while also juggling the taxing demands of having a home life with her partner Nicole, and their fifteen year old daughter. Jordy Ross gave up everything, dropping out of college, and leaving her family behind, to join the Coast Guard and become a rescue swimmer cadet. The extreme training tests her fitness level, pushing her mentally and physically further than she's ever been in her life, but it's the aggressive competition between her and another female cadet that proves to be the most challenging.

For a Moment's Indiscretion by KA Moll. With ten years of marriage under their belt, Zane and Jaina are coasting. The little things they used to do for one another have fallen by the wayside. They've gotten busy with life. They've forgotten to nurture their love and relationship. Even soul mates can stumble on hard times and have marital difficulties. Enter Amelia, a new faculty member in Jaina's building. She's new in town, young, and very pretty. When an argument with Zane causes Jaina to storm out angry, she reaches out to Amelia. Of course, she seizes the opportunity. And for a moment of indiscretion, Jaina could lose everything.

Never Let Go (Never Series book 1) by Graysen Morgen. For Coast Guard Rescue Swimmer, Finley Morris, life is good. She loves her job, is well respected by her peers, and has been given an opportunity to take her career to the next level. The only thing missing is the love of her life, who walked out, taking their daughter with her, seven years earlier. When Finley gets a call from her ex, saying their teenage daughter is coming to spend the summer with her, she's floored. While spending more time with her daughter, whom she doesn't get to see often, and learning to be a full-time parent, Finley quickly realizes she has not, and will never, let go of what is important.

Pursuit by Joan L. Anderson. Claire is a workaholic attorney who flies to Paris to lick her wounds after being dumped by her girlfriend of seventeen years. On the plane she chats with the young woman sitting next to her, and when they land the woman is inexplicably detained in Customs. Claire is surprised when she later runs into the woman in the city. They agree to meet for breakfast the next morning, but when the woman doesn't show up Claire goes to her hotel and makes a horrifying discovery. She soon finds herself ensnared in a web of intrigue and international terrorism, becoming the target of a high stakes game of cat and mouse through the streets of Paris.

Wrecked by Sydney Canyon. To most people, the *Duchess* is a myth formed by old pirates tales, but to Reid Cavanaugh, a Caribbean island bum and one of the best divers and treasure hunters in the world, it's a real, seventeenth century pirate ship—the holy grail of underwater treasure hunting. Reid uses the same cunning tactics she always has before setting out to find the lost ship. However, she is forced to bring her business partner's daughter along as collateral this time because he doesn't trust her. Neither woman is thrilled, but being cooped up on a small dive boat for days, forces them to get know each other quickly.

Arson by Austen Thorne. Madison Drake is a detective for the Stetson Beach Police Department. The last thing she wants to do is show a new detective the ropes, especially when a fire investigation becomes arson to cover up a murder. Madison butts heads with Tara, her trainee, deals with sarcasm from Nic, her ex-girlfriend who is a patrol officer, and finds calm in the chaos of police work with Jamie, her best friend who is the county medical examiner. Arson is the first of many in a series of novella episodes surrounding the fictional Stetson Beach Police Department and Detective Madison Drake.

Change of Heart by KA Moll. Courtney Holloman is a woman at the top of her game. She's successful, wealthy, and a highly sought after Washington lobbyist. She has money, her job, booze, and nothing else. In quiet moments, against her will, her mind drifts back to her days in high school and to all that she gave up. Jack Camdon is a complex woman, and yet not at all. She is also a woman who has never moved beyond the sudden and unexplained departure of her high school sweetheart, her lover, and her soul mate. When circumstances bring Courtney back to town two decades later, their paths will cross. Will it be too late?

Mommies (Bridal Series book 3) **by Graysen Morgen.** Britton and her wife Daphne have been married for a year and a half and are happy with their life, until Britton's mother hounds her to find out why her sister Bridget hasn't decided to have children yet. This prompts Daphne to bring up the big subject of having kids of their own with Britton. Britton hadn't really thought much about having kids, but her love for Daphne makes her see life and their future together in a whole new way when they decide to become mommies.

Haunting Love **by K.A. Moll.** Anna Crestwood was raised in the strict beliefs of a religious sect nestled in the foothills of the Smoky Mountains. She's a lesbian with a ton of baggage—fearful, guilty, and alone. Very few things would compel her to leave the familiar. The job offer of a lifetime is one of them. Gabe Garst is a police officer. She's also a powerful medium. Her work with juvenile delinquents and ghosts is all that keeps her going. Inside she's dead, certain that her capacity to love is buried six feet under. Anna and Gabe's paths cross. Their attraction is immediate, but they hold back until all hope seems lost.

Rapture & Rogue by Sydney Canyon. Taren Rauley is happy and in a good relationship, until the one person she thought she'd never see again comes back into her life. She struggles to keep the past from colliding with the present as old feelings she thought were dead and gone, begin to haunt her. In college, Gianna Revisi was a mastermind, ring-leading, crime boss. Now, she has a great life and spends her time running Rapture and Rogue, the two establishments she built from the ground up. The last person she ever expects to see walk into one of them, is the girl who walked out on her, breaking her heart five years ago.

Second Chance by Sydney Canyon. After an attack on her convoy, Marine Corps Staff Sergeant, Darien Hollister, must learn to live without her sight. When an experimental procedure allows her to see again, Darien is torn, knowing someone had to die in order for this to happen.

She embarks on a journey to personally thank the donor's family, but is too stunned to tell them the truth. Mixed emotions stir inside of her as she slowly gets to the know the people that feel like so much more than strangers to her. When the truth finally comes out, Darien walks away, taking the second chance that she's been given to go back to the only life she's ever known, but she's not the only one with a second chance at life.

Meant to Be by Graysen Morgen. Brandt is about to walk down the aisle with her girlfriend, when an unexpected chain of events turns her world upside down, causing her to question the last three years of her life. A chance encounter sparks a mix of rage and excitement that she has never felt before. Summer is living life and following her dreams, all the while, harboring a huge secret that could ruin her career. She believes that some things are better kept in the dark, until she has her third run-in with a woman she had hoped to never see again, and gives into temptation. Brandt and Summer start believing everything happens for a reason as they learn the true meaning of meant to be.

Coming Home by Graysen Morgen. After tragedy derails TJ Abernathy's life, she packs up her three year old son and heads back to Pennsylvania to live with her grandmother on the family farm. TJ picks back up where she left off eight years earlier, tending to the fruit and nut tree orchard, while learning her grandmother's secret trade. Soon, TJ's high school sweetheart and the same girl who broke her heart, comes back into her life, threatening to steal it away once again. As the weeks turn into months and tragedy strikes again, TJ realizes coming home was the best thing she could've ever done.

Special Assignment by Austen Thorne. Secret Service Agent Parker Meeks has her hands full when she gets her new assignment, protecting a Congressman's teenage daughter, who has had threats made on her life and been whisked away to a Christian boarding school under an alias to finish out her senior year. Parker is fine with the assignment, until she finds out she has to go undercover as a Canon Priest. The last thing Parker expects to find is a beautiful, art history teacher, who is intrigued by her in more ways than one.

Miracle at Christmas by Sydney Canyon. A Modern Twist on the Classic Scrooge Story. Dylan is a power-hungry lawyer who pushed away everything good in her life to become the best defense attorney in the, often winning the worst cases and keeping anyone with enough money out of jail. She's visited on Christmas Eve by her deceased law partner, who threatens her with a life in hell like his own, if she doesn't change her path. During the course of the night, she is taken on a journey through her past, present, and future with three very different spirits.

Bella Vita by Sydney Canyon. Brady is the First Officer of the crew on the Bella Vita, a luxury charter yacht in the Caribbean. She enjoys the laidback island lifestyle, and is accustomed to high profile guests, but when a U.S. Senator charters the yacht as a gift to his beautiful twin daughters who have just graduated from college and a few of their friends, she literally has her hands full.

Brides (Bridal Series book 2) by Graysen Morgen. Britton Prescott is dating the love of her life, Daphne Attwood, after a few tumultuous events that happened to unravel at her sister's wedding reception, seven months earlier. She's happy with the way things are, but immense pressure from her family and friends to take the next step, nearly sends her back to the single life. The idea of a long engagement and simple wedding are thrown out the window, as both families take over, rushing Britton and Daphne to the altar in a matter of weeks.

Cypress Lake by Graysen Morgen. The small town of Cypress Lake is rocked when one murder after another happens. Dani Ricketts, the Chief Deputy for the Cypress Lake Sheriff's Office, realizes the murders are linked. She's surprised when the girl that broke her heart in high school has not only returned home, but she's also Dani's only suspect. Kristen Malone has come back to Cypress Lake to put the past behind her so that she can move on with her life. Seeing Dani Ricketts again throws her off-guard, nearly derailing her plans to finally rid herself and her family of Cypress Lake.

Crashing Waves by Graysen Morgen. After a tragic accident, Pro Surfer, Rory Eden, spends her days hiding in the surf and snowboard manufacturing company that she built from the ground up, while living her life as a shell of the person that she once was. Rory's world is turned upside when a young surfer pursues her, asking for the one thing she can't do. Adler Troy and Dr. Cason Macauley from Graysen Morgen's bestselling novel: *Falling Snow*, make an appearance in this romantic adventure about life, love, and letting go.

Bridesmaid of Honor (Bridal Series book 1) by Graysen Morgen. Britton Prescott's best friend is getting married and she's the maid of honor. As if that isn't enough to deal with, Britton's sister announces she's getting married in the same month and her maid of honor is her best friend Daphne, the same woman who has tormented

Britton for years. Britton has to suck it up and play nice, instead of scratching her eyes out, because she and Daphne are in both weddings. Everyone is counting on them to behave like adults.

Falling Snow by Graysen Morgen. Dr. Cason Macauley, a high-speed trauma surgeon from Denver meets Adler Troy, a professional snowboarder and sparks fly. The last thing Cason wants is a relationship and Adler doesn't realize what's right in front of her until it's gone, but will it be too late?

Fate vs. Destiny by Graysen Morgen. Logan Greer devotes her life to investigating plane crashes for the National Transportation Safety Board. Brooke McCabe is an investigator with the Federal Aviation Association who literally flies by the seat of her pants. When Logan gets tangled in head games with both women will she choose fate or destiny?

Just Me by Graysen Morgen. Wild child Ian Wiley has to grow up and take the reins of the hundred year old family business when tragedy strikes. Cassidy Harland is a little surprised that she came within an inch of picking up a gorgeous stranger in a bar and is shocked to find out that stranger is the new head of her company.

Love Loss Revenge by Graysen Morgen. Rian Casey is an FBI Agent working the biggest case of her career and madly in love with her girlfriend. Her world is turned upside when tragedy strikes. Heartbroken, she tries to rebuild her life. When she discovers the truth behind what really happened that awful night she decides justice isn't good enough, and vows revenge on everyone involved.

Natural Instinct by Graysen Morgen. Chandler Scott is a Marine Biologist who keeps her private life private. Corey Joslen is intrigued by Chandler from the moment she meets her. Chandler is forced to finally open her life up to Corey. It backfires in Corey's face and sends her running. Will either woman learn to trust her natural instinct?

Secluded Heart by Graysen Morgen. Chase Leery is an overworked cardiac surgeon with a group of best friends that have an opinion and a reason for everything. When she meets a new artist named Remy Sheridan at her best friend's art gallery she is captivated by the reclusive woman. When Chase finds out why Remy is so sheltered will she put her career on the line to help her or is it too difficult to love someone with a secluded heart?

In Love, at War by Graysen Morgen. Charley Hayes is in the Army Air Force and stationed at Ford Island in Pearl Harbor. She is the commanding officer of her own female-only service squadron and doing the one thing she loves most, repairing airplanes. Life is good for Charley, until the day she finds herself falling in love while fighting for her life as her country is thrown haphazardly into World War II. Can she survive being in love and at war?

Fast Pitch by Graysen Morgen. Graham Cahill is a senior in college and the catcher and captain of the softball team. Despite being an all-star pitcher, Bailey Michaels is young and arrogant. Graham and Bailey are forced to get to know each other off the field in order to learn to work together on the field. Will the extra time pay off or will it drive a nail through the team?

Submerged by Graysen Morgen. Assistant District Attorney Layne Carmichael had no idea that the sexy woman she took home from a local bar for a one night stand would turn out to be someone she would be prosecuting months later. Scooter is a Naval Officer on a submarine who changes women like she changes uniforms. When she is accused of a heinous crime she is shocked to see her latest conquest sitting across from her as the prosecuting attorney.

Vow of Solitude by Austen Thorne. Detective Jordan Denali is in a fight for her life against the ghosts from her past and a Serial Killer taunting her with his every move. She lives a life of solitude and plans to keep it that way. When Callie Marceau, a curious Medical Examiner, decides she wants in on the biggest case of her career, as well as, Jordan's life, Jordan is powerless to stop her.

Igniting Temptation by Sydney Canyon. Mackenzie Trotter is the Head of Pediatrics at the local hospital. Her life takes a rather unexpected turn when she meets a flirtatious, beautiful fire fighter. Both women soon discover it doesn't take much to ignite temptation.

One Night by Sydney Canyon. While on a business trip, Caylen Jarrett spends an amazing night with a beautiful stripper. Months later, she is shocked and confused when that same woman re-enters her life. The fact that this stranger could destroy her career doesn't bother her. C.J. is more terrified of the feelings this woman stirs in her. Could she have fallen in love in one night and not even known it?

Fine by Sydney Canyon. Collin Anderson hides behind a façade, pretending everything is fine. Her workaholic wife and best friend are both oblivious as she goes on an emotional journey, battling a potentially hereditary disease that her mother has been diagnosed with. The only person who knows what is really going on, is Collin's doctor. The same doctor, who is an acquaintance that she's always been attracted to, and who has a partner of her own.

Shadow's Eyes by Sydney Canyon. Tyler McCain is the owner of a large ranch that breeds and sells different types of horses. She isn't exactly thrilled when a Hollywood movie producer shows up wanting to film his latest movie on her property. Reegan Delsol is an up and coming actress who has everything going for her when she lands the lead role in a new film, but there one small problem that could blow the entire picture.

Light Reading: A Collection of Novellas by Sydney Canyon. Four of Sydney Canyon's novellas together in one book, including the bestsellers Shadow's Eyes and One Night.

Visit us at www.tri-pub.com